Pictures of Our Children

Pictures of Our Children

Peter Kirk

Peter Kirk
2020

Copyright © 2020 by Peter Kirk

All rights reserved. This book or any portion thereof may not be reproduced or used in any manner whatsoever without the express written permission of the publisher except for the use of brief quotations in a book review or scholarly journal.

First Printing 2020

ISBN 978-1-71695-252-4

Peter Kirk
peterkirk_2000@yahoo.co.uk

To Michelle

Pictures of Our Children

Chapter One

There is a stage in the growing intimacy of others that I can almost stomach. It is right at the start, when they are making discoveries about each other and everything is rich and promising. This is happening in front of me now as I sit in the John Lewis coffee shop. A couple on the next table are telling inconsequential stories about themselves and getting things muddled and out of order. Films, hopes for the future, pets, family. I think that they are teachers because this is the middle of the day but outside of term-time. Perhaps they are teachers of very young children as they seem relaxed and enthusiastic and innocent. I look at my watch and wait for her. She is not late; I have come ridiculously early. The couple on the next table press on. There is promise here, a future that I can see perhaps even before they will admit to it. A richness before they become insular and self-obsessed; holding hands in public, grasping shoulders in crowds, sharing headphones…

A figure looms above me and I look up, ready to defend the seat opposite. But it is Victoria, and I had not noticed her buying her own coffee.

"I'm sorry, I meant to treat you."

"That's OK… yes."

She sits awkwardly. Muddy green eyes looking at her tangled feet. She is dressed smartly and has taken the trouble to paint her nails blue.

"Hello."

"Hello, Drew."

"Good to see you."

Pictures of Our Children

"Thanks."

She is small and delicate. Her brown hair is pinched by a plain band into a ponytail. She has a pretty mouth, but it is set and open. Eventually she raises her head and looks straight at me for just a second and smiles.

I say, "Victoria, I'm going to have to take a few notes of this meeting."

She bridles minutely then recovers.

"OK, Drew."

I take out my file. This girl's future is now marked out on a squared grid. In the days when these interviews were conducted in a private office her progress was recorded in a series of plummeting graphs and cold statistics, damning in their indictments of her failings. Now things are less certain, and I will have to talk to Dan, or God help me Clare, about what to do.

"The purpose of our chat is to see when we can get you back as part of the team." She bridles again. "Just tell me a bit about how you have been feeling," I say uncertainly.

She is pale. I can see through her makeup to the foundation. The foundation, I mean the bedrock, and it is chalk white. She shakes her head.

"I don't know. I can't explain. I can't tell you what's going on." Her eyes widen. "Sorry."

"From when we last met. On a scale of one to ten." A violent shake of her head. "Is it better now you are not at work? Is there less pressure?"

"Yes," she falters, "but I don't matter..."

"You've seen your doctor again, like we discussed?"

Sometimes, I have heard, it is a good technique to leave a silence to be filled. Eventually she whispers.

"It's not the job, Drew. I could do this job if..."

She has become distracted. "The doctor," I prompt.

A shake of her head so violent I think that it may dislodge the ponytail. I become aware that people are looking at us now. Our earnest purpose is spreading like the cold draught of a business call in a railway carriage.

"Don't worry, Vicky. But you've been having some counselling too? Tell me about that."

Her head is still this time.

"Mindfulness," she croaks. "My counsellor gave me a glass of water and asked me to sip it silently, giving my mind over only to that…"

Something I think know a little about.

"Ah, yes."

"…As if water could distract me. I do this to please people, that's all…"

"I've seen those colouring books, adult colouring books where you fill in the spaces with crayons."

She bites her lip. "I was at the National Gallery yesterday."

"Really?"

This is something new and worrying. Should she be going on a jaunt to London when she is classed as sick? I need to talk to Dan or Clare. It will have to be Dan because he might be more sympathetic.

"I looked at Vermeer's *Woman Standing at a Virginal* for hours. I could live in that painting."

"In Holland?"

"No. In the calm, the light, the feeling… Well done for Holland though." She is making fun of me, gently. Good for you, Vicky. "Yet standing there in front of that great art things are reflected back at you." I have to stop myself thinking that she means her own scrappy image in the glass. "Your own inadequacy and weakness…" she says.

"Vicky, it won't be like that for long. We'll make efforts to work together to get you back with us."

"I'm not sure I can do that. I don't have the courage, and I have no voice, I'm nothing."

"Everyone is valuable, and it's like your favourite painting. Being an insurance administrator can be as noble as being an artist or musician. Yes!" I say, making it up. "I sometimes see myself as a conductor directing the team to deliver the symphony. Everybody has their part to play so that the whole is great…" Nothing at all on her face, a perfect blank. A long silence. I try to think of something to say.

"Victoria, no one blames you for your absence. If you had broken a leg it would have taken a long time to heal." Her alarmed expression tells me that this was misjudged. "Well, Clare has told me you have underlying health issues."

She nods slowly. "That's a very private thing."

"You can trust me, Victoria."

"What she means is I've had Crohn's Disease since I was seventeen."

Now she talks, her mouth animated rather than gaping. All about it. Symptoms, panic, prognosis. Her eyes are fixed not on me, but as if on an imagined opponent over my right shoulder. She is going too fast for me to keep up, and I lay the folder down on a tray. I will look this up later. Her hands are mobile, moving over the table in the circles of a hopeless caged animal. Almost an excitement stirring her previously listless body. The soon-to-be couple are fiddling with coats, but they left me a long time ago with their secret smiles and weak private jokes.

"Blood."

"Blood?" My full attention is back with her.

"Blood when I have a flare-up."

Now her eyes pierce me.

"Drew, but that's not it! I've given you something to write, that's all. You think I'm doing this to myself? But I need to trust you!"

Eventually she subsides and bows after her performance, her hair shiny like nylon, brushing the table.

In this spirit of trust, all I can think of to do is to lay down the weapon of my pen. But now she says nothing. In the pressure of the silence left by her I can only say what has been most on my mind.

"Vicky, there's some exciting news at work."

She looks up as if startled.

"My team, our team, has been given a special project. I really would love you to be part of it." At once I regret telling her this. I haven't told the team yet, and I need to get in first to explain. Clare has made this clear. Who is Victoria in contact with? Chantelle perhaps? "This is top secret, Vicky."

"Really?" she shrugs. It is much more likely that she is alone and isolated.

"It's very important because it's to do with the pension reforms."

"A change from business as usual," she says, not really interested but suddenly trying to please me.

"Well, it will be that as well…"

"Oh…"

Christ. I remember that I am totally reliant on Gav here. I can't go back to Clare on this. I need my deputy to have a grasp of what is going on. The protocols, the logistics… Victoria is gone as abruptly as she arrived, her valediction an agonised look of panic. I clutch my clumsy folder. Please God let me be able to help her. Please God let me not fuck up the project.

It is seven in the evening, and I am writing up my notes. I do not want to think about Victoria's problems and future in my flat, and so I am in the office where I can experience imposter syndrome properly. People have left fans on, and every so often the movement catches my eye and I am convinced someone's head is bobbing behind a distant desk, but I am alone and have no one to supervise. The walls are decorated with meaningless slogans. The word TRY has been painted only to be crossed out and replaced by DO in fuzzy stencilled letters. I have asked Dan whose idea this was, and he had said the originator was no longer employed and had laughed.

Victoria is in a very distressed state, and we must be cockwomble in order to help her.

Pictures of Our Children

I am stupidly confused, and then I am angry. I open the menus to see the carnage that Jim has wrought on my autocorrect.

priority—arsebadger
proactive—cockwomble
project—fandango
pushback—baboon
resource—palaver

I know that it is Jim because he is clever, and he has it right. These booby traps cannot have been on my computer for long else I would have triggered one sooner, because I have quickly learnt the language of fitting in here. For a minute I make up my own jokes and snigger at them and am grateful to Jim.

Dear Clare, Me and my team are now concentrating all our efforts on the fandango.

Everything I write about Victoria is about as meaningful and useful as this. There is something she cannot tell me and I cannot guess at, and I decide to go home. There is a way of setting computers so that white text types onto white paper, but for once Jim's machine is locked as it should be, and so I cannot try this. Instead I Sellotape the bottom of his mouse to the desk, so for a second it won't move for him in the morning. Sometimes I can do this office banter.

Chapter Two

All my team have something to give—except perhaps Victoria. They look at me now, quiet for a moment, stilled with anticipation. They were not expecting this. I have let the routine business of the daily meeting run its course, and only now have I caught their full attention.

"I have some exciting news."

I look at Jim's babyish face hoping for banter, and of course I rehearsed my own banter last night. Instead what he does is to pointedly echo my announcement, picking up the brutal points one by one.

"We will be responsible for updating the whole department's files."

"Overtime will be available at the usual rate of time-and-a-half."

"This is an acknowledgement of how well the team has performed in recent weeks."

Jane looks at me fiercely, her face not jolly red but raw red. But I see at once that she is entirely resolved to us working our arses off: only if someone slackens will I be savaged. Chantelle has her mouth open, probably not quite understanding. Lucie's mouth is open too, but wide in an ugly gesture of shock. It will probably not close all day with all the gossip she has to spread. I smile at Jenny, Sam and Sally, the new entrants. JenSamSal. A troika of risk. Not an immediate threat here in this meeting because they do not know enough, and are not confident enough, to question me, but they represent a future liability.

Suddenly Gavin speaks. "So, you are saying that this is our reward for working hard? More shit."

Pictures of Our Children

Shut this down at once. "Gav, we'll take this offline." I need to see him urgently. "Now something I had forgotten, something pleasant. Does someone have a birthday soon?"

But discussion of Lucie's birthday night out does not spread the joy that I had imagined. Everyone has other plans for the day I have chosen and the conversation descends into plain admin.

I meet my second-in-command on a corporate sofa, behind a blue fabric screen I am not convinced is soundproof. The military analogy seems appropriate, because I am talking to a man with cropped hair and full sleeve tattoos and the end of some sort of ugly text poking from his collar.

"I need you to back me on this."

"Drew, I will." Then he sniggers. "Somebody really doesn't like you though. What the hell have you done to Clare? This isn't great."

"No."

It is going to be so much easier for him to do well out of this than me. I speak quickly, without thinking, in order to sound decisive.

"Right. If we can divide the resources in a smart way it might not be a problem. I propose Chantelle and one of the new entrants for the project."

"Just two people?"

"We can't afford more. The service standards for business as usual mustn't slip."

"You won't get any overtime out of Chantelle."

"Who is the weakest of the new entrants?"

"Sam, definitely."

"Sam and Chantelle to stuff the envelopes."

"But you do know it's more than that?"

"I'm not worried. There must be an easy way to identify who we have to write to."

"You know what state the records are in?"

"We can't worry about the records."

"I've spoken to IT, and they can't produce an effective report for what we need. Some birth dates have been incorrectly input, and some didn't survive the migration to the new system. Some have defaulted to the last millennium and some to the first century AD."

"Fuck." I am grateful and pissed with him at the same time for taking the initiative on this. I try to appear decisive. "But all we need is an indicator on the records, an indicator in a field that isn't used for anything else. All Chantelle and Sam need to do is to identify those people coming up to retirement and put that indicator on. Nice little job."

"OK, Drew, but you may be underestimating this. You haven't known the years of cock-ups that some of us have known…"

"Gav, I may be relatively new here but I'm on this."

"We need to be careful of the details."

It is certain that I am being tested by being given this task, and perhaps no one believes that I can do it. I have known Dan for such a long time, and yet in this organisation I can feel like an outsider even when he is at my side.

"What should be in the letter, Gav?"

"Exactly what Clare said."

This is barbed. He must know that my attention had wandered during the meeting and that I didn't quite understand everything in the instructions. I say,

"Draft something, and I'll look over it."

"You realise that we'll need pick and mix paragraphs to cover the different circumstances? Maybe more than one indicator?"

"Fine. Then it can be automated. That's what computers are good at."

I think I have got away with it and that he has no choice but to support me. But then he says,

"So, Sam and Chantelle's career development will be sacrificed for this?"

"They will save our arse. I don't know what other fulfilment they need." I look into his intensely mean face and know that I have misjudged it this time. His tone does not mirror my flippancy.

"Drew, how are you sure we can get away with just two people doing this?"

"We can't compromise business as usual."

"This is a disaster waiting to happen. Don't be a prick, Drew. If it goes tits up you'll lose the goodwill of Jane, and she is holding the team together at the moment—and have you noticed how Lucie is being more furtive about the website she looks at on her phone? It's more likely to be *Indeed* rather than *Hello* nowadays."

"I've decided what I want, Gav."

"You need more experience in the project. I could lead it."

"No."

He looks at me with narrowed eyes. "Sam and Chantelle are going to have to be separate from the team, definitely. Otherwise they will get distracted."

"That's obvious."

"They can put headphones on."

I am not keen on this. Myself, I cannot work to music. When Gav wears headphones the music leaks like ugly thoughts escaping from his skull. 180 bpm. This is the man my future depends on. Recklessly I test his goodwill.

"Gav, do you know what's the matter with Victoria?"

"She's a sad snowflake?"

"I can't reach her. You've known her longer than I have."

"If we could manage her out of the door it would be so much better. We could get a replacement who is some use to us."

Something strange happened today. In the revolving doors before reception, if someone gives a self-important shove from behind you can drag a heel and the thing stops dead. It didn't happen like that, I'm sure. The woman in front of me simply stopped moving forward. I got a clear impression of her, imprisoned within the glass compartment. About forty, jet black hair and darkest brown eyes, consumed by an unhappiness that had rooted her to the damp rubber mat. I waited and then gently leant against the metal bar and came closer to her and the intensity of her despair. Slowly this mad carousel moved, and she was propelled into the lobby. I accelerated past her.

Chapter Three

Well over to the centre, tearing down Unthank Road, eyes flicking left and right. Wide of the car doors and the dozy pedestrians. Wide of the shit and the stones in the gutter. Holding the commanding position, scarily fast and assured. Anonymous and shielded—but then a car cuts too close and there is the unmistakable rasp of Dan's voice.

"Prick!"

I know he rides a 500cc motorbike at weekends but I do not know where to find these videos, if they exist.

I have given Victoria the choice of the place for our next meeting, and she has told me she wants to go to John Lewis again. Perhaps this is encouraging, as if she is chasing back to a happy time, or perhaps it is a lack of imagination, or perhaps she is trying to please me. She has, though, suggested an impossible time. Twelve-thirty, and the coffee shop is full of people on their rushed lunch breaks fighting for tables and women socialising with retired friends, in intermittent fits of laughter about nothing. I am early again, but she has arrived before me. She has secured a precious table, but has not been able to defend one of the seats against a middle-aged man who is resolutely sipping coke and eating cake. What must he think of us, though, nervous and silent? Eventually I say,

"Have you been anywhere else interesting?"

"I'm not saying!"

I don't know whether this jolt extends to the cake and coke man, but it strikes me hard enough to disregard him for a moment.

"Vicky, anything that will bring you back to us sooner I'll live with. Have you been to London again?"

"It might count against me!"

Silence again. After a long time, perhaps giving up on ever understanding us, the man sucks up every ice cube in his glass and leaves us, still crunching them.

"OK, Victoria," I say sternly, "what else can I do to help you? How can we support you through this? We need a plan."

"I don't want to come back."

This is like a criminal making a full confession to her defence lawyer, and I must quickly do some fancy footwork to avoid the issue.

"I understand how your illness is making you feel."

"It's not my illness! How dare you say that!" This broadcast to the elderly friends enjoying tea and cherry scones. "I don't want to ever go back to that place!"

I cannot take this at face value or the game is up for her.

"Vicky, be careful and think about this. How will you live if you give up your job?"

"I'm not being forced out."

"You must tell me what's in your mind. I can't help you otherwise."

"How can I trust you?"

"Is there another member of the management team you would rather talk to?"

"No! I just need a little more time, and then you'll see. You'll all see!" She says this as if I am the one who is confused and deficient. I try to look kindly on the girl, but my gaze seems to reach her like a destructive laser from my ugly face. A feeling I have always known.

I have seen the woman who was caught in the revolving door again. She is apparently in my department, but I do not know her name. Perhaps she is new, or has been sick or seconded. In front of me she still gives the air of utter desolation, but proving that her face is not set in fierce distraction like mine, she gives the ghost of a smile as she holds the fire door.

I do not like this place. I feel exposed and unequal to its purpose, the celebration of bonhomie. It is Dan's local and he is at home here. Throughout the evening people call to him, ignoring our quiet conversation, and all I can do is look on and smile as if in total admiration.

"Drew, what do you consider your greatest threat?" Dan says.

"So it's revealing that you see my life as a series of threats, as if I'm in a lifeboat in a storm in a sea of sharks."

"I don't at all." His dark, wise eyes twinkle, and he strokes his immaculate beard. In any event I am not in the mood for this conversation, and I wonder whether to tell him about the woman in the revolving door, to try to identify her. But my portrait would rely more on a mood rather than a clear description and I cannot be sure he would be interested. "Come on, this is just an exercise. What is your greatest threat?"

I want to say that my greatest threat is Gav, but I say what he knows I will say.

"The retirement project."

He laughs. "The poisoned chalice. The poisoned coffee cup. The poisoned coffee cup with pictures of kittens handed to you by Clare." I laugh too, and watch him switching between a smile and seriousness in an instant. "Drew, you'll have that covered I know. You're doing fine. No one has died. I'd tell you if you weren't OK. I have your back covered." Again a smile. "My protégé."

"Fuck off."

"No, I've learnt loads from you too. We learn from each other." I wonder what he has learnt from me and am flattered. "How long have we been coming to this place?"

"Eighteen months?" I shrug.

"To places like this. I was thinking of the Rose, before it shut."

"Twenty years."

"Think back to those days when we used to meet after work. Now is exactly the time you can find some of that fun and mischief again."

"We have responsibility now."

"But we're in charge. We decide what is important. Anyway, projects come and go. What should you really be worried about? What will matter in the long term?"

"Do you know Victoria Samuels?"

"Yes, I do. I know that she's having problems at the moment."

"Well, I had an absence interview with her this afternoon." I have not taken the pages of A4 from my jacket pocket, and I produce them now. On the pub table they seem inadequate, and I know that if he deciphers them it will make Victoria look even more deranged.

Dan stares at the paper amongst the beermats and says, "Explain it to me."

"Well, the first thing is that we have to meet in the John Lewis Cafe. She won't set foot inside the office."

"How long has she been absent?"

"Four months. Since just after my time. Dan, this is escalating quickly. She's sliding into total paranoia. I looked into her eyes this afternoon and realised that I was her enemy."

He thinks for a while.

"That's not surprising. When you become a manager you choose which side you are on. In trying to help someone in a friendly way you may be doing them a disservice. Like a teacher, the relationship needs to be elastic. Close and then not so close."

"You mean exert my authority?"

"It's not quite that, but I do think that you must insist that the next meeting is in the work environment."

"She'll hate that."

"The easiest thing isn't always the best thing. I'm not thinking of you here, Drew. This could go on pretty cosily, and I'm sure that over time you'd become more relaxed about it. But it wouldn't be the most positive outcome for Vicky. This needs to be forged on a harder anvil. Let's give her a good life story, eh? And this is more important than any fucking project. You must ensure that she has the proper medical support."

"Of course."

He looks alert and attentive as if he is waiting for something more from me, but he is thinking.

"Drew, I can help you here."

"You already have. I'm more confident of where I'm going now."

"What if I took Victoria Samuels from you?"

"For your team?"

"Yes. I think she could be a good fit."

"Is it possible?"

"Of course. You're a manager now. We make the rules." But I know that Clare will want an intense explanation from me. "I'm thinking strategically. For now, because your urgent need is bodies to manage the project, she isn't much use to you. But if this is handled well she might, in time, become a motivated and productive worker again. My team are good with such things. Your team are a shade more edgy and on it."

"OK."

Again he looks at me. Have I fallen into a trap? Was I being tested?

"Drew, I'll go further. We'll do a swap."

Am I being offered a new entrant? If so I don't want them.

"Who are you thinking of?"

"Hennie. She's a good worker. Steady."

I don't know her. "Fine."

I try to think who this woman is. Has the deal been done? It does not feel right. There should be more to it than this. Some formality or documentation like a house purchase, or more like a settlement.

"We'll exchange files on Monday. Don't forget to add your notes." He looks at me and smiles, "You'll enjoy Hennie, you really will."

"I'll put her to work on the project, rather than sacrificing my new entrant's development... Will that be OK?" This is my attempt at something sensible and professional. As I desperately try again to think who Hennie is I feel a strange sadness, but an inexplicable excitement as well.

Henrietta Moncrieff has long ash blonde hair and is tall. I have seen her about the building but had not known her name. She is working with Chantelle. These women are in purdah, separated from everyone. They are wearing headphones.

"How is it going?" I ask, and Hennie gives me an intense, quizzical look which continues even when she has slid the headphones down her shiny hair and I have repeated the question. I do not know what Chantelle is listening to, but she is bobbing her head slightly like a parrot, in a vapid happiness. Hennie taps her on the elbow, and she puts a hand to her mouth and fumbles with her headphones.

"How is it going?"

"Fine," they chorus.

"Well," says Hennie still looking at me intently. "I've had a couple of cases where there has been something in the indicators field already. A *d*. I've made a note of them."

She has written a list of numbers in immaculate handwriting in a spiral-bound book.

"That's brilliant, Hennie. I don't think it's anything to worry about. I think we should overwrite it if necessary." I say.

"I have already," smiles Chantelle, and her hand goes to her mouth again.

Chapter Four

The videos speak for themselves with the additional prompt of the channel's title, Dickhead Drivers. I am, though, compelled to scroll down through the circular comments.
Get in the gutter if you don't pay road tax
Nobody pays road tax you retard
I ride a bike and I drive a car...
This repeated in an endless, mesmerising chain. Perhaps I am trying to find a comment by Dan himself, but he never adds anything. The new film is hair-raising because Dan is cut up at a roundabout by a white van. He yells, and the driver blares his horn and then deliberately slows right in front of him. Amazing to top and tail your day with peril like this. If I came to these things without knowledge I might have a different opinion. But this is another dimension to a character I know so well. Perhaps it is not enough to live your life as steady and wise, or perhaps it is heightened reality like this that makes you whole. Ploughing through the gaps, careless of your life, but screaming at those who might kill you.

I don't mind this place. It is an impersonal warehouse. The vast carpet mops up spills and gossip, and people exhale into a cavernous space. It is not like Dan's pub where the atmosphere remains defiantly choking and claustrophobic decades after the smoking ban. We are, though, a tight little group, borrowed chairs jammed into tables.

I look at Lucie and smile. She smiles back. Two weeks past her nineteenth birthday. Constantly talking. Constantly talking about herself. How easy it would be to pick that bubble of self-belief, but I admire her. A good fit for the current ideal model of entitlement and ambition. Sailing true to her own compass, bountiful and kind on her own terms.

Intelligent too, able to drill to the core of a problem in seconds. She would have eaten up the project of course, but I needed her on the phones, keeping people happy. I must not think about these things now. This is nice: my team. Dan says that it is not worth it if you don't enjoy the job as well. The insurance family. I watch the new entrants, relaxed and laughing, Lucie looking after them. Jane has already had a fight this evening and a victory of sorts. In the pizza restaurant the service had been relaxed. Jane had begun to voice dissatisfaction; first to herself, then to me at the other end of the table, and then to a waitress across the room. This had got us two free bottles of wine. Making complaints in a restaurant always has me feeling uneasy. While the meal is in progress they always have the upper hand and might concoct their own disgusting triumph.

Chantelle is not here. She must have a simple existence with her family in North Norfolk, rattling back to Cromer in an old train; not troubled by the day's events, shaken back to her uncomplicated life. Sea and sky. Dashing away from the city to the same unsophisticated table she sat at as a child. I had, shame on me, looked at a timetable. I was curious to see if she could have travelled back later, and I found that she might have spent quite some time with us had she chosen to, but perhaps she lives a long way from the station. For fuck's sake am I becoming like Clare? There is no compulsion to join these jolly team building always-on-duty events. Perhaps I am concerned that Chantelle should have a break from the arid North Norfolk evenings, and yet perhaps I do not love the city as much as I pretend to.

I must watch Gav. The word is that he gets drunk easily. In that state his loyalty might dissolve completely, and he could become an embarrassment to me. I must keep an eye on Jim for different reasons. The legend is that on one occasion his night ended so close to his morning alarm call that he felt compelled to go into work without changing, and he slept under his desk. I would not be sure how to deal with this and do not want it again.

I had forgotten about Hennie. Not really mine or a part of the team, but now she waves and trips across the carpet to us. I had forgotten about her just as I had not cared for her development and had put her to work on the project. But she squeezes into a small space next to me.

"Sorry I couldn't join you for the meal, Drew!"

Thirty-five years old. Stylish in black slacks and orange top. She struggles to take off her faun coat. Tall and slim. Grey eyes and long blonde hair. Aquiline nose and high cheekbones. Posh, cultured voice. I go to the bar to buy her a white wine and Jim a pint. We didn't invite Victoria to this, and maybe we ought to have done. Hennie for Victoria. A strange bargain. But how grateful Victoria will be never to hear from me again. A cheery, optimistic, even cheeky email from Dan will have been a fresh start for her. When I get back to my table it is my turn to squeeze into a tight gap. I check on everyone. Gav and Jim behaving themselves, Lucie laughing. I try to hear what she is saying but cannot. She is probably burrowing down to the core of some innocent gossip, and I must not worry about it. Jane is showing off, going through her whole routine. The manager of the restaurant had been fawning, and the waitress had cried. Beside me Hennie is seemingly happy but apart. Sometimes a distant smile crosses her face like a thought tailored for the occasion. Perhaps she can hear Lucie's conversation better than I can because sometimes she does a theatrical widening of her eyes. A meaningless message for people she barely knows because I have separated her from them. Gav amiably asks me if I want another beer, and I say yes. I am beginning to feel a little light-headed because I had my share of the blood-money wine, but thank God this looks like being a short evening, not a restless chase from bar to bar.

Suddenly I feel Hennie wiggle her hand, bring it up past my ribs and wave. Her face melts into a genuine smile. In the door I see Dan and I take advantage of my freed left arm to wave too. He smiles and waves back. A nice picture for him: my brood happy. I knew that he was out with his own team tonight, but we had no plans to join up and someone must have messaged him. He has one of his team with him, Jake. Dan puts a hand on the boy's shoulder, and Jake blinks at everyone, dazed, waiting to be entertained. I happen to know that this Jake is on a pathway that will oust him from his job. The protocol has dictated that everybody acts normally around him when he is not in escalatingly awkward interviews, and somehow he has tagged on to Dan as if he was his best friend. Hennie seems enlivened by Dan's arrival but shows no inclination to move to be nearer to him. A glass clinks against my still full one.

"Thanks, Dan."

Hennie's straight hair brushes across my lap as she reaches to take her new glass of wine.

I watch silently, noting the slow and subtle change in the evening's dynamic. More talk of the work that unites us and yet strangely feeling a little less like a family with the new arrivals. As soon as I reasonably can I will buy Dan a drink and leave him to this. But before I can manage to escape, lightly and casually my friend touches my arm and the social obligation is turned up like a dimmer switch.

"Drew, I have something for you. Something you'll love. I'll catch you later."

I run through the orders at the bar and wonder whether to add myself. Whatever Dan has for me it will not, I suspect, thrill me. Like all my fellow managers he has a gift of hyperbole, and if the news is about work it may well be underwhelming. But if by some chance it could lead to some interaction with him more intimate than the usual rushed drinks in his horrible local then I would be happy. I buy myself another pint.

When I return with the tray Dan is speaking loudly into his phone, and everyone is listening.

"Can I ask your name? Well, Lauren, what I want to know is how busy your establishment is just now. Say on a scale of one to ten where ten is millennium night, and one is the day after the Queen has died..."

Hennie seems inexplicably receptive to this stuff. She is giggling, and has wriggled further into my place. She looks at me as if she genuinely wants me to share the laughter and pats the cushion next to her.

"Lauren. One other question. How attractive are you? We'll use a scale of one to five where five is Tuppence Middleton, and one is... Anne Frank..."

Hennie lays a hand on my arm and rocks gently.

"Lauren, I'm willing to bet you are much more than a three. You have a lovely voice. Anyway, we'll see you very soon, Lauren."

Everybody quietly explodes with the release of Dan pushing the button to end the call. I resign myself to drinking up quickly and pressing on to some poky, trendy bar with bicycle parts suspended from the ceiling or whatever it is tonight.

"Dan, you are so funny!" Hennie says.

Before we leave I do a quick audit. Jim well on the way but a shared responsibility now. Everybody else in good spirits. Gav, the most important element, completely sober.

On the trek to the new bar I try to be with Dan, but Hennie has him. I hang back and walk on my own. Hennie and Dan are closer than I thought. She leans in to him as if to share a private joke. Suddenly there are fast steps behind me, and I find myself nervously spinning round, not used to being in the city at night. Gav falls into step with me folding notes into his wallet.

"Drew, well done. We've smashed the project."

"Not quite finished but I think we'll get away with it. I think so."

He has surprised me, and I should thank him for the part he played, but instead I say,

"Gav, be honest with me. Are the team... happy?"

"At this moment I would say they are."

"But I mean... generally. Am I doing OK?"

"They work hard and they're happy Drew."

"Thanks Gav. That's what's important, that they're happy. Happy, happy."

The new bar isn't the one with bicycle parts but the one with cobbler's tools. Strangely whatever the result on Dan's crowd scale the group formation has been held, and I am squeezing in beside Hennie again.

"Thank you for your work on the project, Hennie. You smashed it." No murmur of dissent from her.

"Drew," she says, "I know almost nothing about you."

"Hennie, I am very boring. I just work and sleep. Sometimes you come in early and find me in the office, and yes, I have slept there."

This produces no laugh which is worrying. But I don't know what I am trying to do here; to deflect her questions or to impress her with my sense of humour. How attractive is she? Very, objectively, but I must not think that. And I am safe because I am resistant to brittle, arch personalities like hers. Neither are her coolly elegant looks my favourite.

"Where do you live, Hennie?"

"On the Broads."

"Lovely."

"I have a boat."

"Really? What kind?"

"A wherry."

This can't be true. "Really?"

She laughs at me, knowing I don't understand boats. We are attracting attention. We are not the centre of attention, but there are several oblique glances, refracting into gossip. I think I see a camera, but no, it is the blank of a powder compact.

"You must come and see. Then you'll know."

"Does it have sails?"

Somehow I have not been able to halt this conversation, though I hear the brakes screeching in my head.

"Yes it has sails. You'll see Drew."

Maybe she is a water gipsy, though she commutes into Norwich by train and sometimes in a Volvo. I try not to dwell on this and check my team. At this moment Gav is sliding a beer across to me. He is affable and sober. Good. Now Hennie stands up to go to the toilet with exquisite apologies and an excruciating careful grace. Dan is almost immediately in Hennie's place.

"Congratulations on delivering the project. I understand you pushed the button for the mailing today."

"Yes." Now that Dan has said it I go through it again in my head, trying to remember if I got it all in the right order. "But I don't know how much of the follow-up Clare expects me to do, if she wants me to keep ownership. Thank you for Hennie, by the way."

"You seem to be getting along well."

"She's great."

"She is. Things should quieten down for you now."

"It was easier than I thought… Are you saying that you want Hennie back?"

"Absolutely not. But if you can share a bit of resource in the future, then I'd take it. I won't deprive you of Hennie—she seems to have fitted in. Who worked with her?"

"Chantelle?"

"Yes, perhaps I could borrow someone like that."

"Is that what you needed to see me about?"

"By no means, Drew. This is something really exciting that I wanted to share."

He hands me a thick, shiny leaflet. Pictures of young people with toned bodies. Too lazy even to read, I say, "Dan, you're not going to get me to the gym. Ever."

"No, look at it. It's a business opportunity. Shakes."

"Shakes?" I try to process this, but it is meaningless. "Shakes," I say again as if everything is clear.

"Protein Shakes."

"OK."

The bright, busy, font is too much at the moment.

"Read it at your leisure."

"I will." But to please him I don't tuck it away immediately and wave it about gently.

"Drew, I'll leave you with that. See you later."

Hennie is back at my side.

"Shakes," I say to her. "Shakes."

She is disappointingly and obstructively earnest.

"That is a fantastic opportunity for you, Drew."

"You're in, are you, Hennie?"

"Platinum level."

"Shakes."

The drink has made her eyelids just slightly heavier. Her hands are fumbling at her throat for her peach scarf and are just a shade more careful. Her hair a touch more untidy.

As we leave Hennie takes my arm and keeps it all the way to the fast-food place. We are all hungry again because it seems like a week since we met. The business of ordering burgers is insurmountable, and I am in a plastic chair, counting money. I do not want responsibility. Raised voices. I instinctively stand up and Hennie's hands are on my shoulder, and I let her believe that she is saving me from a glorious fight. Only now do I take in what is going on. Jake is opening and closing his mouth like an automaton. Some random insult or obscenity must have come out of it because three youths are squaring up to him. Now a cacophony of sounds. The taunting of the youths. Jim, now also robotic, braying something unintelligible. Jane yelling, "Cunts!" at the top of her voice. I feel Hennie's hands press harder on my shoulder, and watch Dan move into the space between the yobs and Jake.

"Move, fuckwits!" he says simply. Not a reconciliation then.

"Move!" Hennie echoes right in my ear.

But is only Dan who has any authority now. How has he judged it so perfectly? Just the right number of steps into no-man's-land. Just the right menace in his voice. It is not clear at once if he has defused the bomb but, staying still and silent, I am able to watch the retreat of the youths, glacially slow but certain. Like me Dan is quiet, standing firm, knowing he has done enough. There are empty, meaningless calls as the situation resolves. Hennie's grip now prevents me from moving into the glorious space occupied by Dan. I have lost count of the change and sit down.

"Will everyone be OK?" I ask Dan earnestly. Jim has sunk below the robotic stage to a mute insectoid twitching.

"The rule is that everyone always gets home," says Dan, "no one knows how it happens."

I am on a bridge over the river, throwing up into the dark water below. Dan is at my side. Trying to be professional, I say, "Look after Victoria."

I don't know why I was worried about Jim because he is still with us, doggedly following our steps. I look at the river. Wherever I end up tonight it won't be on Hennie's boat because I realise that she has gone.

A cracking where you are not sure whether it is tooth or bone. I put my hand to my mouth and push the plate away. This can't be Dan's home because it is small, with a cold, damp bathroom smelling of acrid plaster and mould. Even so he is making coffee for us while Jim lies flat on the floor. Dan has also provided the plate for my food. The burger, though, has not improved through Dan's intervention. There has been some application of heat, enough to excite the bacteria, and a refreshing of the salad contents. As I decline the rest of the meal Jim is suddenly enthused to go on a hunt, the significance of which I cannot understand, though I laugh along with Dan. It involves cupped hands and an expedition to the bathroom.

"Can we make them look more like cockroaches? Some sort of disguise is in order." Jim says this in a very considered way, and Dan and I are hysterical. Chili powder is applied.

I frame the plate. One woodlouse has apparently expired on the exposed meat, and the other is attempting the Everest of the propped-up bun. I push the button, and the night is represented by bugs on a burger.

Chapter Five

What room am I in? I know the number, having returned flustered to my desk to check it, much to Gav's amusement. But I have no idea where the room is or where I am in this maze of corporate carpet, and I am late for Clare without excuse. Now two things at the same time, distracting and difficult to process. The door just ahead of me opens, seemingly not pushed enough for someone to slip through, but then Victoria does it. I dive to hold the door away from her. Any new urgent agenda would be welcome. Through the glass of the door I see another figure approaching. My heart leaps, but how surprised should I be to find the woman with the black hair and eyes wandering this space like a spirit, lost like me. She is at just the distance to make any business with the door awkward. I think she is shaking her head slightly, but I do not let go of the handle. Now a strange ballet. Victoria, suddenly inhabited by the transparent story-telling grace of a dancer, does not know whether to bolt or to try to hide behind the door I am holding. Soft footsteps come towards us, speeding with the obligation of taking the handle from me. Nothing between the women. Then the small steps accelerate, dark intense eyes focused on the next set of doors. Victoria starts to creep along the wall like a nervous cat. Before she makes her spring to get away I say,
"Good to see you, Vicky."
She is still slowly moving.
"Clare forced me to come here!"
"She shouldn't have done that." But Victoria's head swings like the closing fire doors in the distance. "What room is Clare in?" I ask.

Pictures of Our Children

"It's so cold in this room, Drew," says Clare and fiddles with the thermostat as if we were going to live in here. "Did you get caught in the A11 traffic? I think there was another fatal accident."

I nod though I had walked in this morning, not trusting myself. Finally we sit down opposite each other, but there is nothing yet, just a drip-feed; a slow injection of syrup into my veins from a raised up clear bag. I think of it like the sludge boiled down from a fizzy drink.

"How are you, Drew?"

"Fine, Clare."

"I just wanted a little chat. I hope you don't mind."

"No, Clare. "

I watch her smile and feel the drip, drip, drip.

"Not your finest hour, Drew, last night."

"No, Clare."

"I think one thing that we might take from this, for a start, is not to arrange a party on a school night."

I decide to be bullish before the drip paralyses me completely.

"Everybody is here and raring to go. Well not Jim, but we got him home, and I'll ring him now. I'll tell him he will have to take today as holiday."

"I have already spoken to Jim, Drew. He was here at seven. Do you remember any incident from last night?"

The night had become a telescoping series of incidents that I now want to forget. Clare hands me a piece of paper.

"OK, Drew, that was posted by Jim at four-twenty this morning."

The caption says, "*look what we were seved up last night!*"

"You were tagged in the photo, by the way."

The image still has the power to make me want to retch.

"Clare, you can see that he was paralytic by the spelling. He didn't know what he was doing, it wasn't malicious."

"Look closer, Drew."

"Shit!" I say involuntarily. Beneath the bugs and burger, clearly visible, is a McDonald's serviette.

"I pray that I caught it in time."

"It wasn't McDonald's. That's just a random bit of paper."

"Were you there Drew?"

I am pretty sure I took this picture. By then things were just happening to me.

"I'll make sure that's taken down."

"It already has been, but one share, so we wait and see if it goes viral."

I read the comments. This is just the sort of thing to excite people.

"Grooooossss!"

"No way!"

I say, "I'll ring Jim now…"

"That ship has sailed, Drew. I have suspended Jim, and it's out of our hands."

"What will happen to him?"

"That depends on how sensibly he behaves."

Jim operates in a world of stupidity, and should invite help.

"I think I should speak to him…"

"I'd rather you didn't, Drew. The disciplinary procedure will be overseen by an independent manager."

Jim is an idiot, but he has saved me from myself a few times. He has kept the mood of the team buoyant while I have been grimly concentrating on tedious and probably worthless stuff.

"Drew, you should think carefully about this."

Christ, does she expect me to jump? Does she know I was there with Jim? I can only think of going to see Susie with the news: news important enough to visit her. This plays in my head, round and round, and I do not speak. Clare is looking at me as if I am a simpleton to be humoured. What am I to say now to fill the silence?

"I pushed the button for the project yesterday," I gabble eagerly.

"I know you did, Drew," Clare says flatly. "To be honest I was surprised it was ready so quickly, and I was expecting a report."

"I was going to send that today."

"I was expecting a report before we sent everything, in all honesty."

Again silence.

"Well, now we just wait for the response," I say.

"We've already had a response, Drew."

She has another paper. She draws it across the desk, and opens the razor-sharp fold. I take it. The familiar email print. Long. Addressed to me, but sent to the group inbox. I can only bear to skim it.

"You wrote to my husband as if he was still with me, and able to enjoy his retirement."

This is enough. "Oh God, Clare."

Now the vein is truly open, and the syrup can flow, my resistance gone. Clare smiles a sickly smile. "I'm sorry that these things are what we have to talk about today, Drew."

I try to recover and make a list.

"I'll speak to Chantelle and Hennie and find out how this could have happened. I'll arrange for flowers to be sent to the widow and write to her personally..."

"Are we going to be bankrupt by the florists' bills, Drew?"

"I'll investigate and let you know if there are likely to be any more cases."

I know there will be, and Clare knows it too.

"Drew, if you need support..." she smiles.

Support. This is not something to be sought or welcomed. It is a wedge hammered into a fine crack in a delicate joint.

"I'm fine... but can I ask why you brought Victoria here?"

"Drew, Drew, we'll close this meeting now, shall we?" she says sweetly.

Embarrassment has stiffened my step and made me whisper nonsense to myself. I should have fought for Victoria as I should have fought for Jim. Have I accepted so completely that she is Dan's responsibility now? I push the door and walk into the department, and I have to stifle the muttering as Dan is at my side.

"Drew, can I borrow you for a sec?"

"Sure."

I am disappointed when he only steps a few paces from the door, seeking no more privacy than this. Dan, who has rejected Facebook and could not have been tagged in Jim's post.

"What we were talking about last night, Drew."

"What?"

"Resource. Perhaps you could lend me someone…"

"You can have Jim!" I spit out. But then I immediately apologise, and he does not know why as he pursues me to my desk.

Chapter Six

Today Facebook is full of proud parents. It is World Book Day, and a million children are caught against kitchen walls in fancy dress. This is not what I am looking for. I am looking for bugs on a burger, but I am treated to the child as prince or princess everywhere I search. I could free myself from this torment with the few clicks it would take to kill my account. I could have done that a day ago, but now I am compelled to find out whether we are in jeopardy from a global corporation. I keep scrolling down.
"What Disney Princess are you?"
"I instagramed my dog as a dog."
"Proud parent alert."
Dear God.

To conduct my investigation I am in the same remote, cold basement room as I was this morning. It is a sham because I know precisely what went wrong. I encouraged Chantelle and Hennie to overwrite an indicator for death with our own sign. No one was aware of the death marker, but we should have been, or at least should have taken more care. It is not clear to me how many incidents there will be, but it may well be catastrophic.
Chantelle is late and probably lost like I was. I dread this meeting. Eventually there is a timid knock, and her little face peeps around the door as if she is expecting an army of hostile people in this tiny space. She smiles as she sees only me.
"Sorry I'm late, Drew."
"Don't worry about it, Chantelle."
She is small and thin. She has mousey hair, but bright blue eyes. She looks about fifteen. What I must not do is channel Clare, but within a minute the syrup is flowing.

"Are you warm enough? I don't think the heating is working."

"Fine," she says, but she is shivering.

"Thank you for coming to see me. I have to let you know that we have had a serious problem concerning the project."

"Oh no!" I don't know whether that reaction signifies genuine concern for the project or if she knows she is in trouble.

"We've had a complaint."

I am about to show her a copy of the widow's email but change my mind. She seems too young for all of this, almost too unfinished for grief. But I must get some blood from this sacrificial lamb.

"Chantelle, is there any way you could have sent a retirement later to someone who had passed away?"

"The letters were automatic, Drew. We didn't even see them to check."

"I know that, but when you and Hennie were looking at the computer records, could you have altered them in such a way that it wasn't clear if the person was still living?"

She looks confused and unsettled. "We didn't check for that. Oh no! I'm sorry. I didn't know we were supposed to."

This is enough for me, and I say, "OK, Chantelle. Don't worry about it." All I need now is a satisfactory outcome for Clare. Some win. "This may take some effort to sort out Chantelle. I can't at this moment say with certainty how many cases we might have. Would you be prepared to help in correcting the problem if necessary?"

"Another project!"

I wince. "Yes, another project."

"I'd like to do that, Drew."

"Now, if we do need to do this it will have to be done very quickly and accurately. It will be a real priority. I know that in the past you have been reluctant to do any overtime but, in the circumstances, would you be prepared to consider this, at least for a week or two."

I have upset her, and now I notice that she looks tired. I do not know what she was doing while we were out enjoying ourselves, but her eyes are red and puffy. The image of the cheerful uncomplicated girl that I have in my head does not match what I am seeing in front of me.

"Is anything wrong, Chantelle?"

"No, Drew. It's just that it's difficult for me to work late."

"Can you tell me why?"

Then it is as if everything threatening about this meeting has dissolved, and she beams at me, carefree.

"Molly."

"Your dog?"

She giggles. "My daughter, Drew."

I am truly disoriented. Is this a cruel joke on me? But I look into the girl's eyes and smile too.

"I'm so sorry, Chantelle, I had no idea."

"That's OK. Not everyone knows. Someone complained once that I was a bit bubbly about it so I'm quieter now."

"How old is she?"

"Very nearly two. She's everything to me. I can't explain it... but I must do well at work because I'm all she has..."

"Don't worry, Chantelle. Please don't worry."

"Can I show you?"

"Yes, of course."

She takes out her phone and shows me endless pictures of a cute toddler in an idyllic setting; sea and sky. Sometimes Chantelle is behind her, kissing the top of her head, folding her in her arms.

"I can't tell you how much that little bundle means to me. I just can't. I'd do anything for her." The girl's soft, reedy, true Norfolk tones over the authentic Norfolk landscapes. I hesitate, but then I speak.

"Can I show you something too?"

"Of course, Drew."

I fiddle with my phone to select the images, wondering where I will drop in my history. Just a little while to make sure that I am at the right place.

"Drew, they are gorgeous! What are their names?"

"Gabrielle and Philippa. Eight and three now."

Some of the shots of my daughters mirror Chantelle's, on wide beaches, and in front of endless flat fields stretching to the bright horizon.

"Wow, Drew."

"But I don't see them often."

"Oh no!"

Suddenly there is a third figure in the photos because we are going back in time, and Chantelle looks at me.

"My wife, Susie. We're separated now. We had a house near Holt... well she's still there."

"She's lovely."

"I know."

"I'm sorry. I shouldn't have said that."

This is enough before my voice cracks.

"Chantelle," I say abruptly. "This meeting is nothing to worry about. If ever you need a day off to care for Molly, or if you want to leave a bit early, I understand now."

Dan is not having her, and Clare is not having her.

Hennie is here too soon. I need to recover, and to think about how to save myself, because I know that I am about to be found out. I can see the woman's tall frame in the frosted glass that surrounds the door, pacing until the appointed time. I had left twenty minutes to write up Chantelle's interview, but she has only just gone because we were exchanging pictures, and I no longer know what to write to please Clare. Inevitably Hennie pushes open the door on the dot.

"Hi, Drew. Did you get home OK?"

"Hardly. But that's not what we are here to discuss."

When I told Clare that my team were raring to go, I was thinking of Hennie; keen-eyed, immaculate and relaxed after the debacle of a few hours before. She folds her legs under the chair, and her hair brushes the desk as she leans towards me. I hand her a copy of the email without comment. I can watch the import of the text in her face. The initial jolt of the first paragraph, knowing that we got it wrong. Then the escalating anger and grief of the widow reflected in Hennie's widening eyes and frown. I sigh as she lays the letter down, not giving it back to me but keeping it as her own. My hand goes to my head, and Hennie does the same. We are talking less in this meeting than we should be. I hardly dare speak now because I know that she is going to spear me. She closes her eyes for a few seconds and then looks straight into my face.

"Drew, I'm sorry. I know exactly what has happened here. Chantelle and I ignored a field that indicated that a member had died. In fact we may have overwritten it. We should have checked, and it was careless. It frightens me that there may be other cases. If you let me help to sort this out I'll do anything I can."

A feeling something like elation. Why has she made this so easy for me? She has given me a nugget that I can present straight to Clare to get me off the hook. We sit in silence as I eagerly write up her confession. She smiles when I have finished.

"Drew, I hope I didn't embarrass you last night."

"No, Hennie."

"And I meant what I said about coming to see my boat."

Chapter Seven

I know that this is a pyramid scheme. Perhaps it is somehow legal, but its structure and language are rooted in the honest old days of sending cash to people in the hope that you get a lot more back. I will do this. The thing is to get in early, and I trust Dan and Hennie. People were ruined by early pyramids because they were late in, and there were not enough gullible people left in the world to pay them. The extreme risk of this venture seems to be only that you might be left with cartons of strawberry flavoured powder under your bed and feelings of resentment towards the platinum people whose nice cars you have made a modest contribution to. The actual business of the shakes bores me, and my qualifications for selling a health drink are minimal—every gym membership I have guiltily taken in the new year has lapsed. This, though, is not the point. The website is the thing; people in hot tubs drinking prosecco and posing in front of mid-range Audi sports cars. My enthusiasm will be for the aspirational images, not for the sickly protein. My management role has not brought with it the financial excitement I imagined, because of the escalating expenses of separation. Let me make some money. I have not heard of this stuff before, and so it will be fresh to the company. At any rate I will insist on exclusivity within my team, and I potentially have solidly ambitious people like Gav and Lucie for the tier below. I will see Dan quickly and let him know that I'm in. He is looking out for me. I stare at the paper in front of me and make a large decisive tick. Yes, a list, and even before the tick I had amended the first item to read *Dan's offer* rather than the casual and disrespectful *Shakes.*

The next thing is a name. *Henrietta Rose Moncrief* I have written. The milkshakes brochure survived the turbulent evening, but folded, stained and crumpled. I look through it now, and it works the same way as it had last night. Not all the same woman, but the same look. Tall and graceful, self-assured with shiny hair. In front of cars, swimming pools, and sometimes with children, whose faces have been artistically blurred by sunlight for privacy. This leaflet is almost a prospectus for the woman who Dan gave me in place of Victoria. I am sure now: Dan has done this for me. If it had been Henrietta I had found trapped in the revolving door would I have loved her completely? But in that cold room she saved me, and thinking of that meeting, with her legs folded under her chair to lean closer to the pain of the widow's letter, I find that I love her a little bit. It would be a fortuitous union. The company does not permit those in a relationship to work closely together. If it was me who was moved to accommodate our attachment I could say goodbye to the project and all its fallout, to Gav, and to worrying about Victoria and Chantelle. A political marriage. I stab at the paper not to make a decisive tick but to pierce it. What have I become to live by lists and action plans? I think of the months since my separation when I have been adrift with no help, and now my closest friend has done this. His motive is clear, and it is almost too wonderful and too easy. I even allow myself to imagine Hennie nudging him to do it. With Susie it was so different; what felt like a whole lifetime of becoming closer to her, being as kind to her as I dared to be. Gentle and excruciating, and ultimately all taken away from me. Now I must relax, be grateful to my friend Dan and seize this chance with Hennie. This will be fun. The next item on my list, *Gav*, no longer seems important enough to worry about.

Gav and I sit on the corporate sofa and discuss the project. He enjoys these sessions and asks me trick questions.
"Hennie has settled in well hasn't she, Drew?"
"Yes, she has."

"But we must be careful, going forward, that she doesn't attract resentment within the team."

I look at him, and he grins sardonically. I decide that he means the threat to his own militarily precise ambition. Me being parachuted in was bad enough without this switched-on woman following.

"I don't think there will be a problem."

"But you're fucking glad Victoria has gone, aren't you?"

He laughs when I don't answer.

"Gav, what do you think should be in the automatic apology letter?"

"Do you have a copy of what was in the letter when we replied to the complaint cases?"

"Clare wrote that. I'll show you the letter, but it's crap. She can't string two words together without sounding fake."

"How will they be addressed?"

I hadn't thought of this. "Trustee/Personal Representative hashtag. I don't know."

"OK."

"Gav, I'm thinking that we can't say we are distressed. Everybody we've offended would have complained by now. Let sleeping dogs lie. Most of the addresses will be wrong, but the returns from the first mailing haven't come in, or haven't been actioned."

"I'd say there was a time limit on feeling distressed so we can't do that now."

"What do we feel then Gav?"

"Disappointed."

"Irritated."

"Fucking pissed."

"Something like that."

"Devaluation of the language, eh, Drew? Still, if the company mission statement insists I have to find delight in my work perhaps we should allow ourselves to be devastated."

"I don't know how attached Clare is to her bloody letter. I want to do this automatically. The death markers will be back in place. Hennie and Chantelle have put a temporary indicator on the complaint cases, so we don't write to those bastards again, and it should be easy. We know it works."

"We do know it works because we are getting loads of calls from legitimate, undead people. The team's number shouldn't have been on the pension letters—I understood we were going to direct queries to dedicated people."

I wonder whether, behind my back, he has told Clare about this, and seeing his smirk and wondering what message his hidden tattoos carry I decide that he definitely has.

"The new letters will have to have our number on," I say forcefully as if it affected my previous mistake.

"I'm happy with that, Drew, because there will be fuck all response, like you say. The other stuff is crippling business as usual, and we are a man down. What is going on about Jim?"

"I can't do anything about that, Gav. I mean I did all I could."

"But you'll fight for him?"

"Of course."

"Have you spoken to him?"

I parrot Clare. "That's not a good idea because an independent manager is doing the investigation."

"Have you spoken to the investigator?"

"No, but nothing will happen because the McDonald's post was taken down early. Jim will be fine."

"But it's true that you were there when it happened?"

Instinctively I want to mention that Dan was there as well, but instead I say,

"Listen, I'm in the firing line here Gav. Today I need to see Clare with a draft letter knowing that she'll shred it and dismiss every idea I have. But I'll try to get us finished with this whole bloody fiasco."

"Well you won't do all of that today, Drew, Clare is on holiday until next week."

"Really? She didn't tell me."

"Last minute. Bitch. Don't you check her online diary? Bound to be something for you to pick up."

"Shit! That's brilliant."

I sit back and smile at Gav, happiness and relief coursing through me.

I am in a Victorian corner. Hennie and Chantelle are sat on the floor, and dust is falling on them. Some of the files they are looking at are crisp and new, and some are yellowed and tearing. Death is no respecter of this, and they have to check each one for a certificate and the process of paying the claim. If people are very dead the women might have to spend time in the nineteen-seventies, squinting at out of focus microfiche, just to be sure.

"Guys, I'm so sorry it has to be like this," I say. "If you wanted to you could carry the files to be with us."

Hennie shakes her head. "No, Drew, we are having loads of fun, aren't we Chaza?"

Chantelle grins. I do not even know whether this exercise is necessary because the people they are looking for possibly have no one left on earth to complain about hurt feelings. All of those sort have flowers now. Chantelle giggles as if she really is having fun, and I smile at her. There is something between us now. For myself I do not mind being in this room for a few minutes, grim as it is. There is something between Hennie and I too. I dare to look at her, and she grimaces. She unfolds her long legs and stands; I think she is walking off in a quest for another file.

"How is Molly?" I say to Chantelle.

"Beautiful. Just amazes me every day, how much she learns, how much must be there already, somehow."

"It is incredible isn't it?"

Totally transparent she frowns because, remembering my circumstances she pities me for a second, and then she beams again.

"Thank you, Drew."

I stand up. "Let me know if there is anything I can do to help."

Incongruously she gives a little wave as I walk away.

I stalk Hennie through the rows of tall file cabinets. I peer around each corner, but at the last musty aisle she surprises me as if she meant to arrange a near collision and laughs.

"Drew, how are things for you?"

"Fine. I mean they are starting to turn around. Very positive."

"Really?" she smiles.

We whisper even though there is no one in the room except Chantelle, a long way away behind the files, and probably lost in her own little world. Because of the dust Hennie is wearing old jeans, and I like her more like this. Her phone traces a tight rectangle in her back pocket.

"Thank you so much for what you're doing, Hennie."

"No problem. You just get on with it don't you?"

We have done a little pirouette during this conversation, and the woman is now leaning on the corner of the aisle and I am in the gloom of the avenue of cabinets. She has already started to read the file and now turns, holding it in front of her like a processing chorister. I summon all my courage and say. "Hennie, can I buy you dinner some time?"

She looks up and speaks as seriously as if she had a head full of the file's contents.

"Yes, I'd like that, Drew."

I walk very slowly back to the department, my head full of the smell of decomposing files and Hennie's subtle perfume.

Chapter Eight

A new day. The sun is shining, and I walk to work, buoyant. As I cross the ring road my phone vibrates. This is usually a bad omen as it means that one of my team are texting me to say that they are ill, or will be late. It is Chantelle, and my heart sinks because I was hoping that reviewing the records would be finished before Clare returns, so I could notify IT to do whatever they do to send the letters. There is no message from Chantelle, however; she has sent me a picture of her daughter. Molly is standing beside a huge steam train. I recognise the setting at once because it is Holt station, and that is why she has sent it to me. The tiny child seems unconcerned by the beast behind which is belching steam, and judging by the reaction of others in the photo, making quite some noise. There is just a hint of jeopardy as the girl is not held; but she seems brave and unconcerned, smiling at Chantelle taking the picture, and probably the woman just to the left is her grandmother who looks unconcerned too but perhaps a little bewildered. I imagine Chantelle now sitting on her own train rattling into Norwich, and somehow thinking to do this for me. I reply with a photo of my daughters. Chantelle may well have seen this one when I was flicking through my phone in the cold room, but it is also at Holt station, in this case at the model railway there.

Something is desperately, terrifyingly wrong. I want to go no further than the threshold. People are huddled by the walls talking in hushed voices. Those you would expect to be working on, the stoic or socially inept, are isolated at their keyboards staring blankly at the screen. I know that I will not get three paces into the department before someone intercepts me, and I do not want to do it. Eventually, with people pressing behind I move, and it is Dan who accosts me.

"Drew, can I have a word?"

Redundancy or death, and it is death because the walls seem to reflect sadness as well as shock.

"I'm afraid that we've had some very terrible news."

Dan is surprisingly clumsy at this, hesitating as if he's doing a reveal in a game show; in reality I suppose he is choking with the responsibility. But I am overwhelmed that he is safe, the most precarious life in the department... not quite the most precarious. Oh God not Victoria...

"Nadia was killed in an accident last night."

This means nothing to me, but I frown and shake my head. "Oh no..."

Then, as I feign shock I'm overtaken by growing certainty, replacing embarrassment and confusion and sham concern. Somehow I know that Nadia was the woman in the door. I rudely push away to my desk and sit down, and my team, seeing my distress, say nothing and avoid me.

A richness of details during the morning that escaped me when the woman was alive. They come from an internet search, overheard snippets of gossip and the direct questions that I dare to ask. She had a son, aged five or six, who she lived with in Wymondham. She was nominally in Dan's team but had been mostly absent for the past four months. She died in a car accident on the A11, the Norwich road; she was thirty-eight.

I climb up to Hennie and Chantelle in the Dickensian attic. I'm afraid that somehow the news might not have reached them, but they're sitting cross-legged, talking quietly, and when I approach they become silent as if not only the news, but also reports of my sensitivity, have found this outpost.

"Drew, this is a difficult day," Hennie says.

"Did you know Nadia well?"

"Not really. She was having problems and wasn't about much. She was lovely."

"I knew her a little bit," Chantelle says. "Her son is gorgeous—what will happen to him? Poor mite."

"Thank God he wasn't in the car though," says Hennie.

"It certainly brings things into perspective," I say.

Hennie looks at Chantelle and me with her grey eyes.

"But all we can do is to do this job as well as we can. It is very important to some people."

"Do you need any help?"

"That's fine, Drew."

I would have welcomed spending time here in this muffled sanctuary, but I have to return to my restless team.

I call a meeting and speak briefly about Nadia's death, borrowing what Hennie said about carrying on with work that is important. I have another duty to perform. I have to ring Jim to let him know the news. There is an office protocol that managers must inform absent team members of even the most trivial corporate developments. This will be more difficult, but I welcome the excuse to speak to him.

"Jim, we've had some sad news in the department. Nadia has died in a car accident." This is awkward as he was expecting the call to be about him, and he clearly has no idea who Nadia was.

"OK, Drew."

It is difficult for him, like a leaving collection landing on your desk for someone you have never heard of, but here the currency is grief, not two-pound coins. I help him out.

"She wasn't around in the department much for the last few months. Thirties, jet black hair, tiny." I say it, "beautiful, lovely." The smuggled compliment brings me closer to her.

"Drew, I'm sorry if she meant something to you."

The only time I've heard Jim say something sensible or sympathetic, and it is worrying.

"Jim, I'm not really able to speak to you about your disciplinary."

"I've only got myself to blame, but I know that the managers are out to get me."

"You owe Clare something; she fought the fire, stopped the fallout."

"I would rather have the weight of every one of McDonald's lawyers down on me than that lot."

I sit in the garden with the sun on my back. Scent from the flowers I do not know the names of might fix this moment in my memory. I hope not. Everything is lovely except for the chimney and the smoke. There may be a place where the idea of minute traces of ash falling on soil and vegetation is poetic and comforting, but in the sight of the industrial church and its chimney, it never can be for me. Why am I here? Obviously I'll take any chance to escape the department. Dan put pressure on me to stay to cover, but I resisted, and he did not know why. I am here very early too, just to be alone, and perhaps I can get away with it. I wish for solitude, but it is not good for me. I am stalking this woman through death, yearning to learn more about her. I am not happy with this garden, and I am not happy with my thoughts. Perhaps I could bring myself to go back to the office to spend most of the afternoon with Hennie and Chantelle, finishing up the project. But that could be counted as an even clearer dereliction of duty. I close my eyes and think of Nadia in the door. A slight spring of the wooden slats against my back. I look up and Clare is beside me.

"Hello, Drew."

"Clare, I thought you were on holiday."

"Only to Dorset, and we came back with the news."

I must have scared her off a little way because I was sitting with my eyes closed, but now she moves closer. Irritating, like Dettol on a cut. Good for me, I suppose, smothering me in concern.

"Are you OK, Drew?"

"Fine."

"This is so sad," she says, but I can tell that she is eager to move on to something else. I do not doubt the depth of her feelings—she is younger than me and still experiences these things with a fresh keenness. But perhaps they light on her for a shorter time, like black moths, before fluttering off. Incredibly, what her mind is really on is cover back in the office, though she does not raise this directly.

"So you knew Nadia well, Drew?"

"I felt I did. I know she's been having problems."

"Are any more of your team coming?"

"I don't think so, no."

"I think all of Dan's team will be here. All the managers too, but we didn't think you knew her, Drew."

Her concerns are now absolutely clear, and I say, "Gav is in charge of the department, a safe pair of hands."

"That's good, Drew."

Perhaps it is worrying that she is happy that Gav is in charge. Even now that we are sitting in silence I hate the fact that she is beside me, pressing on my private thoughts. I know too that there is something she is keen to raise, even above office cover, but she thinks that it would not be decent to pursue this agenda in a crematorium garden. When I look up from the ground I see that she is staring at me. After ten minutes she says.

"Had we best be making our way inside, Drew?" Oh God, will I be yoked to her through the whole service?

As we wait outside the door to the chapel, there is a strange moment when we almost collide with the mourners from the previous ceremony. This does not feel like shared grief, more like confusion and resentment. I cannot shake Clare off, and she follows me to sit on the fourth row, leaving space for however many family members might come.

Nadia was too young to be thinking of death, but someone must have known her wishes. The music is Elgar, comprehensively ruined by the sound system. Then the ominous motor of the hearse. A young priest takes the service—so she was Catholic. It is clear to me that he did not know her well, but he has been carefully briefed, and he is sensitive. With each phase of the address comes a new pang. The greatest tragedy I knew about of course: she had a son called Luca. Six years old. Too young to be here, and probably being cared for by a family member, depleting the front pews further. Her husband, an Italian, died three years ago which I also knew. She had, however, rallied from the grief according to everybody. He had been much older than her, and that must have added poignancy to the vows at their wedding. She had not been left rich and had to return to work to support her child. She was kind. Somehow I knew this because of the effort of the half-smile she had flashed to me. She was funny. I have no evidence of this, but I imagine a gentle, self-deprecating wit. For most of her life she had worked as a legal secretary; everybody had liked her, and the humour must have been robust enough to make some sort of impression on the insurance industry as well. She adored animals, and had two rescued greyhounds and a fierce parrot that only she could approach. She collected waving cats. What? I have to imagine a shelf of cheerfully kitsch oriental ornaments. She was beautiful. Perhaps the priest means that she was a beautiful person, but I take it at face value. Jet black hair in a tiny ponytail. Dark eyes... As I am thinking about this Clare's cold, damp aura falls on me again, and I can no longer picture Nadia's delicate features, only the ruin of the accident. Clare seems to be muttering something banal, like, "such a shame." She seems closer to crying than I am and keeps up an inaudible mantra until the coffin slides forward, and Nadia disappears through the little door. I need to escape Clare soon. I turn around to look at Dan, and he is chatting amiably to one of his team as she makes sure of her handbag, and the *Pines of Rome* plays. I notice that all the rows behind Dan are empty... but now I see someone. Right at the very back is a woman in the act of rising, but head bowed right over. A glint of dusty sunlight as the door opens, and I follow; pushing past

Clare, and passing Dan's team who swivel their heads as one. I take long steps over the tiles and reach the door as it is swinging shut. A few seconds to locate the fleeing figure and now I run.

"Victoria!"

I shout this before the door creaks back to muffle it. I pound over the rough concrete of the car park and gain on her and can see that she is wearing jeans and a black blouse and dark glasses as a poor disguise. We're both all instinct as I accelerate through the garden, jumping borders and trampling flowers, water from the damp grass splashing my suit. The paths are narrow and wind crazily so that it feels like speeding over a model village, but now every time I catch sight of her she is further away, and I feel my heart pounding and my breath coming in gasps. But for a short time I have run as fast as I have ever run in my life. Away from the crematorium, away from Clare and work and cold reason. But Vicky has lost me; scurrying away as if she was hunted. My breath fails, and I have only chased her from where she wished to be. I no longer know why I have done this. Now I must walk back to the people coming from the chapel. I do not wish to speak to anyone, but if I must explain myself then it should be to Dan. The members of his team with him melt away at my approach.

"Let me give you a lift back." He says simply.

"No, I need a little space to think, to clear my head."

"That's fine then, Drew. What happened just now?"

"Did you see who that was?"

"I heard you call."

Slightly dizzy and unbalanced on the rough grass I lean towards him, and we embrace. Sharing our grief, me grateful to him for Hennie as a replacement for the troublesome Victoria. And I know it is for protection too; but the hug cannot last long enough to shield me from Clare. As Dan breaks free, I turn my back on her, but she tugs at my coat.

"Follow me, Drew," she says gently, but I know that she will lead me to nothing but her crappy car. "You walked here," she says in a tone between concern and accusation. "I'll give you a lift back."

The worst thing is when you are in debt to someone for a kindness you did not want. I follow Clare and hope that I do not throw up because of her old wallowing Vauxhall and erratic driving. I sit beside her all smiles and gratitude. There are no questions about my behaviour at the crematorium yet. That is deferred. The concerns are on a conveyor belt of difficulties to be dealt with in order.

"I understand that you are pressing ahead with the apology letters."

"Yes, I am."

"I thought that you might have discussed the wording with Dan because he was covering for my holiday."

"I discussed it with Gav."

"With Gav?"

She stabs at the brake, and the seatbelt digs into my chest. The unexpected traffic light changes, and we spurt forward.

"Well I definitely don't want these letters to go out automatically, considering what happened the last time."

Thinking about this and dealing with the changes in acceleration is like some aptitude test for astronauts.

"It would be a lot of work Clare, and I am confident things are all set to go."

"I'm anxious that we should be cautious and delay. I'll be back in on Friday and we'll review it then."

We lurch around a corner. "OK, Clare," I belch.

"Another thing. Was there a problem with the telephone numbers on the original letters?"

"No problem, Clare. We can cope with the queries."

So, Gav has had the chance to skewer me after all. Also, I have pressed the button to send the letters already, or rather I have had the slightly intimidating phone call with the confusingly precise guy in Document Solutions—or whatever they are called this month—to let them know what is to be done. Clare grinds to a halt to release me, and I sprint away to make another intimidating phone call, but first to find the nearest toilet.

Chapter Nine

Speeding into the night, lashed by the driving rain, the blurred lights ahead are beacons leading me to a risk that it is impossible to calculate. I swing out of the roundabout again and put my foot right down. Trust the lights.

The most terrifying experience of my life was a minor car accident. I was driving with Susie beside me and Gabby and Pippa in the back. We were on a country road close to home, a road I know well. I had slowed to a crawl, cautious of the blind bend ahead. Then somehow a growing sense that we were in danger—perhaps a streak of black had closed up the gaps in the trees ahead, or perhaps the engine noise had risen above the radio and my daughters' chatter. Once I saw the car all I could do was to lurch forward trying to drive further and further into the hedge. Then I waited to be hit. Violence is something we watch on film, distant and sanitised. When you actually feel it, Jesus, you know that you are mortal. I might have been thinking of Susie and the girls just before, but in the moment of impact I was concerned only for myself. A screech of brakes was the accompaniment to the pain of the seatbelt scoring my chest as I was jolted left and forward. My neck was locked, but behind me I heard Pippa crying and Gabby comforting her which broke me as surely as the crash. Susie climbed over my shaking legs and snatched open the back door. I remember stumbling out later to see her, smeared with the powder from the airbags, arms around her girls and confronting the car driver. He was a man in his early twenties and I shouted at him too, to connect with Susie. He was more willing to engage with me than my wife and daughters, and said that I had been in the middle of the road. When my voice suddenly failed he called me—in front of my family—weak and a festering pussy. In all of this the Multipla was not written off, and patched up and devalued, I still own it. It is my way back. To my colleagues' amusement I hardly ever use it, walking to work most days.

I do not like driving in the dark. Nadia had been travelling at about seventy when she had slammed into the bridge, according to the paper. Not the first bridge as she raced away from home, but I think I have the spot as I flick my eyes to the left, although there is nothing to mark it. One last time. I accelerate out of the roundabout yet again and overtake a lorry. Three bridges. One, two, three. What would it take? An insanely fine adjustment to the wheel, a movement controlled by the ghost of a thought, the twitch of a divining rod... Fuck! My wheels shake across the line, and I overcompensate, swerving back into the lane. Horns blare behind me. Sweat slowly cools on my back as I crawl home, my ears ringing with the sound of horns remembered and real. I park and freeze for twenty minutes outside my flat, and know that thought, that twitch on the Wymondham road has become the most terrifying moment of my life.

I make myself drive the next morning and arrive at work very early. I do not know on which desk Nadia would have placed pictures of her son; people and teams are constantly being moved and churned—to what purpose I'm not privy—but I wander into Dan's team's seats, and think about the woman. I am almost sure now.
"Morning, Drew."
Gav has got in even before me on his fucking fixie, and he has caught me, eyes closed, clinging to a foreign desk. I guiltily turn to him as he says,
"Drew, I've just taken a strange call from a good old Norfolk boy. He said he just wanted to let us know that he wasn't dead as far as he knew. He said that about five times, laughed like an idiot, and put the phone down."

"You got the details?" I bark.

"Of course, Drew, I did all the security checks before the call descended into farce."

He still has the member record on his screen. I look at the date of birth but have to do the calculation on my fingers. Within our range, one of our retirees. My blood freezes. But it may still be OK... I find our marker field, and it is empty.

"Fuck!"

"Do you know what's going on, Drew?"

"No."

"You look as though you might do. You look scared."

"I need to think... Have you touched the record?"

"Of course not."

I glare at him as if he has orchestrated this conspiracy.

"Well," he says, "perhaps we can legitimately say that we are distressed now."

Chapter Ten

Clare has her head in her hands.

"So, Drew, let me get this clear. We have written to six hundred and seventy people in terms that suggest they are dead."

"Yes, we have. Document Solutions got the instruction the wrong way round."

"I can't contemplate this. I really can't contemplate this at the moment."

I can't contemplate it either. What did it mean that Victoria ran from me at the funeral? Was she there because she recognised and understood Nadia's uncorrected flick of the wrist? Had she considered such a thing herself? But even these unnerving thoughts are not enough to shield me from Clare's intensity. Her head is in her hands not because she does not understand what has happened, but because she understands perfectly; the process and the consequences. I make my play.

"Clare, what we need to do is this. I'll speak to Document Solutions and ask them to do another run tonight, but this time sending letters to the records that show markers. My team are fully briefed as to the situation and are handling all the complaints very sensitively, and I am available to take over any calls if necessary. Unfortunately, the nature of the error has meant that the original complainants have received another letter and I'll be proactive and ring those people this evening—"

"Drew, Drew, with respect and apologies I'm taking this out of your hands. Dan can mop this up."

"I'll brief him."

"No, Drew, he's up to speed already."

The interview does not end here, but Clare is apparently lost for words, and we sit in silence. I want the chance to ring Document Solutions because I had prepared what to say to them, and had boldly told my team what I intended to say. I think back to what I talked about with Victoria in John Lewis. Is it possible that being in insurance can ever be as noble as being a musician or artist? If you do the right thing it could be. The right thing might be to resign now; but perhaps, for me, not to fight and to say nothing will be as dignified. Eventually Clare whispers,

"Go back and look after your team, Drew. We'll talk more about this later."

Her calmer tone hardly registers. Why is Victoria so afraid of me now? What is happening here beneath the surface?

"Drew?"

"Sorry, Clare, sorry."

I am surrounded by fog, a dense white vapour. Dan breathes this in and out with impunity because it is supposedly clean. Even so, he is exiled to the smoker's corner, and I am not entirely happy about sharing my lungs with his. The stuff is a pointless, tasteless cloud; pure glycerine, but Dan pretends he is savouring it. I am, though, grateful to be sharing these few minutes with him. As he talks the cloud around his face becomes denser.

"Drew, we might have to have another meaningful chat about resource."

"OK. Are you saying you want Hennie back?"

"Not especially, no."

Dan says this absolutely flatly. I want more from him: I want some mischief as if I was a schoolboy.

"That's good... What have you given me there? I can't make her out—"

"The girl who worked with her upstairs."

"Chantelle."

"I can use Chantelle if we have to start the project again from scratch. She has some knowledge of it."

"Well, yes."

"Thanks, Drew."

"I don't think it will be necessary to start all over again."

"It might be. Clare thinks so."

"Listen, I'd prefer to keep Chantelle. I have some resource issues of my own since we lost Jim, and all the phone calls are coming in to us."

"Let's see what happens."

"Dan, you can have Lucie."

He raises his eyebrows and blows more fog at me.

"Can you explain exactly what went wrong with the letters?"

"Clare told me that you knew," I say, resentful that he is not as up to speed as Clare believed. My understanding of the project was hard-won, and somehow I do not want his path to be easier.

"If you can share that would be good, Drew."

"OK," I say grudgingly, "what happened was—"

"A memo would be great. Just a one-pager."

"Dan, do you know why I ran from the funeral?"

"To find another bridge to throw up over? We heard you call to Victoria so I assume it was that."

"Did you know she was there?"

"Not a clue."

"She had dark glasses on and was trying to avoid everybody; I was worried about her."

"Drew. She had a perfect right to be there and a perfect right to privacy. She's mine now, and anyway are you a truant officer? A child catcher?"

"I thought that it was a dangerous situation for her to be in alone."

"Are you even sure it was her?"

"Of course."

This is a doubt too far, but Dan has confirmed my confusion about my reaction that day.

"Drew, have your free samples arrived yet?"

"There was something, a box of something, yes."

"Then get to work! Good times!"

I see that Dan is having a meeting with Document Solutions at his desk, all bonhomie and sketched flowcharts. No reference, apparently, to my complaint about their disastrous misunderstanding of my instructions, which was half of my one-page memo. A cacophony within my team. Phones ring relentlessly, and as people answer each call there is a rising volume as stress takes hold. In the brief lulls caused by unfathomable laws of probability a grumbling dissatisfaction amongst my people. I take the calls passed to me from the most insistent complainers, and after the first few I scarcely know what I'm saying, and my apologies are hollow. After a while I feel obliged to answer new calls, and feel the anger and indignation before I have the protection of saying that I am a manager. Sometimes the calls are about ordinary things, business as usual, and I have no idea what to do. I have to pass on these queries, diverting them to others who have been enjoying a brief respite from the pressure. Jane is a red, hissing mass of resentment. Chantelle is pale and panicked. I have lost them. Only Hennie works on, calm and unperturbed. I watch her type every detail of each call as she listens, intense and yet relaxed. She is my hope, the still centre, and her mythical boat has made an appearance in my dreams.

Chapter Eleven

A wherry is a type of antique sailing barge once used on the Norfolk Broads, but long extinct. It is highly unlikely that Hennie has one. What was sweet in the pub is bitter now.

"These shakes taste like fucking shit, Drew," Gav shouts across.

"What did I give you?"

"Strawberry."

"Try the vanilla." I throw a sachet.

"Anything else?"

"No." Pink or yellow shit, not that I have got beyond smelling them. "Try snorting it," I say.

Clare has intervened, and I have lost Chantelle. I can see her sitting with Dan's team. She has a permanent look of confusion on her face although this does not necessarily mean she is unhappy. In all of this Hennie has a holiday. It is annual leave agreed with Dan before she came to me, and I cannot resent it. It is an embarrassment because I misinterpreted her effusive goodbyes to the team on Friday, and thinking they were ironic had echoed them to everyone, having no memory of the arrangement. She had laughed at me. Yet I cannot be sorry she is not here to witness my failure, though perhaps she might have prevented it. In the masochistic corporate logic that embraces change I have been given Jake from Dan's team. He looks just as he did on the night out, neither more nor less intoxicated, and still waiting to be entertained. His slow exit from the company is my responsibility now.

"Jake," I say to him, "at nine those phones will go ballistic. Are you going to be on it?"

As if to emphasise this my own phone rings and interrupts us, although I suspect I would never get more than an inane grin from Jake. I have stopped taking calls from the team's phones because it seems to cause more problems than it solves, and no one picks up this one for me.

I once had a telephone conversation with a cat. I had answered a colleague's phone and a voice had announced,

"Mr Rupert Jolly wishes to speak with you."

Then silence. Not quite silence because I could somehow sense a presence on the line, that someone was still there, waiting. I got nothing from the cat, and nothing from his PA, my colleague's mother, but I held onto the call, waiting too. This is similar except perhaps more of a hint of a human presence, a breath like a fine sandpaper on wood and possibly a hand on a mute button.

"Hello, hello," I say, maybe wanting to prolong this easy work, or to relive the innocent hilarity of the call with the cat. Then a faint woman's voice.

"Drew…"

Then by the law associated with such things we talk at the same time, perfectly co-ordinated.

"Lucie?"
"Sick—"
"Are you OK—?"
"Ill, Drew—"
"What—?"
"Throwing up—"
"Today? —"
"All night, Drew—"

Another strange silence, although both of us know the other is there, then I say quickly, "Look after yourself, Lucie."

During this Gav has been preparing two lines of yellow powder in front of me with his entry card. The contents of the call have been obvious, and as soon as it is finished Jane spins around on her chair and says,

"You better not have poisoned her with those fucking shakes!"

And as soon as she says this and does not spin back I know that I have done just that. Gav realises this at the same moment.

"Brilliant. I have just drunk two."

I creep round to the bank of desks where my precious trainees sit and attempt to confiscate the sachets I handed out yesterday. I can only recover two and I think that I dealt six.

At nine-thirty my phone rings again, and I expect more news of the carnage wrought by my shakes. Instead,
"Hello."
"Hello."
"It's Jim."
"I know who you are, Jim."
But this is only met with a flat, "OK."

I am flustered because I had resolved to call Jim days ago but had not had the courage to do it. Whatever he has rung me for my nerves ensure that I launch into my prepared speech.

"Jim, I'm going to be there at the hearing next Tuesday. Clare can't prevent that. It's your right. We ought to meet up before to go over things if you can manage that—"

"Too late, Drew."
"Jim, I'm sorry. I'm sorry, I feel so bad about this"
"I mean that I'm not going to the hearing"
"You've got to."
"Not if I quit."
"Don't do that, Jim, we'll fight."
"It's no good. I'm not sure who I can trust."
"We could do with you back here, it's grim without you."
Then he says,
"By the way, I know who Nadia is now."

I hold the phone long past the time I am sure there is no one on the line. There is a paperwork problem for me now too. I am not sure I have all the details needed to process the resignation—I will need to talk to Clare. I almost call straight back. Something in Jim's tone has upset me and might change if I speak to him again.

Once Victoria had been sitting at her screen making small repetitive circles with her hand over the zoo cage of her workstation; opening and closing her mouth to vocalise alarming intakes of breath. Jim had come up behind with a spider he had crafted out of paperclips suspended from a chain of staples. That had done it. At once she had beamed at him and giggled. Always he gets the small things pitch-perfect, the spider just crude enough to be funny, and the gasp of shock stilling the automatic tics of Victoria's anxiety for that afternoon.

Surely Jim will be OK because he has the blessing of not caring about things. I grip the phone tighter and feel something beyond my failure and my concern for Jim. *I know who Nadia is now.* What did he mean by that? I put the receiver to my ear again, and protected by this, think about those words as I replay them in Jim's hollow, scared voice.

When I walk to see Clare there is always a fluttering in my stomach. This is different; all the butterflies are dead, sitting heavily. For now I know precisely what am going to confront. I push open the toilet door and call. Gav has been missing for twenty-five minutes, and Janet has told me to find him.

"Gav?"

Nothing at first then, "Drew, you bastard," then retching.

This is too technical and too difficult for me.

"I intend to embark on a course of Optimil Shakedown! *and have a few queries concerning nutrition."*

Somehow this has been diverted to my Facebook newsfeed, presumably by Dan, who has promised to find new leads for me. I have to hide my screen for this, but I need a relaxed, stress-free evening to survive, and so I must get this milkshake admin out of the way at work.

"Could you please outline what steps, if any, I need to follow to ensure:
1) an optimal calorie intake
2) daily recommended consumption of vitamins B12, C and D."

My friend, these will be the least of your concerns.

"In addition my father, aged 60, is a type II diabetic and is considering Optimil Shakedown! *as a means of weight control..."*

Clearly I am being set up here, and I will not answer these questions about my sugary toxin. There are easier queries.

"Is there a discount on bulk purchase? Emma."

Certainly there is Emma. I grab the screen as Jane looks in my direction. Perhaps she caught the reflection in the window; pink, not insurance corporate blue.

There is a way out of this. I know enough of the symptoms, crude as they are. The department can function without me for a day or two until I gather strength to defend myself and to resume looking after my team properly. When they are all well again I will stand with them. I run through it in my head,

"Clare, I've woken up not well...", "Clare, I've been throwing up all night, and I have diarrhoea too..."

But can I adequately mimic Lucie's sorry squeak or Gav's anguished rebuke? Wait. Something else. This is a mad idea, and I am afraid of it a little. But it is not a huge deception, rather a forcing of events to help myself—to save myself even. The consequences will not matter much, and the future will not diverge greatly from what might have happened anyway. The shock of the plan is never as great as when it first came into my head, and within half an hour I have accepted it as normal and easily done.

I lump the milk bottles about in the fridge until I find the one marked *D* in bold marker pen. It is just in date but disappointingly not as full as I remembered. As I pull it from the back there is a shower of possessive post-it notes. The sachet has no mechanism to open it, and I attack it with a keyring penknife then shake the pink contents into a plastic cup. There is not enough milk for a proper dilution, and I run the unpromising emulsion under the tap. The viscous contents coat the sides of the cup as I tilt it. Can I do this? "Hennie." I say out loud. In my flat, with crisp proseccos and bitter, hoppy beers I have toasted Hennie; revelling in the name and the sensations on my tongue, more alive to the moment than Victoria ever was in her mindfulness exercises.

"Oh God... Oh God!" I say as if I was in in my flat, private. I cannot get one-quarter of the way down the cup. This stuff tastes evil, as if it wants to do you harm. How can people be so desperate about health or body image that they inflict this on themselves? I wait one minute. "Nadia," I call and down the suicide cup to its gritty dregs. I feel as if I could legitimately leave work now. The stuff has not properly done its work on my digestive system, but it has a slimy finger on my gag reflex.

Queasy, I listen to my phone ring. Still no one will answer it for me. But when I pick it up I am overjoyed for a second.
"Hennie, I thought you were on holiday—"
"Well I am, Drew, but not away."
"Where..?"
"Norwich—"
The same collision of words as with Lucie.
"You're on your mobile."
"Yes."
"Where?"
"Norwich... Norwich, Drew."
"Good."
"Do you want me to come in?"
"No, not at all."
"I just rang to check whether there had been any news on my course."

Another treacherous diversion. I take a breath, and she lets me collect myself.

"What course is that, Hennie?"

"Preparation for Management?"

Another thing I'm supposed to know about, left over from Dan. I feel stupidly resentful of her ambition for a second, but then I have to think quickly.

"Hennie, I think that releasing you in the next few weeks is out of the question—you know the situation. But it should be possible to fix something up for next month."

"That's great, Drew."

This is a hollow conversation, echoing down the delayed line and distorted by my cheap office handset. I have an overwhelming desire to rescue something from it. She has been easily diverted from talk of the course, and perhaps that was just an excuse to ring.

"We're missing you here, Hennie," I say. Jane, sitting beside me, stirs from her work and tosses her head.

"I would come in—"

"That's not what I want—"

"Well I've cleared up all I need to do here—"

"Hennie, can we meet?" I whisper.

"Meet, Drew?" She says this as if it is a new idea for her.

"Supper," I say.

Silence lasting beyond the pauses of talking to a sick Lucie, who was possibly vomiting even as we spoke, and in my mind stretching into the realms of conversing with a cat. Then,

"That's kind, Drew, but I'm busy evenings this weekend."

"Fine."

Another pause. "Actually, I could do tonight—are you up for that, Drew?"

"Absolutely! Seven at the Star of India on Magdalen Street." I do not know where this ready-made invitation or command has come from, but I am anxious not to let her change her mind. "Bye, Hennie."

Now the line is dead, and I want to ring back to confirm the arrangement. How much have the sorry remnants of my team been able to pick up from my side of the conversation? Everything; and if I asked them they would be able to attest that I had a date with Hennie. Oh God. A churning in my stomach indistinguishable from excitement.

This is a game of who blinks first. I glance at Jane, and she is still working, eating through the paperwork now that the calls have stopped. There is no sign of any of her leaving rituals like the filling of a spreadsheet to prove how much she has done. I want to be away to get ready for Hennie, but I do not have the courage. Jane knows that she is pinning me here, I am sure. Across the room I notice Chantelle is here too, the rest of her team having left her. This is very strange and worrying, and I wonder what is behind it. I leave the silent rebuke of Jane and walk to stand over the girl. She is working quietly for Molly, her hair sweeping the document she is looking at.

"Chantelle?" She jumps a little then looks up at me and beams. "Do you want to be here?" I say.

"It's fine, Drew, " she smiles.

"How are things going in your new team?"

"Great!"

"I'm so glad you're happy."

"Yes, brilliant! She is not artful enough to modify her reply to save my feelings.

"I'm pleased, Chantelle." So, my cautious protection of her was excessive, but it has harmed nothing. Jane has been watching and listening to all of this and now resumes her work. I may not be on top of things technically, but my pastoral care is sound, and it is that I am mostly paid for. I walk back and stand beside Jane.

"Jane," I say gently, "how are things going?" She ignores me. "Jane?" Still nothing. I raise my voice, "Jane, talk to me." Silence, during which I notice that the pain in my stomach has reached a new level. "I'm sorry it has to be like this, Jane. We are all doing our best—"

If I thought her stony concentration on a work screen was a sign that I could take time to explain myself I was wrong. She spins around on a chair and spits out,

"You fucking prick, Drew, you lazy, weak prick! This is your fault! You're a fucking incompetent idiot!" No general announcement or pep talk for the department has been louder than this. "We are working our arses off, and you don't care. So much for the team!"

Chantelle here, no one else about as far as I know. What would Dan do? I want to retreat, but instead I take a step closer to the woman and bend forward.

"Jane, think about what you just said. I'm going to ask for an apology for that—"

A slap explodes across my left ear, and I reel backwards. When I recover Jane has turned around and is pretending to study the screen. Perhaps regret and embarrassment are at work, and I give them enough time.

"Jane, I don't blame you for your views." I whisper, "but you understand that—"

A lightning-fast hand and a stapler jack-knifes through the air to hit me in the mouth.

Chantelle's hair still touches her desk—I do not know what reaction I missed when I was in shock or waiting for a sign of remorse. Jane walks calmly past me, and whether she intends to return I do not know. I wait long enough for her to have barged her way through the revolving doors.

I take the stairs two at the time, but someone blocks my path down.

"Hi, Drew."

"Dan."

"Are you OK, Drew?"

"Brilliant." My pat on his elbow almost overbalances us down the stairs.

"Something good going on tonight? You seem in a rush."

Peter Kirk

My sickness he cannot see, but my injuries he might, and I turn and hurry away.

Chapter Twelve

A small cold pipette dripping. My nerves controlling the flow as surely as if my thumb was pressed against the stem. This cool sensation in my gut in contrast to the rest of my feverish body. I look at the tepid food on my plate. As I push the cubes of chicken from the shiny sauce bugs emerge in a small procession. They parade in size order, first woodlice and progressing to cockroaches. I blink and stuff the chunk of meat into my mouth.

I had been late. Always I'm early; to savour the excitement of anticipation, or else perhaps it is superstition, believing that I can squeeze the time back into the meeting allowing me to relish it properly, or think more clearly. No kiss on seeing each other, and in the moment I did not care because I was focused on my growing discomfort. A confusion of words as if we were still on the delayed phone line.
"Hennie—"
"Shall we ask for a table by the window?"
"—I'm sorry—"
"Drew, how are you—?"
"—Fine—"
Then I was paralysed, playing Jane's attack back in my head. I realise that almost certainly I have lost my job.

Hennie has hardly touched her food either, and I think that it must have arrived cold like mine. Not just cooling against a burning throat, but objectively cold, stone cold. She will think me weak for not complaining. Now that the pretence of enjoying good food together has gone the conversation is firmly anchored to milkshakes.

"It's all about this, Drew—I like this quote—'I'll give up a little of what others are enjoying now to find what they can only dream of later.'"

Is this to be all about self-help? Seeing my distress she smiles and says,

"It doesn't feel much like sacrifice. It really doesn't. I want this for you, Drew."

I am a project for her. Annoyingly she has driven here and is drinking iced water. Alcohol takes the edge from her sharp, analytical mind and softens her. She looks straight at me for fully half a minute. I do not know if she is seeing what I saw when I looked in the mirror straight after I arrived; my unruly hair, my reddened cheek and bloodied lip, my confusion and weakness. I think that she has found something even worse beyond these failings because there is a fierce intensity in her grey eyes. Then she does not say anything. An excruciating silence. It is most like the silence at a job interview when the board are waiting for your answer, though I have no question to respond to.

"Drew, remember that an arrow has to be pulled back before it can fly."

I have found nothing more than this sort of thing on her Facebook page. Slogans telling people how to live their lives. Nothing; as if there is a hidden profile somewhere where I might discover her weaknesses and fears, and pictures of her in unguarded moments, and clues as to how she lives her life.

The remorseless flow of the pipette has been slowed, but not stopped by my sitting down. Perhaps, in this cool business meeting, my companion has not noticed my growing physical discomfort, concerned only with my financial and intellectual well-being. There is a reassurance every time she looks straight at me and smiles, but also a jangling of my nerves and the chafing of what feels like a wound in my stomach. I can stand it no longer and push back my chair.

"Excuse me, Hennie," I say, but I am not sure whether I mumble this when I am close to her, or if I only voice it as I pass by cosy candlelit diners.

There is a trade-off between the time I spend in this cell and the time I can be with Hennie. Previously I don't believe I had the imagination to understand Victoria's struggle with Crohn's, but if it is this, lived out in a succession of public toilets, no wonder she is anxious and depressed. I must think about what I'm going to say to make the most of my time at the table. I need to start again, and I think back to the innocent couple in John Lewis getting to know each other in their amateurish way. I want this with Hennie.

She is wearing yellow linen trousers and a cream blouse, perhaps nothing very different from what she would wear to work. But there is the glint of a gold watch on her wrist, and maybe this has been specially chosen for this occasion, and I want this to be the case. Perhaps she is wearing a different perfume too.

"Do you like dogs?" I say. To back this up I have Poppy, Susie's chocolate Labrador, and a fund of inconsequential stories that I might be able to remember.

"Not particularly, Drew. I was savaged by one as a child."

"You're a cat person then?"

"Not that either, really." She bites her lip, and now it comes. "Drew, are you OK?"

Her voice is quiet, and she has laid her hands flat on the table, slowly opening them out, and she nods once to encourage me. But I squander this chance with an automatic response.

"Fine, Hennie."

"Are you sure? You seem stressed."

"I just hate that I was late for you. I was the only manager there, and I had to supervise Chantelle, who showed no sign of leaving."

In fact, I realise now, I had deserted her. Thank God Dan was on his way back.

"That's odd then, Drew. She usually flies home as soon as she can."

"You got on well with her, didn't you?"

"She's great. She looks about fourteen." I am reminded that my fate is in Chantelle's hands. "What, Drew? What do you think about Chantelle?"

"She's lovely."

"Very innocent. She likes you."

Is this the closest Hennie has come to teasing me? She waits for a reaction with an odd intensity.

"I've lost her, Hennie. Clare has taken her from the team."

"Dan told me. She'll be fine with him."

"She needs looking after a little bit. Did you know she has a daughter?"

"Yes. Extraordinary, lovely… And, Drew, I know that you have daughters too. Dan told me that as well."

Now my mind races along the wrong track, trying to catch the rogue thought that Hennie might be very close to Dan indeed. Then I realise that she is leading me to something that might be rich.

"Pippa and Gabby."

"How old?"

"Three and eight."

"Wonderful."

"It's just the most amazing thing to watch them grow…" Even in this I cannot trust myself to make sense, and I have to borrow from Chantelle about Molly. "So much they learn every day, so much that must be there already somehow."

Hennie smiles at me. I want to tell her every last thing about my daughters, but in this moment I cannot think of how to describe their beauty, their felicitous comments and achievements.

"I don't see them as often as I'd like," I bleat.

"I'm sorry, Drew, that's terrible."

Susie not altogether to blame for this of course. In my head I hear Dan gently suggesting that I am being stubborn, and I know that it is true. When I am ill, even more than when I am well, I understand that my default position is a passive-aggressive self-righteousness, and a drive to punish my wife through my children. It is a strange thought that Hennie may know this too. Dan's portrait of me may not have been painted just with the broad smears of my marriage breakdown, but as his relationship with Hennie, whatever it is, deepened, with fine dots coalescing to reveal my true nature.

"It's not an ideal situation."

"Oh, Drew."

I try to gauge her reaction to my family. Is it the instant delight of Chantelle, or a feigned interest to please me? Quite possibly things have escaped me. I know almost nothing about her, and this is more basic than pets.

"Do you have children, Hennie?"

"No."

"You're very young."

A cold silence, and I wonder in what way I have gone too far.

"Drew, I can't have children."

Brittle, she stares at me for a reaction. I do not know whether she wants a quick apology or slow sympathy. A waiter is at my elbow.

"We need a little more time," I say. I cannot leave her now, but I feel discomfort rising.

"Show me a picture of your family, Drew."

I do not think she wants this. "No, Hennie."

"When will you see them again?"

Panic. I have no time for this.

"Gabby's birthday is on Friday. Binoculars for bird watching."

"Smart girl. The wildlife is so rich on the Broads where I am."

"Excuse me, Hennie…"

I wonder if she was leading to an invitation, but I am already passing the cosy diners again and sensing their renewed resentment.

A pipe runs across the wall above me, covered in many layers of paint, so that it touches the wall along its length in beads of dirty cream. There is a drip from the pipe, seemingly coming from one of these beads, but close to a brass nut by the cistern. Once every twenty-three seconds apparently crystal-clear water falls onto the lino floor, and there is a brown accretion there. My time is being measured by this clock. Perhaps anything under that flow might be petrified like the slow process of a dropping well coating everything in chalk. The pipe must have been dripping for a long time, perhaps even for nine and a half years. Yes, I have been here before. Perhaps the toilet was not as rank then, or perhaps I did not notice it, or I did not visit. It was on that night that mine and Susie's love became perfect and unstoppable. Whether I could have said this with certainty on the long walk home I doubt for it was an excitement added to half a dozen thrilling after-work meetings, but looking back after hundreds of priceless days and nights the meal in this crappy restaurant was the turning point. We became relaxed in each other's company and easy with silences. She teased me mercilessly, and every time it was a new thrill. In summoning this place I had forgotten that the magic was not in the food or the decor but in what passed between Susie and I. So subtle and sensitive was the understanding between us I cannot remember any of the countless stupid little things that cemented our friendship and love, and it might have been that the dire surroundings was one of them. I have now bought Hennie here, and I do not think she finds me funny.

Heavy footsteps and the lock is rattled. I panic because I have not thought of anything else to say to Hennie and spontaneity is dangerous.

The sweet which we ordered is no more palatable than the main to me. As the silence grows again it is a matter of chance which of my current concerns I share with Hennie to try to establish some common ground or sympathy. Everything has equal currency in my febrile mind. I am about to tell her that two hours ago Jane hit me as we worked, but then something seems easier to form into a sentence and presents itself as a more generous gift to her.

"Hennie, I know that Nadia's death was suicide."

She looks at me, incredulous.

"Drew, we all believe that, but no one wants to say it. It doesn't need to be said. How difficult would it be for her family, her son in later years? Don't say it Drew, don't."

"I don't mean it as gossip. I just want to know what was behind it."

"Depression, Drew, but I feel uncomfortable even saying that."

"But she had a son."

"Luca was safe back in Italy, thank God."

"I mean what pushed her to leave him?"

She looks at me as if she is explaining death to a child.

"Drew, it's something we can't know. No one understands what can go wrong in people's minds. There doesn't have to be any reason, these things can just overtake you, and everything looks black."

Is this some sudden hint of vulnerability? My hand moves to cover hers, but she withdraws it.

"People blame her," I say. "I want to correct that."

She still talks to me as if I were a child, a naughty one.

"Drew, nobody blames her. Please stop."

Discomfort rising an alarmingly short time after my return. Not urgent yet, but I need to escape.

"Excuse me, Hennie."

The rate of drip from the pipe has increased when I was sure it would remain constant. Almost four times a minute now. By this clock time runs faster, and it makes me more anxious. For the first time I am sick, and I am reacquainted with the bugs. I must think of something to say, and I must make sense. I must tell Hennie about Victoria at the funeral and Jim's comment about Nadia. But I cannot escape this foul room yet. How much of this is the work of the milkshake and how much my own mind? I have to make it back to the table or else the woman will think she has been abandoned, but the drip of the pipe has been synchronised with the pipette in my guts, and I do not know how I will ever leave this place. My phone vibrates on the floor. It is Hennie. The insistent buzzing somehow enters my stomach, but at the same time it makes it imperative that I go back and throw myself on Hennie's mercy. I reject the call and stand. As I stumble into the restaurant my way is blocked. Hennie has her coat and mine.

"I've paid, Drew."

"I didn't mean you to do that. Let me give you something—"

"It's OK."

"I'll buy the next one."

It was raining when I arrived. Which way will things have gone, worse or clearing? Torrential. She walks quickly as if she is trying to lose me, and I find it difficult to keep up. I want to kiss her. At first I absolutely wanted to kiss her more than anything in the world. Now that the fast walk has jarred my guts and I am looking for an escape, to kiss her is a box to be ticked. Perhaps it is something to be enjoyed in retrospect, or perhaps her damp cheek and dripping hair will wash away thoughts of this horrible evening.

We reach her car and she says, "Can I give you a lift, Drew?"

This is out of the question; it is as much as I can do to stand still without giving away my distress, and I shake my head. She opens her car door, and I step forward. I am aware of her face screwed up against the rain, and the sodden wool of her coat and my chance is gone, and on the long walk home it seems impossible that I could have kissed her.

I am in the sanctuary of the file room. If my subconscious is really in control of my sickness then it is now punishing me by abating the symptoms. I woke at four and knew at once that I was well enough to come into work, and that I would have to come into work. Gav and Lucie have been resurrected too, and this would have been enough to condemn me for malingering. No fall-out yet from Jane's attack, but I am getting ready to defend myself. The sound of the door opening, and I flinch. Purposeful footsteps; not searching hesitantly for an ordered file but hunting for me. The long strides are advancing on me, past the avenue of racks, and I imagine eyes turning left and right. I reach for a file as my excuse and spin round. It is Hennie who has found me.

"Morning, Drew."

In my hiding place my mind leaps to some sinister conspiracy.

"Why are you here?"

"I thought you might need some help."

She steps a little way towards me. "Thank you for last night," she says, and I shake my head. "I don't believe that you were very well. And the text message was lovely."

At ten past five I had sent her the photos of my family she had asked for. I was trying to get back to that moment. Like a save point on a computer, the last good version before everything went wrong.

The only warning I have is that she gives a little glance behind her. Then she walks towards me and kisses me on the cheek. The kiss is so unexpected and illicit that I cannot savour it, but then her arms fold around me in a tight embrace.

Chapter Thirteen

Going home, scarily fast. Up to the red light and then no brakes, but a hop onto the pavement. A sharp noise which at first I thought was interference, then a confusion of sounds and images. A sudden, unexpected impression of fabric, right up close to the lens. Blinding sky then more rushing disjointed flashes; hard pavement, curb, car. This resolves itself into the clear road again, but then Dan, safe, spins his head and the camera finds the fast receding figure; standing firm, angry and staring straight back. In the last frames Dan spits the whistle from his mouth and roars, "Wanker!" These streets must be where he lives, but the camera is always turned off before he steers the bike to a shed or wall, leaps off and goes inside his house.

Hennie has done something remarkable for my recovering team. I do not know whether I discovered it by accident or if it was left for me to find, but on a desk was a pencil portrait of me. I think I have found them all now. Lucie on the phone, just a hint of exasperation in her averted eyes; Sam, seemingly completely baffled by a piece of paper; Gav smiling menacingly. These are not cartoons, but real likenesses, drawn with a remarkable economy. I think of my conversation with Victoria because they dignify routine work, not diminish it. Hennie has now moved on to groups, the composition and shapes somehow emphasising the team working together. She has told me with a grin that she does these at home, but I have caught her making darting movements over scraps of paper as the phones ring. I suppose that it is important that the team believes she is fully committed to the effort, but for my part, I would pay her to do this like a war artist. Everybody treasures their picture, even Jane. She has been caught in a flattering portrait showing her speed and diligence; mouse under her right hand and left fanning papers. Her hawkish eyes scanning the screen.

Jane has not spoken to me since she threw the stapler, nor I to her. Somehow the work gets done as it always did. I cannot tell how much she has shared with the team and how much they are acting as intermediaries between us to make sure that things go smoothly. This cannot go on: it is a time bomb. If my team become aware of the nature of our fight, or if the tension becomes obvious to Clare, then it is only a matter of time before I lose my job. For the moment, though, I am happy and relieved. To my surprise I have survived this, and perhaps I could survive much more. I am a good judge of character, I think. I knew that Jane would not go to Clare immediately like some sneaky schoolgirl. She is strong and self-contained, and it will be a much more considered thing for her. I do not, however, know if my fate is in my own hands or whether it depends on some whim or strategy of Jane's. I think that Chantelle is sound. She would be shy of getting me into trouble, of course, but I think that it is deeper than that. She has an innate sense of loyalty—I might flatter myself here. She might be first of all loyal to Jane or scared of her, but she seems to have a truer moral compass than some of those who at first sight more obviously belong in the adult world.

I have stolen my portrait from the whiteboard where it was pinned high to inspire the team. It is not unflattering. I am giving a briefing to everybody. My eyes, though, seem to slip between caring, concerned and downright worried. But it is something that Hennie sees in me, and I would hate it to be defaced. I want something of her too.

Chantelle is alone in the breakout room when I enter to get a coffee. It is one of those situations where you resolve to do something, but when the clear opportunity arises you are paralysed by second thoughts. She is hunched over a table, head bowed, and I do not know whether she is supposed to be here. I almost creep out without disturbing her, but I need the reassurance that she is on my side. I wish I had Jim's paperclip spider.

"Chantelle."

Not cathartic shock, not a momentary automatic reaction, but genuine, considered alarm from the girl. She throws her head up and stifles a cry. Alarm for me too because she is paper-pale, and her eyes are raw. She has been overtaken by a debilitating illness rather than the joyous exhaustion of caring for her daughter. I do not ask her how she is but what is wrong. At this she twists and attempts to push her chair further away, digging her back into the edge of the table. I say,

"I just wanted to thank you Chantelle."

A look of troubled incomprehension comes into her eyes as if she is panicked about my meaning. She tries to push away further and would push me away too, if she could. She is like a little girl herself; big tears begin to fall, and she draws a huge breath. It is an alarm call I cannot be associated with, and I leave quickly.

Chapter Fourteen

You, sir, are an entitled cock.
Prick giving cyclists a bad name.
Cunt suddenly realises he doesn't pay road tax and rides the pavement.
These opinions, and scores of dislikes, sully Dan's page after his last video. The supportive comments are no more decorative.
Wanker pedestrian owned.
Kill the fucking peds.
I watch the video again and almost comment; just two words. *Stay safe.* I have never commented before and have never even discussed these films with Dan—perhaps that would feel too much like stalking. "Stay safe.", though appeals to me in its reckless support of his hop onto the pavement and tangle with the aggrieved pedestrian. I do not type. Perhaps this is something I can talk about with Hennie, and we can make our mark together.

The gossip storm blows over me. I see averted stares and hear unfinished sentences as I arrive. Perhaps I can detect some code in the conversations I catch, and I try to piece them together and gauge how far they are from the truth. Hennie is completely unaffected and carries on as normal. She is warm towards me, but we have hardly seen each other alone since she sought me out in the file room. In my growing panic I need her, and she is the only person who might help me, but she has postponed one drinks invitation, and I dare not ask her again. And yet she has given me the most remarkable token. She has told me that she was orphaned at the age of six in South Africa; this in a whispered conversation at the printer. Perhaps she had meant to head off any clumsy enquiries from me, protecting herself from hurt during a discussion of weekend plans, but I treasure it as a precious confidence. A quick smile and she had gone.

When I pick the phone up I know immediately that there are new horrors ahead. Even before Clare speaks there is a hostile echo. The wretched woman has me on speakerphone.

"Drew," she says with an opening civility that barely conceals venom, "can I have a little of your time?"

"I'm busy at the moment," I say as an experiment. Perhaps I am bullish because I am ready to fight if this is about Hennie.

"Drew, I do need you up here now."

My impression is that there is more behind the echo than an empty office. She is sitting with her special team, showing her authority off to them.

"What's wrong, Clare?" I try to sound unconcerned. Obviously, I am not relaying this conversation to my own team, but I sense a growing interest. The woman's amplified, distorted voice booms, "Drew, have you heard of a BBC radio programme called *Money Box*?"

Clare's very special team are less adept at concealing their curiosity than mine, and I, whose roasting was broadcast to them a few minutes before, do a slow walk of shame to her desk. Dan has pulled up a chair beside Clare and exactly mirrors her concern as they pass letters to each other. I sit down in front of them. Clare has modulated her voice to a whisper, but it is not hard to determine that she would put a megaphone to her lips if she could, to gratify her expectant troops.

"Drew, was there another indicator on the records? I mean besides the retirement and death indicators?"

I struggle with this, but then say, "Yes. There was. A letter *C*. It meant—"

"And what did that denote?" she hisses.

"I think it was used for those people who have written to us initially." *C* for complaint. *C* for Chantelle. *C* for cockwomble. *C* for cockroach. It might have been any of these things.

"Would it not have been a good idea to share that information, Drew?"

In the impossible corporate aspirations of quality control, aeroplanes and pilots are often invoked as the model of unthinkable failure. I am more at home with the idea of trains and signalman. In my box, I had passed the express on to Dan, and it had been accepted. The signals and points had been set, and it was now up to my colleague to send it on its way safely. I feel I am on solid ground here because my offer to help Dan had been firmly rejected by Clare. I wait for Dan to say something in my defence or for Clare to realise that she is being unreasonable.

"The outcome, Drew, is that we have sent a third, nonsensical letter to the original complainants." My nerves are stretched tight, and I stifle the urge to laugh. I do not know whether she has caught me in this, but Clare's voice is rising steadily.

"The outcome, Drew, is that I have had an email from the BBC financial program *Money Box* asking for a response. This will go much higher than us, much higher."

If her words are still restrained for now, her gestures are not; a stab at Dan and I try to think what I had written in the one-page memo to him, which had ended with being much shorter than one page.

"This, Drew, is going to cost us a lot more than a few bunches of flowers." Her voice is back to unprofessional BBC broadcast levels. "If this is malicious, I will have your career!"

I look Dan straight in the eyes and will him to speak. I do not want to absolve myself from all of this; I want the fellowship of shared blame. He looks down and then resumes the synchronised pattern with Clare, frowns, and head shakes, perfectly in tune.

"Are you distracted in any way at the moment?" Clare resumes.

"No."

"Are you sure?" I do not think I could function away from Hennie now, however tenuous our link sometimes seems. "Are you sure, Drew!"

Dan, perfectly calm whispers, "Clare, I think we had better take this off-line." Never has this stupid phrase being put to better use. I leave, but Dan stays where he is, right beside Clare.

I do not know whether Dan got me this job. At the time I held this rather pleasing possibility in a fine balance with the satisfaction of believing that I might have won it on my own merits. Dan was not on the interviewing panel, but Clare had been, and I sensed that she had been fed information about me beyond my plain application. After months of watching them, I cannot work out the dynamic between Dan and his superior. She can show a strange deference to him sometimes, and yet in private he joins in with the cautious mockery of her by the rest of the management team, like children ridiculing a teacher. There is, though, a mutual respect there. When Dan and I worked together at Norwich Provincial we had no respect for anyone and were confident that we could do better than any of the fools in charge. This palls when you get older, of course, to be replaced by proper disappointment and ambition, and I was happy to catch Dan up in the real world.

I look across the desk at Clare, and a day later she is back to her unctuous self which is a hundred times worse than when she is properly angry. Perhaps I can understand her outburst because she was clearly stressed, but her usual two-faced self is largely unforgivable. She will by now have seen much more than she wanted to of the people she reports to, and perhaps she has encountered men and women whose reality is usually founded on terse email announcements sent to the whole company division. We do not touch on the mechanics of the new disaster, although I am curious. It is, though, so much worse than everything that has gone before because it has real financial implications and so it must have implications for me.

"Drew," she says, "I have to think what is best for you now."

I am silent and wait to hear what is best for me.

"I think that we can agree that these past weeks have not seen you at your finest. We have yet to see that. I still have confidence in you, Drew, and believe that you have a lot to give the company and the department, but... perhaps we need to release the pressure valves little bit. Short term. I think it would be a good move for you to get a broader view of the department's work—the nuts and bolts. That will be so valuable for your long-term career."

I know what this means.

"Clare, this can't be with my own team."

"No. It will be as a part of Dan's team."

I want to cry out. "Clare—"

"Drew, this has been decided. My reasons are that you have a good working relationship with Dan, and you will be very useful to his team. He will also be able to help and support you. I know that you are close personally."

Yes, we are close personally. When my marriage had begun to fail, I had confided in Dan and in no one else. This had seemed entirely natural, although our relationship has been strangely compartmentalised. He has met Susie and the girls once or twice, but I have never met Freya, and find it hard to imagine her existence. When I am reminded of her I can only bring to mind an exotic affair conducted behind the wall where he leaves his bike, and yet I know they have been married for nine years. When I confided with Dan about the rift in my marriage, it marked a new phase in our relationship, a leaving behind of our laddish past. Dan's response had been extraordinary. He had been quiet for the whole evening and then had shocked me with his sense and understanding. It is a platitude to say that a marriage should be saved for the sake of the children, but he went further.

"Drew, don't give up unless someone is going to get hurt."

"I might get hurt."

"Well, obviously, but that doesn't matter. Don't you see your wife in your children? Isn't that the idea that brought you together, even if you weren't consciously aware of it? Everything leading there. Don't you imagine that your wife sees you in her children? You're all the same stuff. If you can't communicate with Susie, then you are on the same wavelength as your daughters and they with your wife."

The idea of little Gabby, wise beyond her years, acting as some sort of unconscious emissary between Susie and I was so beguiling that I sometimes think about it now, and it is disorientating to realise that it is no longer relevant to my life.

I do not know what I am doing. The simple everyday tasks which make this business work are beyond me. Across the room I watch Gav. He is always on his feet, talking easily to Team Three, my team. When he calls them together I strain to hear him, and he veers effortlessly between the menacing and the relaxed, and I watch Hennie laughing. In team Two I sometimes ask for help, trying to explain myself affably and calmly. But often there is an assumption that I know more about the computer system than I do, and I must ask the same question again of someone else. I do not feel part of Dan's team. There is an assumption that I know more about bonding and social interaction than I do. Dan scarcely acknowledges me, and probably embarrassment is at work here rather than any management strategy. One person I do not go to for help is Chantelle. She is a zombie, a ghost who sits amongst us. She is less use than me. Over the past few days

Pictures of Our Children

I have watched her decline. When I was first dumped here I occasionally caught her smiling weakly at her colleagues, but now she stares at her desk, whether there are papers there or not. Today she has had long meetings with Dan and with Clare. It is inevitable that her collapse will lead to a catastrophic absence from work. Just like Victoria.

Dan has been unfailingly kind to me over the years. He is an extraordinary force within his team; they love him, and he gets the best from them. He is knowledgeable and can break every problem down into its un-scary component parts. He uses an ironic charm which seems to make him untouchable. "*You beautiful man!*" he will say of a new entrant who has done something well. He cares about everybody, and every indiscretion endears him more to everyone. There is a winning disconnect between his unguarded words and his actions sometimes. I have never doubted him.

I do not know what I am doing. I put frozen boxes into my trolley; a basket would be less mocking and ridiculous, but I cling to this. It was always a trolley with Susie, of course. I used to enjoy this, every kindness to make sure that Susie had an easier time of it. I pushed the trolley and distracted the girls from toys and sweets. Today I scarcely take note of what I am buying; it is mean, subsistence stuff, that is all. Cheap. As I back away from the freezer, not caring where I go, a woman stands in my way. She looks just long enough to give the impression that she recognises me, but I'm sure that I do not know her. Her eyes are into my trolley now, and her familiarity brings me back enough to register that she is about forty; plump and dowdy. I move out a long way to avoid this weird shopper, but she raises her eyes and looks expectantly, not initially in my direction but along the aisle. She wants someone else to see me, and when her eyes come back to mine it is almost as if she is trying to delay my progress with her stare. Is this a friend of Susie's? As I try to escape Dan joins us.

"Hello, Drew."

He had been dispatched to buy milk, and he clutches this now rather than toss it in with the other shopping.

"Drew, this is Freya."

She smiles at me, and probably she knows me well from photos and gossip. I had imagined Dan's partner as cold and steely; always, except for him. She extends a hand, wet from frozen peas.

"Drew, you must come and visit us and bring your little family."

Perhaps she is not as up to speed on my life as I thought. Dan is still clutching the milk, and she takes it from him and examines it.

"We need a better date. I'll take it back, and you can talk to your friend."

Dan has nothing to say to me, and I cannot make small talk. I grip the handle of my trolley. I never use the new handrail on the stairs at work now, though when it was first installed it was smooth and tactile. On the evening that Jane hit me I needed it and felt the silky aluminium spotted with unidentified sticky gobs.

"Dan, what have you done to Chantelle?"

"Drew?" A moment before he realises that this is not playful.

"The night I saw you on the stairs. Did you touch her?"

"No, Drew!"

"Are you pursuing her sexually?"

"Fuck off, Drew... Drew, Drew!" He takes my hand and squeezes it.

"Swear it, Dan!"

"I swear I haven't done anything to Chantelle and I'm not interested in her."

A flood of embarrassment as I cannot think clearly, and our grip is corrected to a handshake. A torrent of remorse as I look into his eyes. He says that he has not touched her. What else? Perhaps he has blamed her for the escalating farce of the retirement letters. Perhaps he has ensnared her in the pyramid scheme, which she certainly cannot afford. But I know in my very soul that there must be something more. Dan senses my doubt.

"Drew, I have not touched Chantelle, and I have no interest in her sexually."

An avalanche of excruciating mortification. But I do not believe him.

Chantelle, Victoria, Nadia. I am sure that some access and privileges have been electronically denied to me in a fury of un-ticking boxes. For one thing, I could not get into the building at ten to seven this morning and had to hang about waiting for the green light. I think I am early enough to avoid people, though, and I still have the physical key to the staff files cabinet. I have Chantelle's and Victoria's files in my hand, but Nadia's not there. This is strange; Jim's file remains even though he is no longer employed. But he is not dead of course. Much of Chantelle's file I wrote. That is not to say it constitutes a convincing biography. My predecessor felt no need to document anything, or else nothing happened. There is no reference to her child—she joined the company just six months after Molly was born. My own notes are clearly aimed at scapegoating her for the retirement project fiasco. Her reaction, reported by me of course, is apologetic and dignified. Then there is nothing. It is extraordinary that Dan has not documented the meetings which I know have happened recently. The last thing is a sick note. Depression and anxiety. Maybe Human Resources have more, and perhaps this is just the skeleton of the file. It is shocking that Victoria's file started off normally four years ago. She had previously been a trainee Legal Executive—I'm not sure what that is. Then for some time, as far as we were concerned, there were just notes of courses taken and tedious tick-box annual appraisals. I skim through the escalating symptoms, which culminate in my bleak assessments. Then nothing again. As with Chantelle there surely must be another file—perhaps Dan has his own, locked in a desk. Here is my relieved handover against the plastic clip, but no receipt. OK. I flick through the pages again, and my thumb pushes down hard on a little financial memo. Fifty pounds paid to Victoria for something or other. Probably not significant, but it can stand for Dan's grubby purchase of her. I now believe that my only friend abused all three women.

Chapter Fifteen

It impossible to pin Hennie's eyes down to blue or green. She smiles and opens them wide as if she knows I am engaged in this puzzle. It is amazing to watch her eat; not health-conscious, not faddy, not picky, not timid. Eating up life in my company. Large Wetherspoons' breakfasts at The Queen of Iceni. Cheap, and a free view of the river increasingly hedged round by luxury flats. I have eaten almost nothing for three days. Perhaps I am eating now to please Hennie, or perhaps my appetite has been tricked by this heady situation. There is no agenda for our meeting, and it was Hennie's idea. No milkshake business to be discussed, no self-help banalities and not the hideous pressure of a first date. Yet, when I am not distracted by Hennie's beauty, I agonise over whether I should reveal what I know about Dan. Sharing this secret might release me from the hell of isolated worry, but just to bathe in her company for a few hours might relax me enough to make the decision alone. Hennie goes upstairs to the toilet. I watch her as she climbs the open steps, graceful and smiling. When she comes back it will be a new conversation. I squirm as I remember the conversational cycles of our disastrous dinner. If I am as timid and inept now as I was then I will get no other chance. I have just a few minutes to decide what I will say... An excited flurry of pointing by the elderly couple on the next table. The waitress serving them looks at the river too.

"An otter," they all say to me.

I struggle to see it, but perhaps there is a circle of ripples near the opposite bank. Hennie is already standing by the table, and I divert her attention from the old couple to my own pointing.

"An otter," I say.

"Wow! So close to the city!"

Otters must be small currency for her on her boat, but she seems genuinely delighted and watches the creature as it brazenly emerges and walks along the bank, now certain of the appreciation of its audience. My first otter. A strange longing to be on Hennie's boat; but of course, here she is with me, laughing as I wave to the otter.

"Where now, Drew?"

Elation for me. The otter paddles his way towards the Broads and Hennie's mythical boat, and we head upstream to the Compleat Angler.

When Dan and I worked on this side of the city this pub was a place of birthday drinks and leaving parties—so many people I have never seen again. This morning it is a bright station on the river, the simple glazed annexe flooded with sunlight. We drink fruit cider. Hennie looks at her watch and says, "We have some entertainment if we want it, don't we?"

I have to make some adjustment for this as I realise that she is talking about a worry that has been blown far from the storm centre of my thoughts.

"Yes," I say. "Twelve, after the news."

"Are we going to listen? A big day. A big day for all of us, Drew." she declaims with mock gravity. I shake my head. "It might help. It can't be any worse than you imagine."

"No, Hennie."

So it takes place without us, a wound to be confronted after the anesthetised operation.

"Drew, don't worry. Everything will be OK."

I am overwhelmingly grateful to her, pretending that her words are meant to soothe a worry she knows nothing of. We sit in silence, and I wonder at the transformation that has left us completely at ease with each other, and has meant that when she touches my arm it is as natural a gesture as a shake of her head or a nod. Fifteen minutes after twelve and I know everything will be finished on *Money Box* because our story will surely have headlined. We still sit quietly as the aftershocks from lesser financial earthquakes vibrate unheard about our ears. This is comforting.

All of a sudden she drains her glass and stands up. I still have a lot of cider left, and trace patterns on the cold glass as if it is immovable from the table, as if it will keep her with me. She smiles and says,

"Come on!"

We are back in the pub with cobblers' tools hanging over our heads. The last, long swig of cider, when I realised that Hennie was not fleeing home, has given me a delicious hit. "Not your finest hour," Clare said, but I would live or die by that night now, for it is a night on which Hennie knew me and accepted me. Almost a language of touch with Hennie now—short taps for reassurance and longer touches to draw things out of me. Sometimes she reaches out, and I raise my arm to catch her touch. A squeeze of my wrist so emphatic that I want to tell her everything.

"Hennie, I need an amnesty on this, what I'm going to tell you. If I say anything stupid..."

"OK, Drew."

"Do you want to talk about Nadia again?" she says.

"Yes, partly."

"Well, that's fine, Drew."

Perhaps it is best to go from the start. A strange dissociation from it here.

"I watched this from the outside," I say. "I had no idea who Nadia was until just before she died. I didn't know her name until she died." Hennie listens intently but says nothing. "The first time I saw her I followed her through the revolving door at reception. She simply stopped. We were trapped there... I don't know how long that lasted. She had such an aura of sadness..."

She swigs her blood-red wine.

"Did you fall in love with her a bit?"

I sense she is not teasing me, like she did about Chantelle. "Yes," I say. "I don't know how that happened."

"Did you ever speak to her?"

"Never. She half-smiled at me once. Another door..."

"Oh, Drew."

"I want to understand why she took her own life on that road."

"We may never know; I mean that there may be no reason."

"But do you know Victoria who used to be in my team? You replaced her. Dan swapped you..."

She frowns, "Yes, I know who you mean."

"I've changed my mind about her. I doubted her a bit. More and more I get a sense that I've failed her..." My voice cracks.

"Drew, Drew." She kisses my forehead, and I stop talking.

In the light of the pub with bike parts on the walls Hennie's eyes are definitely, ridiculously green. I have been led here by Hennie, who took my arm through the Saturday crowds. We drink crazy orange cocktails, syrupy and bitter. Pedals cogs cables. Neither of us cycle, and I do not think we know why we are here. It is not clear whether these things are a celebration or ironic. Sword of Damocles lasts have been replaced by dangling handlebars, and it does not mean anything. I watch Hennie. Beautiful; animated then still, her spirit as impossible to pin down as the blue-green of her eyes. I will be as kind to this woman as I dare to be. She smiles at me and says the most perfect thing, here amongst the deconstructed bicycles and the deconstructed pub.

"Drew, nothing matters."

I test her, "Hennie, I poisoned my team with the milkshakes."

She rolls her eyes, "Don't talk business now! Aspirations are for another day!"

"I poisoned my team!"

She laughs and lays a hand on my arm. "Nothing matters, Drew."

For fifteen minutes nothing does matter; not my guilt, my isolation, not Dan's denial. It does not matter that Hennie doesn't understand about Nadia and Chantelle and Victoria. Then I am at the bar. I feel the reassuring shape of my wallet, but then I touch the other pocket. I look back at the table, and Hennie senses my unease.

"I've left my phone somewhere," I mouth. She does not understand, and I go back to her.

"I've lost my phone."

"Drew, don't worry, we'll retrace our steps."

"I don't care that much…"

"It will have slipped under a table."

"Nobody texts me except you. I'll get the drinks."

"Do that, Drew; I'll stick with you till you find it."

A slight air of panic, but we have almost managed to maintain the sense of unreality and dissociation. But I am desperate not to lose her.

Hennie looks into my eyes with an intensity that thrills me.

"Drew, I think that they have treated you shamefully."

We are not rushing this. "Your phone will be behind a bar somewhere," Hennie has reassured me, and we have ordered more red wine in the pub with cobblers' tools. It is not behind this bar, but I am more and more certain that I had it at breakfast and that we will walk lazily all the way back to Wetherspoons, calling anywhere that may or may not harbour my lost property.

"I brought this on myself."

"I don't know," she says thoughtfully. "But I can see that you are quite prepared to take the blame for all of it."

"How are the team?"

"Drew, I wish you were back."

"How is Gav doing?"

"Gav is a likeable prick, as he always has been. It's all a bit serious and intense at the moment. Gav and Lucie are at each other's throats a lot of the time. Lucie is a likeable, ambitious bitch as she always has been. You were a mediating figure."

"You mean that I was mediocre, lowest common denominator."

She grins. "Yes, exactly that, Drew. And we miss Jim for his stupidity. And we miss Chantelle for her gentleness and humility."

At Chantelle's name, my face has betrayed me because she says,

"Drew, what is really worrying you?" I shake my head, "Is it about Nadia?"

I prepare to defend myself, but she says, "And Victoria too. Somehow these women are linked? I understand now that you are concerned for Victoria."

I feel overwhelming happiness.

"Tell me if you can."

But in this moment, I draw back. An admirable coolness in her that makes me fear I will make a fool of myself again in trying to explain things and ruin this perfect day.

I watch as Hennie charms the boy behind the bar, asking about my phone and the Wi-Fi password. The Compleat Angler is as bright as it was when we left it and it is sweet cider again. When Hennie returns, she holds out her iPad.

"Let's listen; nothing can be as bad as what you've already been through."

I desperately want to please her, "OK," I say, though I am afraid of the grieving widows who may be lined up against us. She makes a determined face as she prods deliberately at the icons, pretending to be surprised when the announcer says, "And now, at just after midday *Money Box.*"

"Twelve. I would go back and change nothing."

Pictures of Our Children

What she means, I realise, is that she does not regret spending the time with me. An extraordinary use of words, playing with our back-and-forth Odyssey, which has me reappraising her as I did when I found out that she could draw. "Remember this is all us," she smiles. "All us."

Yes, we are the headline item, Hennie and me. The grave presenter intones our company name and Hennie gently takes my hand. I lean closer to hear the tiny speaker. It is inevitable that there should be an outraged member of the public, and here he is. Not a widow then, but his voice does climb to an alarmingly high register as he becomes more enraged, making him wonderfully ridiculous. Even now I am struggling to understand what has happened. Hennie shrugs and shakes her head too. He must have been an original complainant so there would have been a death somewhere and his record would have been marked with the infamous *C*. This plague cross would have subjected him to an assault by the relentless logic of computers and quirky human intervention.

"In one letter I was addressed as Mr Cuthbertson, deceased."

"Standard," I say solemnly. Hennie bites her lip, and I realise that she is trying to suppress giggles. It is, of course, Mr Cuthbertson's wife who has died. We had started all of this off by resurrecting her.

"It seems to me that the insurance company had no idea what they were doing." The man says, and Hennie splutters. "I was bombarded with a volley of increasingly bizarre missives..."

"Missives!" echoes Hennie, almost choking. The sense of inevitable climax is now compelling, and we both anticipate it and dare not look at each other. I hope that the apoplectic Mr Cuthbertson does not become actually deceased on air, or that his voice does not slip above a pitch only to be heard by bats.

"The final letter said..." Hennie squeezes my hand. "And I quote..." I can feel Hennie rocking gently. Now Mr

Cuthbertson adopts a staccato delivery, as if mimicking the printer firing out the letter. "And I quote... Dear deceased Mr insert surname... Please accept my apologies... You have not passed away... Cockwomble ... Pisspot... Valediction... That is all."

I look at Hennie and tears are streaming down her face. She pauses the radio stream.

"Did he say Pisspot! Cockwomble. Pisspot. Valediction. That. Is. All!"

My throat relaxes, and I laugh without restraint too, despite people staring at us; because this has been our show and they do not understand and cannot take it away from us. So, this ghost has been exorcised. By Hennie, and by the accident of a lost phone. I look at her, and suddenly her tears are indistinguishable from those of someone genuinely sobbing.

"Life is so shit, Drew," she whispers. "Everything goes wrong, and anything that can get screwed up is screwed up. All I wanted was to live quietly in the country. All I wanted was a child..."

People look away now, but I am transfixed by her, and by her sadness. Poor Mr Cuthbertson has been the catalyst for this; the strange, tattered fabric of his collection of letters woven on our broken loom.

I have ducked under the table at the Queen of Iceni, and Hennie, her face still stained with tears, bobs down and then up again. We have rehearsed this pantomime three times now in different places.

"I don't care about my phone so much," I call up to her. "Perhaps I left it at home or at work. I never look at it unless you ring me."

I sit down on the dusty carpet and wait. Another fleeting appearance by Hennie's face, upside down this time as if she is playing a game with a baby. So now in my mind, like a well-studied photograph, is the image of Hennie, framed, squinting at me sitting still under the table, tears running back into her eyes. It sits with the picture of Nadia in her glass case, the revolving door. I rise too quickly and bump my head. Hennie takes both of my hands in hers and looks concerned.

"Hennie, you've got to help me," I say.

"Drew?"

"Have you seen Chantelle lately?"

"Well, she cut me dead a few days ago as I held the door for her... No, that's not right. It was as if she didn't see me."

"She's had some sort of collapse, and I know the cause of that."

"Drew?"

"I left her alone. The night we had the meal. Jane had gone. As I was leaving I met Dan coming up the stairs—"

"Oh God, Drew."

Nothing else needed, and a frightening sensation of speed like an aeroplane racing to flight. She closes her eyes as if dizzy.

"Nadia, Victoria, Chantelle. All three?"

"Yes."

"Have you spoken to Chantelle?"

"She's terrified of me because I'm Dan's friend, just like Victoria was afraid of me."

Things fall into place now. One night I walked across the city to the library. Swan Lane. A small figure in front of me. She hesitates, and then an elbow goes up across her face, and she hurries by. It must have been Nadia. So, the last time I ever saw her she had tried to hide from me. That fear can only because she had associated me with Dan... Now Hennie says the most extraordinary thing.

"Nadia, Victoria, Chantelle," she breathes. "Do you think these women were vibrating in sympathy like wine glasses, or were they getting picked off one by one...?" My blood freezes. "God, Drew if we even half believe this then it has to be the police. I'll try to talk to Chantelle—"

"She'll trust you."

Peter Kirk

An overwhelming, mindless relief inseparable from the thrill of being with this amazing woman, and independent of its hateful origin. Fate has worked its way so perfectly. The lost phone, the journey back. At this moment I honestly believe that I have dropped my phone today; but at the same time, like the strange workings of quantum theory, I know that I might find it on the floor of the file room, where I sometimes hide.

Chapter Sixteen

I do not know what I am doing. I am in the middle of my real team, my own team. Bang in the middle measured by the expanse of carpet where I used to hold meetings. I turn three-sixty degrees. A coat over at Hennie's chair, but not hers. Suddenly I am pinned in a fork between Gav and Lucie, both competitively demanding to know what I want. I needed this to be discreet, but now the whole team are interested.

"Is Hennie about?"

"No, Drew," says Gav, "she's on a course."

"Thank you," I say, stepping back, but he wants more.

"Can I help?"

I turn to Lucie, "How long?"

"A week," she says. "It's in Bath. Managing people in an Insurance Environment. Can I help you, Drew?"

I turn and walk away. I am angry with Hennie for not telling me about the course, and with myself for misjudging the limits of her ambition. I stab at my new, inferior phone not bothering to conceal it.

Have you spoken to Chantelle?

The buzz of the phone comes while I am in the daily team meeting, Dan is sitting on his desk, calm and assured. People ask pointless or self-serving questions at the end, and I hate them all. The meeting dissolves into time-wasting stupidity as it always does, and even before Dan's jovial dismissal I dive back to my desk to look at the message. It needs to save me because I no longer know what to do. Short. No signature or kisses.

Drew you need to go to Clare

I no longer make a clear distinction between my professional and personal life. I brazenly check Facebook at my desk, and Hennie has posted nothing, and there is no secret message. On my own profile I am isolated, but it has become the hub of comments about milkshakes. Also, there is a hole in my bank account. Susie has a share, and now, inexplicably, milkshakes have a share. This is out of control. Back in the blue corporate world I compose an email as strident and attention-seeking as I can make it, for my own satisfaction. Flagged as high priority and titled urgent. Irrevocable.

Clare, I must see you ASAP.

"Did you hear the broadcast, Drew?"

"I don't want to talk about that Clare."

She misunderstands me. "It wasn't as bad as it might have been. We managed to retrieve the situation a little."

I wonder how she can possibly believe that the corporate evasion and half-truths of our response can have righted the situation we created. She is pretty. About thirty. Chestnut hair and blue eyes. Her smile, in another place, in different circumstances, might soften my heart. She is, however, contaminated in my eyes as if with the corporate colour blue, with a corporate pox, pockmarking her blushing skin.

"I'm so glad you came to see me, Drew. I've heard very good reports..." I am pleased that she is taking this conversation so far from reality that it will be as easy to deliver my message as if I was an actor. "Dan is very pleased with you and says that you are fitting in well with his crew."

Can there be any more proof that he is duplicitous and wants to divert me?

"How do you feel, Drew?"

"Clare, I just can't do this now."

"OK. On another occasion we'll sit down and chart your course. So it's something personal you wanted to see me about, Drew?"

"Not personal, no." She raises her eyebrows just slightly. An attractive woman who I am bound to by some variation of the master-servant relationship. No less absurd than Hennie and I sitting under the bike parts. Nothing matters and I deliver my lines.

"Clare, I have a real concern about Dan. I think that there might have been inappropriate behaviour towards Chantelle."

This bloodless accusation and the weasel word *inappropriate* seem good enough in the unreal moment, and good enough for Clare. She filters and absorbs the news.

"OK, Drew. "

"It might have been a word, or it might have been something much more than that. You will have seen how Chantelle is now… her behaviour."

Behaviour is a good corporate word. Behaviours would have been even better, but I can never bring myself to use it because it only seems suited to describing wild animals.

"Yes, it has been noticed. What evidence do you have for your feelings, apart from the shift in the pattern of Chantelle's behaviours?"

"One night, three weeks ago, I know that Dan was alone with Chantelle, and her collapse dates from exactly that date."

"You are great friends with Dan."

"Yes. I've asked him about it, and he denies everything. Chantelle, though, is afraid of me. Afraid of me as if Dan is standing at my shoulder."

Clare's reaction in this strange reality is one of quiet acceptance.

"OK, Drew."

"Clare, I also think that there is a link between this and Victoria and Nadia."

She nods slowly, and the poxy veil lifts from her skin, and I am sorry for her because I have shared this, and it is her responsibility now.

"OK. This must have been a burden for you. I am so glad you came to see me."

God, she knows already! Her quiet manner gives her away.

"Has anyone else had suspicions, Clare?"

"I can't tell you that, Drew, all I can say is that you have done the right thing. I'm going to have to ask you to sit tight for the moment. I'll move you when I can."

"Can it be back leading my own team?"

"No, it can't, I'm afraid. You are doing well, and I admire your resilience. I admire you even more now for your moral strength and your courage. But we are not there yet, not quite, and I hope that you understand that. It is a journey for you, but not necessarily a very long one. I have faith in you. You must let me take this burden from you at least. For me, it may not be such a difficult one."

"Do you mean that the police will be involved?"

"I need to look at everything."

"Will you tell Dan I spoke to you?"

"I don't know. I'm sorry."

"But I don't care."

I have the sensation that she wants to hug me.

"Have you been struggling with this alone?"

"Hennie knows. I told her."

"I won't ask the circumstances of that conversation…"

She has stepped out of character just a little way and smiles.

"Let's sit here for a bit, " she says, "Weighty matters."

She has a piping voice, like a child sometimes. I think about her journey from conscientious pen monitor to responsibility for a hundred employees and thousands of clients. I do not know whether I truly want the responsibility. Of course, I want to stick my head above the drudgery of day-to-day work. Sometimes I have an interest in people. When I'm with Hennie or with Susie I am ready to take on a challenge. Now I want the weight to be lifted from me.

A loud knock and Clare flinches, knowing what is coming next. Dan bursts in, used to the door being always open to him.

"Drew," he beams, "so sorry! Well CB what are we to do about the departmental next week? Do you want me to go ahead with the pension reform presentation?"

He uses her nickname. This is a cosy world I never see. Clare recovers well.

"Shelve it for now, Dan, in the light of events... We've been charting Drew's course." The rather pleasing phrase devalued by its reuse, revealing that it was probably not newly minted for me. Dan slaps me on the back. A revulsion and I almost recoil, but I put my arm around his shoulders as I stand up.

"Good man, Drew."

Clare looks on anxiously. Just before the door, I turn. I have the urge to jump over the cliff. Everything now please. Any number of things I could say to provoke the crisis; they flick through my mind as on a card index. I cannot catch them, and I am left with the thought of reciting the names. Nadia, Victoria, Chantelle. Clare looks panicked and says,

"We'll talk again soon, Drew."

I smile to reassure her. I am her creature now.

Hennie can I ring?
tired drew speak tomorrow

My new phone is failing me with emoticons, and my brain is failing me too.

Sure
place came up at the last minute, gav was v good
I saw Clare. She knew I think
oh god
All OK though

I want to tell her about how the ground had shifted a little for me in that meeting.

ring tomorrow drew
Have you spoken to C?
she won't answer
Try on the hotel phone
have done

I sense that she is becoming irritated with me, but in this plodding conversation, I find I love her even more than in her intoxicating, distracting presence. A love founded on dependency and longing, but urgent and real. Perhaps she's finished, but then;

I hate this course and I hate this hotel. Then; *I feel trapped*

Exactly what I was about to type, and I almost send this message and let her believe it had crossed with hers in the air. *I feel the same* isn't enough. An overwhelming sorrow for her, lonely and confused: a sorrow that lets me see myself too.

Sleep well x
xxx
xxx

Elation runs its course. I had wanted to tell Hennie about Clare, about how she had stepped just a little way out of character, and about her support. I had sat in her office and let her emolument wash over me. Now in the middle of the night my skin is cracked and bleeding and raw. I had been pleased with myself, but this does not feel like courage now, to have given everything to Clare. To have let myself be calmed and flattered. It does not feel like the model of the nobility of routine work that I had conjured for Victoria. Of all the appalling images that are in my head, it is the imagined scenes with Victoria which are the most distressing. Vicky. Damaged and vulnerable, not a prize to be sought, but a handy convenience for Dan.

Chapter Seventeen

Jane stands up and closes the blinds. It is a dull day. We are left with a half-light and a chill from the breeze rattling in. No one puts on the lights, but there is a murmur as if people are complaining about the darkness. My team, Dan's team, are on the opposite side of the room to Jane and the windows, separated by a wide aisle of blue carpet. We are all arranged in rows, some people sitting opposite each other, but no place in front of me. Further from the main door are two more opposed teams, and here too someone has taken it upon themselves to block out the light. We are close to the city, and the windows look out onto the multi-story car park attached to John Lewis. It is this that has been eclipsed by the dusty horizontal blinds. People close to me look at each other, and wonder what is going on. I do not feel able to speak or even look quizzically at my neighbour because I have not made friends here. On the other side of the aisle people are up from their seats. They move short distances, and news is being passed between them as in a colony of bees. Somehow, by osmosis, something crosses the carpet divide. People are whispering, and I strain to hear. Eventually I catch it: someone is on the car park roof.

I have not slept properly for days. I have in front of me work—a set of insurance renewal figures which I'm supposed to be reconciling. It means less and less to me now, but I keep returning to it as if it might help me to make sense of what is happening, or protect me from it. Something is going on: the outside is coming in. Dan is on the phone, the handset turned into his collar so that no one can hear what he is saying. He looks at the blinds and back at his collar. Clare bursts through the swing doors and rushes to Dan. They whisper urgently to each other, almost in an embrace. Suddenly Dan grabs his coat, and dials his mobile as he leaves. Nothing has ever looked so decisive here in this palace of false urgency. I am paralysed, looking at the renewal problem, but then I hear the whispers; Victoria, Victoria, Victoria! Hands on my shoulders still me as I try to rise. It is Clare, and she gives me a cold smile. As she releases her grip I am trembling. *Are these women vibrating in sympathy, or are they being picked off one by one?* Some people still work, tapping keys. The phones, of course, do not stop. It is apparent how many calls my old team are taking; they are embarrassing, like a noisy, troublesome toddler. Since *Money Box* they have been answering the avalanche of calls cautiously, but now their words must be particularly hard-won and careful. In less busy teams, teams who escaped my legacy, people have drawn chairs together and chat. An odd sense of excitement. Like Dan giving himself away, people sometimes look at the blinds as if they might suddenly become transparent, although everything is happening so high it would be hidden on our side of the room and only a tragic end would be visible. Clare patrols and polices us, but her little team upstairs will have a grandstand view. I look at my work; the numbers are sometimes meaningless, sometimes have extraordinary meaning. Life insurance sums assured. Whether they are wrong or right I have no idea, but they dance in front of me, multiplying up to become a good pension for loved ones. A phone rings on Dan's desk, and people rush to answer it, but it is all about work. "We have an incident here," someone tells London in a clumsy way. A few people stumble into this and wonder what is going on. Clare stalks up to them and hisses something stern as if everything was their fault. The timid girl clutching a yellow duplicate account form who retreats of her own accord. A purposeful woman dragging a vacuum cleaner who almost finds a power point before being accosted. The insurance family. Other than being on top of that windswept roof we are at the centre of things. For as long as Clare paces edgily about here Dan will have to come back, or at least phone her, and we will know. It strikes me that Victoria should be sitting at the desk opposite. I gave her away, and her's is the empty place. Chantelle is missing too, but her desk is claimed by brightly coloured stationery and a picture of Molly. I think that I would love to have Victoria opposite because she might find my fall from grace funny, and in time we would be friends... What if Victoria came through the doors first, not Dan? The girl receiving kisses and Dan handshakes and applause... I see her, at last breaking free of the embraces. She takes work from the pile, beams at me and picks up her pen... Jesus! I have almost slept.

I count the sirens. This has been going on for too long. The mood is changing. Not impatience, but the flavour of that. I have the impression that something has happened that I missed. If you are to meet someone there is a point when you know that they are not going to come. Suddenly the doors are kicked open. It is the most nauseating, disgusting gesture I have ever known. Dan has kicked the doors like an overburdened waiter. I do not know whether this was considered or whether it came upon him when he saw the waiting department through the long, narrow windows. Dan stands like a gunslinger in a saloon as the doors swing back behind him. It is Clare who must hurry to him. Everyone turns to watch. The second time a cold dread has settled on this space. Tears stand on Dan's cheeks, and every woman in the room wants to comfort him. People hug their friends. I think I hear... have I heard this, or have I synthesised it from the corporate lexicon? I think I hear,

"Not the outcome we would have wished for."

I want to let out a scream.

No garden for me this time. I creep in just before the service and take a seat right at the back. I think see I Hennie sitting with my old team, a long way in front and far over to the left. People bob out of the way, fidgeting or in prayer, and my sighting is confirmed by ash blonde hair spilling over her chair back. No one would guess the link between us, but we talked until three this morning, and now she knows everything. A shock for me as I try to collect myself—I notice that Jim is here, and he is sitting at the very front. An anesthetised numbness has stolen over me in the last few days, but the incongruity of Jim sitting with the family jolts me into thinking properly about Victoria, and I grab the back of the chair in front of me. At a wedding you can object, although it would take nerves of steel to wait for the time and protest. No such call for the truth here, although every word and every action calls out for it. A man turns to me and I must have vocalised something. But if Dan came through the doors next to me I would block his path, and that would be my just cause and my duty. The sinister motor of the hearse rumbles and the bastard has stayed away, thank God. But again, there comes an urge to get to my feet. A woman is officiating. I do not know what she is, a vicar or some humanist celebrant. She is struggling, and her voice wobbles and she coughs. There is nothing here. Words come out of her mouth and she chokes on them; perhaps she is uncomfortable with suicide. More likely she is lost because she did not know Victoria at all. There has been some catastrophic failure in communication with the family, perhaps a trap set by grief, and she has no steady centre to cling to. For a start she has mistaken our profession. If our department gets to deal with real members of the public it is by accident or mischance. Victoria never had the opportunity to be kind to ordinary insured people, bereaved or otherwise. "I'm sorry I can't discuss this with you," she was trained to say. The closest she came would be calls from brokers, and then she was as relaxed and obliging as a cornered hare. The woman has mistaken Vicky's social interactions too. Open and giving. Not so much. Victoria's friends had been worn down by attrition to a faithful few. People she was close to were bound tightly to her by a precious undemanding love. Now the woman falters altogether because she has nothing more. Dust from her restless hands, ash from her stuttering mouth. A reading from my inadequate file notes would have made more sense and carried more meaning. Suddenly a disturbance at the front, an abrupt outbreak like a fight in a pub. Chair against floor. Someone has stood as if to cry out, but then he rushes down the aisle towards me. For a moment Jim looks straight into my eyes; crying, angry, frightened. Now his frantic march is accompanied by blaring, distorted music which has rescued the woman whose throat has been closed by uncertainty. I follow Jim at once, through the doors which have been slammed in my face. In the light nothing as my eyes adjust. I look left and right and then follow the chapel wall, trampling the uncut grass and grazing my hand on the flint. At the corner I expect clear distance between Jim and me, but he has stopped dead, body jack-knifed double, and I almost collide with him. He pulls himself up and we run again, but then his legs fail, and he hugs the buttress of the chimney. His face is a parody of his old self, puffy and sneering, a joke foam mask. But before this descent he had somehow become close to Victoria. His wild eyes make me step back.

"Jim listen to me—"

He lunges at me and grabs my lapel. "You fucking cunt, Drew!"

I yell out, but we are alone. His fist goes back.

"Jim, I know everything! Go to the police!" The fist drops and I wonder whether it could have had the power to hurt me. I want to pull him into an embrace. "I know about Victoria. I know about Nadia. Go to the police, Jim."

"I can't, and you don't know!"

One last look at him before I flee. He is kicking over a patch of soil. I should go back. Perhaps he believes that Dan abused Victoria. I could tell him he did not, but that comfort would be relative.

Jane closes the office blinds on a dull day. She does this to protect us, and to exert her motherly authority. The outside is coming in. Now thoughts strike like bursts of music in the dark, jarring and potent. I have work in front of me, and Dan has given it to me because it is difficult and overdue and will cripple me. As it becomes more opaque and irrelevant, so the moment becomes clearer and more pressing. The team in the far corner begin to haul up their blinds, but Jane stands up and glares at them, and the slats tumble as if the cord had been cut. The crash and the darkness and my mind comes even more alive. I know that it is Victoria on the roof before the whispers. It is not a stranger, but one of us, to teach us a lesson. Dan leaves, the centre of the story. Clare pushes me down into my seat, but I have some authority here, or at least some free will, and I stride over to the team across the aisle. My rightful team. I pull down a slat as hard as if to break it. And I see her. I think I do. No more than an impression of a white dress, or a wisp of hair above the parapet. People lined up to her right, so still at first that I thought they were the posts of a broken barrier. One of these jagged dark shapes is Dan. Then she is gone. "Come away!" someone hisses and I comply. But I saw her, and I see her every minute. A word or a gesture from Dan and she was gone. On her heels like a sprinter from the starting gun. As straight as she could, hurting herself on cars, accelerating over unused parking spaces and roadways. And, when she had come to the opposite wall, no hesitation. The end of her anxiety, her Crohn's, her quiet grace.

We wait. Then Dan kicks the doors. They swing shut behind him as he wallows in the acclaim for his heroic intervention. I want to spit on him: a sin as heinous as murder in this corporate cocoon. If he comes to speak to me privately I will scream into his face that he killed her. As everyone hugs each other I stab at the keys of my calculator. Thoughts hit me now not like bursts of music, but like tolling bells, discordant and deafening.

I remember Cologne Cathedral. How the sound had poured down the cold stone spiral staircase and terrified us.

Susie, yes, but me even more. And Gabby was much too young, and we had abandoned the climb even before the bell had caught us. Huge tears coursing down her face and a single tear from Susie, looking as young as I had ever seen her. We lied to our daughter that this was a once in a lifetime thing, that bell, for us who were retreating from it. But little Gabby knew that there would be other bells, and other shocks, and on the treacherous way down we mourned her loss of innocence as we fought to comfort her.

Are these women vibrating in sympathy? I can feel Victoria trembling as if I had reached out to her across the table at John Lewis. Nadia. Nadia in her glass case, trapped. Chantelle. In the supermarket Dan had denied he wanted her. I think of his hurt, watering eyes and his embrace over and over again. I do not believe him, I do not believe him. But something else. Dan's wife blocking my way, staring at me, staring into my trolley. Dan makes the introduction. Dan and his wife staring into my trolley. Nothing there, hardly. I see my empty trolley and the empty child seat... A bell so loud and deep that it resonates in my gut. They want Chantelle's baby.

Chapter Eighteen

Perhaps they want my babies too. I pull Gabby closer to me. She resists slightly as she is intent on fiddling with her new binoculars. They are lightweight, a smart blue colour, and in a proper leather case. They are grown up, but the focusing wheel and the zoom function have not defeated her, and she trains them on a boat far out to sea. They are not the binoculars I bought. Susie got there first. My childish pair weigh down my rucksack, wrapped in pug paper. Pippa wants a look too, and this early in the day she and Gabby are still firm friends. The angle is adjusted, and the rubber cups gently applied to Pippa's eyes.

"If the sun ever shines again you must be careful," I say.

Gabby rolls her eyes, "I know Dad!"

Pippa smiles at whatever it is she can see.

"Who are we waiting for again?" Gabby says.

"Well, Gabs, we're not strictly waiting for anyone because they're not late." She rolls her eyes again at this semantic nonsense. "Her name is Henrietta. She lives on a boat."

"OK. What are we going to do?"

"Well, I thought the aquarium—but as it's your birthday treat you can choose anything you like."

A slightly troubled look that I have learnt to recognise, but that she would never acknowledge.

"Yes, it's your birthday treat, Gabs, but there is a present as well, and I'm sorry it's so late."

Released from this concern she smiles, and Pippa snuggles up against me, shielding herself from the cold breeze and slight drizzle. This is Great Yarmouth. When Susie and I came here it was always with a knowing sense of irony specially honed for this brash, trashy place. Gabby cannot hope to understand this… but then she seems to come close as she looks around,

Pictures of Our Children

biting her lip, pulling a face and laughing. Pippa, contented and stoical, will put up with anything.

Hennie is beaming and waving as I catch sight of her, and it is possible that Gabby and Pippa noticed her before I did. She has chosen to come by train and has walked from the station, damp but not sodden. Of course, she does not kiss me, and the first thing she does is to extend a hand to Gabby.

"Pleased to meet you, Gabrielle."

Gabby is pleased with this grown-up formality and delights in pronouncing Henrietta very carefully. Pippa wants to be like her sister, and the greeting is repeated several times and turned into a game. Then a hand on my shoulder, and I think that the arrangement that I have regretted and feared ever since I made it might be OK after all. People get on with things because of their children. Grief is properly curtailed, and everything put into perspective. The rawness of Victoria's death has been settled by Hennie's touch. There are many things I want to talk to her about, but they must take second place.

"An octopus!"

I am always wary of hastily interpreting my eldest daughter's reactions, but this is said with some vehemence.

"Are you scared, Gabby?"

"Of course not!"

Something is troubling her though, as she looks at the picture in the aquarium foyer. Like an errant octopus Pippa has her hand in the tray of plastic sea creatures beside us. A smile and a look of intense concentration, and then delight as if she is tasting them with her fingers. I will need to buy her something if Gabby gets her present, and it might as well be all of this. There is nothing suitable for Gabby here, although I would buy her the whole gift shop if she wanted it. Pippa's hands can hold a surprising number of fish, but I do not count them as I pay. I look over my shoulder, and Gabrielle and Hennie are engaged in an earnest conversation. Gabby is using

118

the extravagant gestures of an orchestral conductor, as she does when she is explaining something important. Hennie nods gently and looks intense, as I have often seen her. When I return Hennie says,

"Drew, we have another plan," and smiles at Gabby, "You see, octopuses are very clever creatures, and we don't know whether this one will be happy to see us and all these people."

Gabby nods enthusiastically, and to illustrate the point plucks an octopus from the sea life spilling from her sister's hands and makes it do a little dance. Then it swims free.

"We could take a boat out to see the seals," Hennie says.

"It's raining, Hennie."

"What does that matter?"

"What does that matter!" my daughters chorus.

So, the day becomes an expedition, and the rain is no longer important. Gabby sits right at the front and trails her arm so that her fingers sometimes brush the sea. Then she will place her cold hand on her sister's cheek, or flick water at us, and Pippa will giggle. When we get near to the sandbank, Gabby turns her binoculars on the seals and their pups. Every new natural thing brings wonder for her, and will forever. For myself, I hate water and sit well back.

My daughters are fearless today. They run and launch themselves from the path onto the damp sand below. I fret, but Hennie says, "Relax, Drew." Then she pretends to wince with every leap. She turns and looks at an elderly couple, who might be having disapproving thoughts about my childrens' exuberance. She smiles, and they smile back and return to their cream tea.

"You must go on the Snails!"

A timid little roller coaster, humps and bumps. Too much for me, though. Gabby and Pippa love it, of course, holding on to each other and shrieking. The Snails at Great Yarmouth.

Pictures of Our Children

Every mother in Norfolk seems to claim this as part of their family tradition, but I am from Leeds, so I don't know. Even Hennie says, "You must go on the Snails!" But she was brought up in South Africa, so it is unlikely that they were part of her childhood history either. Perhaps we are building a tradition here. Maybe this day will stretch into the future, and possibly shine its light on generations to come. For the moment I'm thrilled to have Hennie at my side shouting, "Hello!" to my girls every time they come round.

"Drew, things will get back to normal."

"With Dan suspended I'm happy."

"Quite... Wave!"

It is the Teacups now, after the Snails. Hennie and I whisper when my daughters are on the far side of the roundabout, and smile to greet them back again.

"Hennie, I want to write to Victoria's family."

"That would be good, after that crappy funeral."

"What would I say? I feel I could have saved her."

"Drew, Drew!"

"Hi, Gabs! Hi, Willipa!"

"Everybody's safe."

"Chantelle and Molly safe?"

"Every few days I try Chantelle. She won't answer."

"Christ, I hope she's gone to the police."

"The police will have found her. I'll text her a picture of the Snails. She might respond to that."

I do not know whether she is serious, but she holds her phone for a picture of the Teacups too.

"She'll like that, Hennie."

The next time my daughters come round the cup has swung away so that I cannot see them, but Gabby holds her hand over the rim as if to reassure me.

"Did Dan succeed in any way?"

"Nadia's son was safe back in Italy. She protected him."

"Oh God, Hennie."

"Drew, we can't do anything more."
She touches my hand and pinches it.
"I can give a statement," I say.
"Slowly back to normal."
I do not know how long these things go on for, for a fiver.
"Jesus! I need a present for Gabby."
"Wave! No, you don't. The day is complete."
"I'll find a shop."
"She loves you! It's not a competition."
"I promised her."
Hennie brushes her hair away from her neck and fiddles with something under her silk scarf. I do not know what I am holding. It may be gold or it may be plated base metal for which designers can get away with charging the earth. It is wonderful. A simple representation of a shell on a fine chain. I have it just in time for the roundabout to deliver my daughters right alongside us.
"Close your eyes, Gabby."
"Happy birthday!"
I fail to secure the tricky catch before Gabby opens her eyes, and she lets the thing fall into her own hands.
"Wow!"
The beautiful, grown-up jewellery excites her, and she sings.

I pull up not quite outside Susie's house for some reason. When I return after giving back my girls, Hennie says,
"Your daughters are beautiful—and smart."
Nothing back like this from Gabby and Pippa about Hennie, but there had been an immediate, natural acceptance and perhaps a hint of imitation. Pippa a little more gently mischievous and Gabby even more self-assured than normal. These lovely developments would have happened anyway, but certainly both girls kept calling, "We have another plan!" throughout the day.

As for Hennie, she was amazing. But this is killing her. I say,

"Fantastic day. Thank you so much, Hennie. Now home."

"No, Drew," she whispers. "Norwich Station please. Tired."

Perhaps the train was a plan to escape me as soon as possible. But then she recklessly kisses me. And we cling to each other in the dark, while inside Susie welcomes Gabby and Pippa home. But around Gabby's neck, with her new binoculars, my girlfriend's exquisite necklace.

"Drew, are you sure you want this? You have so much to lose."

"Hennie, there's no going back."

"You must see your children more often! Fuck!"

"I know."

"I can give you nothing. You understand that."

"Yes, Hennie."

"I had an operation when I was twenty. I almost died."

I pull her towards me again, my mind flooded with thoughts of her possible destruction before I met her and of the intimate scar I have not yet seen.

Chapter Nineteen

"Hello."
"Hello."
"Hello. Who is this?"
"Hello, Drew, It's Lucie. I'm here temporarily while Dan is away."
This is new. I was expecting Clare, who has been fussing around the team ever since Dan's removal. Evidently the flood of jealous ambition when Gav was appointed in my place has served Lucie well.
"Congratulations, Lucie."
"Thank you. How can I help?"
"I'm afraid I'm not going to be in today." I go through my list of options. Because it is Lucie, I find myself saying, "Sickness and diarrhoea."
A pause as she goes through her list of options too.
"Take care of yourself then, Drew."

Clare is plainly nervous of the man she is sitting next to. I cannot understand this. She has all the mechanisms and tricks for coping with superiors, the hint of deference—never too much—the confident spouting of facts. Perhaps it is guilt, but surely he can have no interest in her private anguish—that she let Dan have his head that morning, allowing him to chase Victoria off the roof. This is an office I have never seen before in my peripatetic career of awkward interviews. Detective Inspector Ulph has been contained here. It is as if he has curated it so that the air of gloom and unreality on the morning of Victoria's death has been preserved, like a crime scene. There are slogans on the whiteboard, to whip up new entrants or to beat the heads of the time served. They die here. The policeman seems oddly at home. Clare does not like him, and I do not like him. He reads my statement as if he means to criticise my presentation, and it takes much less than this now to cause my confidence to evaporate. But I have not offered him some fuzzy, heat of the moment eye-witness account confusing the height and clothes of the suspects. He has from me the description of a friendship, and the final destruction of that friendship. Moreover, I have given him the link between the three women. I have spent the night with this, and each word has been hard-won.

Hennie has been no help. She has answered the phone, often tired and brittle, but her mantra is always *slowly back to normal, Drew.* No. Everything has become strange and disorientating. If Hennie wants to put a brake on our conversation she has only to mention protein shakes. I kicked my boxes under my bed weeks ago and had forgotten them.
"There's a new opportunity, Drew..."
If she means because of Dan, then I am appalled. Last night I had ploughed through this ice, and when I had talked about Chantelle she had said,
"Drew, we must leave this to the police. We can't be sure that everything we believe is exactly true or would stand up in court."
"But you do believe it?"
"I believe something happened."
"Christ, Hennie!"
"Slowly back to normal, Drew."

The sinister policeman looks up when he has finished reading.
 Can I clarify your position?"
"My position?"
"Your position within the organisation."
"Manager." I look at Clare. "Yes, manager."
He knows my job title, and has said this only to discomfort me.

"But without special responsibility at the moment."

"Yes."

"At the time of the incident which forms the crux of your statement, you were indeed in charge of a team."

"Yes."

"This young woman, Chantelle Dowson, was left alone in the department?"

"I thought that a senior member of my team was also working." This is not true. I had every reason to suppose that Jane had stormed through the revolving doors, but it should not be me on trial here. I wonder if Clare should leave us alone to prevent this having the atmosphere of a disciplinary hearing. It is as if she is my tribunal friend, ready to help me out, and I do not want this.

"And in that space you created, some improper approach was made to the young woman."

"Have you spoken to Chantelle?"

"You know I can't tell you that."

"I don't know it..."

Clare looks alarmed, and I stop.

Detective Inspector Ulph. Hollow cheeks and questioning eyes. Tall and lean, about fifty. I had imagined this interview with a bright, sympathetic woman, but I am dealing with someone strangely aloof and distant from the horror of the situation.

"It is the case, is it not, that your direction on this has changed since you first raised concerns to your manager? Then, you were alleging rape or sexual assault of the young woman."

"Now I believe a proposition was made concerning Chantelle's daughter."

"From your statement, this is all a bit nebulous."

"Rape or sexual assault of her baby," I say.

Clare screws up her eyes. Ulph makes an involuntary fist on the desk.

"Whoa!" he says. "What I mean is that the evidence for such an allegation is not clear."

"Everything is clear to me," I say, increasingly irritated, and made recklessly bold by his reactions. "The evidence for court is your job. Many people must have suspected what was happening. Also, I know that Nadia's suicide was as a result of a threat to her child. Dan and his wife were complicit in that too. Victoria, for one, knew what was going on. She was terrified of Dan."

"Ah, we come to Victoria," says Ulph, after a strange pause in which he seems to be catching up, or else deliberately slowing me. He fans his papers, pats them back into his ordered pile, then riffles them like a pack of cards. "She had grave mental health problems, yes?"

"How could she not?"

Ulph and Clare exchange glances, a silent review of the situation. Whatever influence she is having on this meeting Clare should not be here. In the formal interview I will think more clearly.

"When I need more I'll be in touch," the man says suddenly.

Nothing else happens. Clare and the policeman beat me towards the door with their stares. No encouragement, no reassurance. I see now that Clare had managed my expectations for this meeting,

"Just drop by with the statement, Drew," she had said, as if it was business as usual.

Now their business must be to talk about Dan. And about me.

Lucie, in this bright east-facing room is much less deep, and to me, much more transparent, in her role as police officer.

"There are certain issues we need to address, Drew."

"Fine, Lucie." She flicks through her file, perhaps wondering where to start. "Well done again for the promotion. You deserved it."

"But it is only temporary until Dan is back."

I do not know whether she believes this, or is maintaining the fiction for my benefit. If this is subterfuge, then she really will be a good manager. Now she has decided which missile to fire first.

"Your absence record, Drew…"

She is helped and speeded in this by the corporate apparatus, which codifies and clouds the issue. It is a little time, however, before I realise that she really does have her claws into me. There is a little formula which calculates the level of my transgression. I have got it wrong, of course, because the model favours great swathes of absence rather than the little nibbles that I have been taking. She marshals this evidence, and rebukes me in a strangely formulaic way.

"Drew, you understand that this situation is not satisfactory."

With Ulph I had felt the need to rebel just a little, but for Lucie I say nothing. She has another piece of paper, and has actually taken the trouble to hand-write this one. Training needs. This is a category of tasks I have been too lazy or too stupid to master. I listen, and I watch her, fascinated. Toward the end of each prepared section her speech accelerates like the garbled terms and conditions of a radio advert. In the headlong dash towards the conclusion of the interview I catch that my status is now *Not meeting expectations*.

"Are there any issues that you wish to raise, Drew?

"Lucie, if there is any particular thing you would like me to say then I will say it."

I want her to step outside of this, to feel the same thrill that I did with Clare, knowing that nothing matters. No such thing comes back from Lucie. Clare must have sanctioned this meeting, and I suddenly realise that I have lost her protection.

Pictures of Our Children

Jesus. I do not care for myself but for Gabrielle, Pippa and Susie, this might be disaster.

Monday morning, turning back. In early for this eventuality of not being able to face the day at work. Hennie is right, of course; I must collect myself and move on. A new plan. But yet again I have not slept well. Coming up the stairs is Danuta, a member of my new team who has helped me, but I do not want to see her.

"Hi, Drew!" she calls. Always happy, never less than kind to me, patient with my stupid queries. Her life lived as if in a musical, always singing, always singing along to the radio on overtime, even to the adverts. But I do not want to explain myself, and I squeeze against the handrail. And yet when she has gone I do stop and wonder whether I should follow her back up. As I stand stock still a warning. Someone stomping up the stairs in twos. The rail is sticky and filthy, I feel it like snot Braille.

"Drew," he barks, and his briefcase hits my knee. I stumble down, the rail stopping me from falling. Dan's eyes follow me. They look like a tracking CCTV camera. Above me he holds out his palm.

I text as soon as I am clear of the building.
Fuck Clare. What is going on! Dan back?!
The reply comes when I am at home.
Not appropriate Drew.

Tuesday morning early, Victoria's file falls open at the payment slip for £50. I read from that point onward, my notes and HR's notes. I am not looking for explanations, and I am not looking for clues. Victoria is teaching me how to be ill.

Chapter Twenty

I am like a birdwatcher here, at dusk. But while Gabby may look at owls and stars through her binoculars, I am trying to focus mine on a house. It is not raining, the water all comes from the rich, massive fields, the tangle of weeds and the binding routes I am lying on. I think that I have identified the right spot, but the bright maps and Street View images seem a long way from this place. My binoculars are poor. They were not cheap, but I did not know how to tell good from bad when I bought the things, and I am glad that my daughter does not have them. They are nowhere near good enough for her. I struggle to turn the thumbwheel to find any sort of clarity, but they show me something. A tiny detached bungalow. I can tell that with my naked eyes, but in their unsatisfactory way the binoculars resolve a circular window in the front door, or rather they don't really resolve it but suggest the idea, as if the image is following a different route between eye and brain. A pattern of light. Nothing behind the porthole, but a glow in the window to the left and a softer, pinkish glow to the right. Living room, hall, bedroom. Totally isolated. Behind me the road to Cromer with just a few cars every minute; my car in the village half a mile away. Beyond the house must be the coast, but the binoculars are no use because everything in the distance closes to a fog. But the failing light gives an increasing sense that the North Sea is very near. When Hennie and I were drenched with rain in Norwich I had not imagined the water seeping through our skin and muscles, but this is what it feels like now. It feels like my body is absorbing all of the cold damp of the field and will not be dry for a long time. A huge sky. The stars have a clarity I've never seen before having always lived in suburbs, insular and stifling. Here, on clear nights, they have this, and I have to make adjustments for this place, and I have to make adjustments for Chantelle. Not the straightforward life I imagined for her, and I hope that her baby's father helps her. I am always guilty of oversimplifying, taking the laziest route. Suddenly a sense of movement, and now the binoculars might do work. A woman is by the bins at the side of the house. Slowness and heaviness; a strong impression through the lenses that Chantelle's mother is old and infirm. Molly left in her care when Chantelle worked. Chantelle not able to share her fears. No car, motorbike or bike outside, I am almost sure. The third night I have been here.

I must stick to this. Not only for justice, or for vengeance on Dan, but to comfort and protect Chantelle, who I came to know in a meeting when I had meant to chide and blame her. I will stand on her doorstep, bedraggled, to pose as her manager or her friend, once I decide which it should be. I stand up. Dan often boasts of a metal plate inserted to mend a broken leg when he was a child. Every time I move I wince, feeling a grinding pain that might as well be screws and bolts. Was Dan irredeemably corrupted even at the age he fell off his first bike? It is difficult to know how this might have manifested itself, or what infected thoughts could have been inside his head.

Even before the car turns I have a warning, my senses super-tuned for any alarm. I hear a change in the engine which suggests slowing. I turn and catch the faint orange flash of the indicator. The car has not slowed much to turn into the lane, and it is almost on me, recklessly accelerating. I press myself into the hedge, but it does not yield, and branches dig into my back. A turning point: from wanting to hide to a desperate need to show myself. I wave and yell. Not quite slow motion. A juddery stop-go, like mouse clicks on Dan's videos to pause and release them. Car-tarmac-fabric. Even in my panic I cannot believe the car is going to hit me, but now the blow. The sensation of a camera panning along with the car, and I see Dan. Shock on his face seems to turn to a sneer; certainly I see him long enough to register his eyes swivelling towards me. Then I am free. I stumble into the road struggling for breath. My jacket had caught in the mirror, and just for a second that dream of the panning camera and being carried along to study Dan's face must have been real. Then I had smashed into the rear door and fallen. I crawl back to the hedge, seeking shelter. My hand is badly cut, and the sleeve of my coat ripped. Without me knowing the car has parked right up close to the door of the house. Dan has seen me, and that is enough; he has seen me here. Then suddenly the car is coming back at me. I dive across its path and into the opposite verge. The bushes give way, and I tumble into nettles. A freeze-frame of the car as I fall; bumper height, tyre height. No one else in the car except Dan. No one else in the car that I can see...

I hammer on the door, but it is not opened for a long time. Then I am mistaken completely.
"He's gone."
"No," I say. But the elderly woman has taken so long to resolve her confusion into this misapprehension that I let the door slowly close. And upstairs I have heard crying, the utter abandoned helplessness of a child's cry. But it was not a child.

Perhaps Clare is slightly drunk, and I shout into the phone.
"You've got to listen!"
"Party here, Drew but go on—"
"I'm at Chantelle's house, and Dan was here—"
"Pastoral visit—"
"I think he's taken Molly!"
"Take a step back, Drew—"
"You wouldn't let me save Victoria!"
"Drew—"

"Perhaps I couldn't have saved Victoria, but she would have bolted across that roof more slowly seeing me and not Dan!"

To Clare this sentiment must seem deranged. And yet it is considered, and I have used the same words not three minutes before. The words certainly sounded unhinged to Detective Inspector Ulph, judging by the moment of silence they provoked in the hectic conversation. But they ring with urgency, and I have done all I can.

"Tell me you're OK," Clare says kindly.

I have not quite done all I can. This last thing is the most difficult, and I have delayed acting, and it is late. Another door. I have the key, but of course I knock, gently. The house that Susie and I fondly imagined was in the country. A scuffling all along the bottom of the door. Poppy is friendly to everyone. When we walked her as a puppy strangers would come up to pet her without asking, and I was angry, but Susie laughed and said, "No, she must be socialised." A restless energy to Poppy's love. She has no boundaries with me, and her paws are on my chest as soon as the door is opened, as gentle as she can be. I am grateful for this distraction, and I think that Susie is too. The dog has repaid our affection again. I am in the hall without explanation and Susie is laughing.

"Shhhh! You'll wake Gabs and Willippa."

She is tiny. Tightly curled black hair and brown eyes. Not the darkest, rather, hazel. Clear pale skin. No different to when I first knew her, but crumbling tired. Her clothes are casual, relaxed, but she can never relax. Suddenly the dog's attention turns from me. Susie is distressed.

"Look at you," she says, "look at you. What's happened? Where have you been?"

"I visited a member of my team. Pastoral visit."

"You crawled there on your hands and knees?" She cuddles Poppy to comfort the dog and to mask her own tears. "Drew, we'll talk."

She turns the television down though it was already so quiet I could hardly hear it.
"Are you at work, Drew?"
"No, but honestly, I'm fine."
"I'll do anything I can to help you. No rush. I'll make us coffee."
As soon as Susie leaves the room Poppy leaps onto the sofa, and I bury my head in her fur. Unbearable kindness. Susie is an Occupational Therapist. In the good days we would talk about her clients and their progress. Now she is weighed down with administration and management concerns. "Clients, I don't consider them," she will say bitterly. "It's all budgets and office politics at the moment." Susie is the last person to be excited by office politics. "Being part-time, it's all I can do to watch my back." This house is not convenient for her because she is based in Cambridge now. Dear God, Walsingham. Susie and I had found a semi-detached bungalow here early in our marriage. The competing shrines, the dead, atrophied cottages, and the Easter pilgrimages. Candles, and lamps, and the Holy House. An irony too far. During our first exploration we bought an icon from the Anglican shop. Then Gabby wondered what this sinister cross was, and we hid it.

Susie, pressed into the cushions, looks even smaller and more vulnerable. Perhaps it is this frailty that made me decide to fight her.
"Has something happened to your phone, Drew?"
"It's a new one."
"You didn't swap your SIM? I tried your work number as well, but people were a bit strange."
"Was it something urgent?"
"Something awful in the Norwich paper I wanted to ask you about. Then I suddenly had second thoughts about Great Yarmouth... but that worked out fine anyway."
"It was a good day."

Pictures of Our Children

"I heard glowing reports of the amazing Henrietta."

She looks straight at me, and there is the flash of a smile. She is not being wilfully mean. Always with Susie a mischievous edge which makes her gentleness even more delicious. I can see this in our girls too. In Great Yarmouth we sat near to the industrial-looking water flume for a long while. Every time unsuspecting passers-by got soaked Gabby would put her hand to her mouth to hide her giggles. Even Pippa seemed to be slyly calculating the magnitude of the splash by the number of people in the log-shaped boats, and waving her arms in anticipation when someone was on the path. I do not have such a light touch as Susie, or the innocence of our daughters. I cannot prevent myself from saying,

"How is Doctor Evans?"

"Well, we have coffee about every three weeks, so that sustains me... Oh, Drew, why did you always resent my friends? It's who I am and how you and I came to know each other. Do you think I would have agreed to meet you for that drink if I had thought it was a date?" A joke but I have hurt her. "There has been nothing since. Should I ask you about that other girl at work?" She is distressed suddenly and does not look at me. "Lucie, isn't it?"

Just one night. What I needed then. Thrilling ambition. All BMWs and barn conversions on the Broads. Young and bright and shrill. Eating up life. Generous and shilling people on eBay for her friends' fashion items. Taking the low step on my back, but I had nothing much to give her.

"Well, you needn't worry about Lucie because she came close to firing me last week. I think that's what you might call a strictly professional relationship."

"Drew, when I couldn't get your number at work... has something happened?"

"Humiliation, but in the scheme of things nothing."

"Is that what you came to tell me? What does it mean for me and the girls?"

"Nothing. I've made sure of that."
"What then, Drew?"
"Dan."
"Dan? Well, I hope he's OK," she says gently. "Most of my impressions of him come from you who adore him, and I still think he's a cock. But even so—"
"Stop! He's a predatory paedophile Susie! I came to warn you of that! Dan and his wife too!"
Not the thrilling rush of understanding that I saw in Hennie which had swept me with it. After a while, Susie says.
"Are you telling me that Gabs and Philippa are in danger?"
"We need to think, that's all. Perhaps you could spend a few weeks with your mother."
"In Swansea? How the hell is that going to work? I don't understand, Drew. Do the police know?"
"Yes, but I've just seen Dan in his car, and he's at work as if nothing had happened. I don't know what the hell is going on."
"Jesus! This better be right if I'm going to ruin our daughters' innocence."
"Don't say anything. Just take care. And don't post anything about our girls on Facebook."
"I never do! But don't you know, Drew, those two have little antenna that pick up the slightest disturbance. If you were around them more you'd know that…"
Suddenly there is a finger on her lips, and I do not know whether it is for me or for Gabby, who is standing in the doorway laughing.
"Hello, Daddy."
"Oh, Sugarpuff! Don't wake your sister," Susie says, and Gabby immediately mimes greeting me, mimes telling the dog to be quiet, mimes laughing. Susie splutters and giggles. Poppy, overcome with our joy, barks. Inevitably a few minutes later Pippa appears at the door, sleepy and happy, waving at me. If her little antenna has picked up that I am

dishevelled and distressed she does not let it show. Now we are a group Gabby says,
"Have you come home, Daddy?"
And it is as if I have come home, a hero even to Susie.

A sharp pain in my left side. I look at my watch, and it is five in the morning. To my left Pippa is stirring and stretching and pushing her feet against me. Then she sleeps again. On the armchair Susie is curled up, small, her face untroubled. Gabby sleeps on the floor with Poppy the dog, next to a huge brick tower she has built for me. I have woken up surrounded by my family.

Chapter Twenty-one

This feels obscene and yet, I realise, I may have done it to myself. Perhaps it had been an unthinking response during the fraught phone conversation, or perhaps Clare had steered me to it. The full horror had not occurred to me, even as I waited in front of the vast screens and blaring speakers of the electrical department. I was more concerned with finding some strategy to cope with the awkward meeting. In this, I only got as far as treating it as unlikely date, an illicit tryst that no one must discover from our actions or words. This would suit the reticent, cautious, demeanour that might find me. The stupid idea was fixed in my brain by the jab of a customer's finger on a volume button and the flood of sound. But even as I smiled at Clare and offered to buy her coffee, I realised what I had done, and that no game or pretence would help me. Clare had strutted out to find this table. So far in front that I could not call her back or slide into a vacant seat near the counter. A table right by the window in John Lewis. Occupied by two people before us, who had left plates smeared with butter and with two half scones gnawed into matching waxing moons, as if they had found them indigestible at the same moment. I hold back, but Clare urgently shifts this detritus, dumping the plates, the trays, the lipstick-stained mugs onto a table nearby; a table for six occupied by a solitary man who looks up briefly. Our own trays next and he raises his head again. Now Clare brushes crumbs with a serviette and scrubs at a coffee spill, her arc widening as if the coffee will clean the whole top. I flick sugar from my trousers that Clare has swept towards me. She has the upper hand; my only consolation is that I have the place with my back to the huge, cold window overlooking the car park. Incredibly she has ordered food, an apricot Danish. She mashes the jam with her fork and flakes of pastry stick to her lips. She removes them almost flirtatiously with a crooked little finger and a curled tongue. I look away, and when I dare to look back, beside her plate she has a spiral notebook and a little pink ruler, perhaps for drawing grids. In this provocative arena I need to fight.

"Hennie tells me that Dan is still at work."

"Drew, we need to have some ground rules here."

"As if nothing had happened!"

"Listen to me. First, we'll talk about you, and then I might be able to calm your fears a little. I hope so, Drew. Danuta was asking after you, by the way. Everybody is concerned." She smiles at me. Not a cheerful smile. "I know from our phone conversation that you've visited your doctor, so perhaps you can tell me about that."

It had been easy. I had relayed Victoria's early symptoms. Her proxy. Asking for a friend. It had been so easy that I had the space to wonder whether Victoria might have fared better under the care of my doctor. He had listened, quiet and sympathetic, allowing me to recall everything I had listed and memorised. Mild depression and anxiety. The latter, I suppose down to details I had inserted of confusion at my desk at work, caught up in myself.

"You have the doctor's note now Clare."

"I do. Well done for going, Drew. Well done for taking that step. Proud of you."

Perhaps I had expected more than mild depression, but I can escalate this if necessary, in the process of self-diagnosis.

"This is just the first step on the journey, though. Did your doctor discuss talking therapies with you?"

"He did."

"And you are aware of the Staff Assistance Programme, which could help with payment for counselling?"

"I am."

I will not do this, unless I cannot avoid it. I already feel guilty about the expensive pills I will never take.

"Oh, Drew. Please, please consider this step. You've done the hardest part."

"I need to think about it."

"OK. I understand. Tell me, though. What have you been doing with yourself?"

This is a hand grenade. I have not been visiting art galleries. Rather, I have been walking on windswept beaches and at night on the coastal path.

"Mostly at home."

"That's not good. Drew, I wonder if you ought to keep a little diary for me. A record of how you are feeling on a scale of one to ten, say, and a note of three positive things that have happened that day."

I do not know how someone genuinely stricken with mental illness would react to this. Perhaps it would suit someone susceptible to Clare's brand of diet coke replacement sweetness. But did I propose something similar to Victoria, scared and trapped as she was?

"Things take time, Drew. Just as if you had broken a leg."

Jesus, did I write the manual on this? I think of that troubled girl, when we were sitting a few metres from where Clare and I are now, her eyes screwed up tight; I think trying to trust me.

"I really believe it is a good idea to keep busy. Gentle things. Perhaps a little colouring?"

Clare is pleased with this idea and makes small movements with pinched finger and thumb, signing off with a flourish with her hand and lips.

"Above all, you must let yourself be helped, Drew. Are you getting the support you need?" At once my mind goes to kissing Susie awake on that golden family morning, but I say,

"Hennie is staunchly behind me."

"That must be a comfort for you." But she says this as if Hennie was nothing more than a kind colleague. I want to give Clare no more of myself.

"What do you have for me? You said there was something."

She pauses and sighs.

"OK. I spoke to Chantelle last night. I can't tell you that she is perfectly happy, but her issues are no greater than yours, Drew. And to ease your mind a little I heard her daughter in the background."

"Chattering, laughing?"

"Crying, Drew, but that is the way of things, and she was definitely with her mother."

"I don't doubt it. They borrowed Molly. A play date."

"Drew, Drew…" She means to punish me. "Listen, I think that it would be a step forward if we held the next and subsequent meetings discreetly in the office"

"I'm not going back in that building!"

I am surprised by my vehemence in this. It comes from my study of Victoria, and from a strange new wariness of my former colleagues.

"I need to set the direction of travel for this experience, Drew—"

"Never. I'm not going back."

I do not see the change happen, but when I look up from my nervous confusion Clare's brow has creased, and her eyes have become steely.

"Drew, perhaps we need to make this accommodation for you. It's only right that we embrace these allowances, but—"

"What do you mean? Whatever else is going on I'm rational in this!"

A word repeated becomes nonsense. This is happening to my name.

"Oh, Drew, it's not only this. We felt the need to protect you. You've become a little over-focused. I won't say obsessive—"

"Jesus, Clare, it's not me you've been protecting!"

I had been waiting for the moment when Clare stepped aside from herself, to show me again that reality was not as I imagined it, and now it happens.

"Look behind you, Drew."

"I know what's there!"

"She died down there, Drew. You can still see the stems of the flowers… the remains. She jumped in front of the shoppers and their children. Look down."

"No!"

But I have been there when the flowers were fresher. I had looked up to this big window and to the car park roof. I am not sure what I feel about shrines like this, but as I read the notes from strangers, I had wanted to leave something myself.

"You have to ask if we could have done more, Drew."

"I'll never forgive you for stopping me from going to help on that morning!"

"Oh, I meant rather before that." She has become sweet again to twist the knife. "When Victoria was a member of your team. When she was your responsibility, Drew."

"I'll take no responsibility for that while your fucking crony Dan is free!"

I see the change happen this time, her head tossed back, nostrils flaring and brows knotting.

"I can't accept this, Drew."

Then slowly she reaches into her handbag. As precise as an artist she places a phone to the left of her coffee cup. Then she looks up at me, her hand resting on the phone. Christ, she means to fire me here, reporting my failings to HR right in front of me. Just before the long pink nail of her index finger draws the pattern on the screen she delicately turns the phone. Portrait, facing me. My lock screen flashes on. Composition recognised an instant before the subject. Almost illicit. Hennie's photo at some team meal. Not looking or thinking about me. Her hand waving in front of her face, but the wrist bent back away from her eyes. Awkward grace. Instinctively I make a grab for the phone, but Clare's hand closes over it.

Pictures of Our Children

"Lost property."

"It's my phone."

"I know, Drew. Greasy, sticky fingers. Not secure." She traces my lock pattern large in the air as if reading it from the screen. "Drew, your wife was worried about you for a time. Look. Your lonely little phone buzzing in the dark."

I struggle to understand what is happening, but hits me that there can no going back from this for Clare, only escalation from now on. Susie's messages scroll past too fast to read but words snag. *Something upsetting.* Without pausing the flicking of her thumb Clare says.

"Something upsetting in the paper, about your office I think. Ring if you need to."

She has memorised this and chooses to recite it with a nauseating increase in pitch. I try to hear it in Susie's own gruff-kind voice. Each new violation by Clare is shockingly fascinating.

"Is Great Yarmouth a good idea after all?—Disastrous I should imagine, Drew." Then,

"Drew can you ring me?"

But this is something new. A different tone as she reads. Then something different again as she interprets the mechanical words of the phone.

"Please ring Drew—Victoria (Work)"

"Victoria?"

Her thumb swipes up again.

"Drew I have to trust you—Victoria bracket Work bracket."

Then this, but spoken not as a plaintive cry, but in the voice of a robot.

"Help me Drew! Vicky."

I make another grab for the phone, but she holds it to her breast and smiles as she gives me the distressing time of the message.

"Three ten am. Victoria (Work)"

Until now Clare has hardly lowered her voice, careless of people around us as if everything might be interpreted as a game, as I had imagined it. Now she whispers and hisses.

"Pictures, Drew, pictures." Her hand tightens on the phone and her knuckle bones rise, white. Serene, beautiful photos framed by a reddened hand.

"My daughters."

"I know. Now this." Chantelle's daughter, the image she had sent me. "Not quite appropriate, Drew… Next one."

Grainy and horribly enlarged. A boy of about five years old. I had downloaded this. I had made the image—I know the sinister legal terminology. I had edited it too. A work event I had not been invited to. The full picture showing the boy clinging to his happy mother's hand. Nadia.

"Other people's children, Drew."

Then a flood of images that spin past, sickening in their speed, and sickening as Clare's thumb slows and I catch an impression of the images. An unspeakable flick-book. Child after child registering in a succession of standard poses and then giving way to the next wretched boy or girl.

"Not mine!" I cry and people look up.

"Drew, I'll keep this," whispers Clare. "Live quietly."

I do not remember the conversation ending. I do not think I added anything. Clare strode down the escalator before I could grasp any thread of rational thought. The speaker's controls are turned in an unbearable crescendo and shockingly the huge televisions flash children's programmes. The blackmail bargain is no more real or understandable to me than swimming images of a fight in the burger bar and woodlice on a bun. I will myself to hold to this new reality, but I am less in control than when I was throwing up into the black river on that lost night.

It comes to me when I turn off the light. All evening I have been searching for a clue as to what could inspire such

Pictures of Our Children

loyalty to Dan from Clare, and I have scoured Facebook and Instagram. Clare happy, and happily married as far as I or anyone would be able to tell. A lot of pictures of family life. A lot of pictures of seemingly delicious food too, but you never know whether it is under-seasoned or cold. So perhaps it is a dangerous office romance, as heady as mine and Hennie's. Clare is giving unthinking, reckless support to Dan, and I wonder if I could do the same for someone I loved absolutely. My head spins with this. Then I turn off the light and know. Not in a flash of inspiration, but in a flood of darkness. I had been thinking of the wreckage wrought on my phone. Two packs of cards riffled together. The innocent mingled with vile injections of disgusting images. Chains of tedious milkshake emails mixed with incriminating messages… Jesus! This evil has a pyramid of its own, perverted gratification rather than cash tumbling down the layers. Dan and Clare grasping and sharing and swapping with others. I tear off my bedclothes. I know what I am going to find because it is obvious now. On a bland corporate page, a grid of faces like all the rest, I see it eventually. Sheffield and not Norwich. Head of Compliance. He cannot bring himself to smile like his colleagues. The man who had been introduced to me as Detective Inspector Ulph.

Chapter Twenty-two

Hennie has not quite untangled this. "I'm worried about you, Drew."

I have watched her intense eyes as I described what happened yesterday. My sudden realisation of the horror of the meeting place, the animal change in Clare, the lock screen, the desperate messages, the phone full of children. Then the confusion of the blaring speakers and Clare striding down the escalator—no lover's parting more devastating.

"Drew, worried."

She is a day behind, fretting about my adopted illness.

"Hennie, I don't matter. This doesn't stop with Dan and his wife. The thing is a cancer, spreading across the company as far as I know. Across the country to Sheffield. If Clare is involved who else?" I had chased her here to the station after her work. I had called her name, and she had shepherded me into the mean buffet and bought coffee. There is a mild optical illusion caused by long plate mirrors in the window recesses. People outside seem to be walking towards you then rush past your shoulder in the other direction. Hennie seems caught up in this trivial phenomenon. One detail I have not yet described to her: almost too intimate. I had woken this morning warm and momentarily happy. For an instant the infantile security of when my bed was a boat or train. The phone had not woken me, but had rung seconds later, muffled by the pillow.

"Morning, Drew. How are you?" Clare had purred. Absurdly early. Five. I could only think of her lying in bed herself. Coming down from my moment of euphoria it is was too seductive to ignore and I had not hung up. "Everybody is worried about you, Drew. Me, Danuta, Dan, Lucie, Mr Ulph."

"What?"

"Mr Ulph, Drew, Mr Ulph…" It was the rhythm of three that jolted me properly awake. She was taunting me with his bare name. "Drew, you have to look after yourself and think of your family."

It was Clare who abruptly ended the call there. I had a stupid impulse to ring her back, but had pushed the phone to the floor and slept until two in the afternoon. When I look up Hennie is still thinking, eyes closed as if asleep, frozen and beautiful.

"The policeman was fake," I say, making sure she has understood. She tosses her head. "Clare rang me this morning. Completely normal. Recorded for training purposes. But she said Mr Ulph."

"I get it, Drew. I get it."

"Listen Hennie. When I was in John Lewis with Victoria we talked about the dignity and nobility of work. Whether an insurance clerk's life can ever be worth as much as a great artist's, say. Perhaps it can be if you are tested and do the right thing."

"You've decided to go to the police?"

"I failed Victoria. She wanted to trust me, but I wasn't there. I have to stand up to this—"

"Think, Drew, think."

"I'll be dragged down. I know that."

"Your family."

"I'll protect them."

Her eyes widen. "How will you protect them? Lurking outside with your toy binoculars?"

Perhaps I am addicted to women with a cutting sense of humour who make fun of me. Hennie is a harder drug than Susie. But now he rush. Hennie catches my hand.

"Drew, I'm afraid for you. For your wife, and for your daughters. Don't do anything tonight. Give me a day. I'll think of something."

I cannot deny that I was thinking of Clare when I decided to make the phone call. I mean I was thinking of the thrill of the morning when she was breathing comfort into my ear. I lie in bed trying to get warm and ring Hennie's number.

"Listen," I say, "I'm worried because I don't want you to do anything stupid."

"What stupid thing would I do?" Her voice is not the honey I had hoped for.

"Don't go to the police yourself."

"Well, that *would* be a stupid thing to do. The consequences would be exactly the same for you. We're too closely associated."

"What then?"

"Nothing yet. I need time, like I said."

I lie awake and take comfort from how linked Hennie and I are. The fact of it, and how she had acknowledged it.

The locomotive towers above me. It is an ancient class 37, battered and loud; as old as I am. I have walked a little way down the slope at the end of the platform. These things are diminished when you see them in stations, but they are tall and menacing on the tracks. A few paces further and the driver looks down and then back to his signal. He looks watchful and strong. For the few seconds I see him, I can project onto the man who has bought me these few miles a dignity, sense of history and pride. He does not seem unduly perturbed by my trespass, I suppose because he is used to trainspotters, and judges that I do not intend to leap in front of his loco. Yes, I think that I could happily retreat to collecting numbers and names, but would never choose to be mangled by the wheels. I am irritated because Hennie is not here. She has given me a precise time, even chosen the train I am to catch, but she has not met me. Now I doubt what is to happen. I had visualised a short walk, with her laughing and gently reassuring me, and then, on her boat on the Broads, a plan and a way out. Perhaps, though, she lives on a new-build estate and my dreams will be shattered. The motor of the 37 grates louder and I am momentarily pleased with myself for knowing the nickname of these things—tractors. The diesel revs and moves and there are carriages gathering pace and then the agricultural thud of the second unit on the back. The train has pulled away like a curtain in a theatre and there, on the opposite platform, is Hennie. She beckons to me, urgent and insistent. The crossing gates have not opened, and I dash across the bridge to join her.

"What's happening?"

She looks at a message on her phone. "First carriage."

"Back to Norwich?"

"Yes."

She is brittle and distracted, and I cannot explain the minor joy of the class 37, or dare to ask what her plan is.

"It will be here any minute," she says as if I don't know how these things work. I look at the closed gates and the clear semaphore signal.

"Yes," I say.

Hennie peers into the distance towards Great Yarmouth and seems impatient with the humble multiple unit even when it comes into view. She shrugs

"Only one carriage anyway."

"Class 153."

"What? We haven't got long. Norwich isn't far."

"Yes."

She waves me onto the train ahead of her. I know that we must be meeting someone. Some grown-up response from Hennie; perhaps a lawyer she knows, and I will wait for a tap on my arm to identify them. And yet the carriage is empty, empty of lawyers, almost empty of people. Then I see him. The train jolts and I watch the platform slide by, and for a few confused seconds believe that Hennie had engineered this so that I cannot escape. Jim is slumped by a window. Embarrassed I take the seat beside him, sitting slightly askew at first so Hennie cannot pass easily.

"Jim," I say to his reflection.

As soon as Hennie has settled opposite us she seems distressed, and urgently flicks her hand across the table. It is something so unlikely to me that it is only when she hovers above my shoulder and I squeeze past her that I realise what has happened. She is not comfortable with travelling backwards on trains. Jim turns to us with the disturbance. He looks the same as when I saw him at the crematorium, as if he had been living amongst the brambles and ash. When she has recovered herself Hennie, now at his side, watches him like a concerned sister.

"Jim, what we talked about last night."

"That's OK," he mumbles as if this finalises the matter as far as he is concerned.

"Are you still in your flat in Norwich Jim?" I say as an opener, testing his hostility.

"No, I'm staying with Victoria's family in Acle."

They are not looking after him very well.

"Are you still in Norwich, Drew? Why are you travelling from Brundall?"

Hennie looks anxious again and steps in to end us settling where everyone lives.

"You'll get a taxi from the station, Jim?" Another sign directed at me over the table. This time she flashes her watch. I have no idea what her rushed agenda is, but if our conversation is to be timetabled along with the short journey to Norwich then I must say what I need to say now.

"Jim, I failed Victoria."

"I failed Victoria," comes back. In our daily meetings at work Jim would often echo, even mimic my words. This was to emphasise how hollow and foolish I was being. If this is his purpose now it would cut me in two. But there is in his voice a vulnerability and a sense of regret that makes it clear my statement is a reflection of his own torment.

"I didn't get her last messages to me." I say.

"I'd told her she could trust you."

"I'd lost my phone."

"I know."

Hennie says urgently. "Drew, Jim knows everything."

"About Clare?"

"All about Clare."

"Jim, you said you knew about Nadia. Was her son safe?"

Hennie seems exasperated with me, but then railway business intervenes. The boyish guard sells Hennie a return. She is annoyed with the whole idea of the train and with the fact that she is the only one holding things up in this way.

"Do you need a ticket, Drew?" she says, and I shake my head. Before the transaction is complete Jim begins to speak.

"Have you ever loved anybody for a fault?"

So far we have just about understood each other above the grating motors, but this is so off course that I have to ask him to repeat it several times, even interrupting his repetitions.

"I think so, yes," I say when I am sure what he means.

Hennie, waving her card at the guard's machine, looks up anxiously.

"Well, you might understand, Drew. I never knew if there was any chance of her getting better, but that made no difference. I just had an irresistible urge to be good to her. Is that some sort of perversion in itself, given how damaged she was?"

Hennie looks distressed and tugs at his sleeve.

"Jim."

"And now this. The culmination, the consummation. The fall."

"Jim, Jim."

I listen to the noise of the engines and rails overwhelm the voices of Hennie and Jim.

"But something good will come of this," Hennie says.

"I know she was controlling and selfish, but I loved her like I never thought would be possible for me…"

Hennie leans across to me.

"Jim is in the same position with Clare as you are, Drew. Exactly the same. You confided in me last night, didn't you, Jim?"

"I don't care. I really don't care." Jim says.

We pass the Carrow Road football ground, and I look at Hennie to see if she is content, and if this is all I should expect. She sits back and blows out her cheeks. But then the hint of a smile for me.

The strange, edgy sense of urgency continues over to the end of the journey, and we say our goodbyes to Jim before the ticket barrier. Hennie squeezes his hand and I embrace him. I bury my head into his shoulder and smell the must of his uncared-for clothes; brambles, and ash. We watch him race ahead to his taxi and our sloppy, unconcerned driver climb down from his cab with his little black case.

Hennie propels me into the buffet, and we sit in the same seats as yesterday. Jesus, is this crappy place going to be significant to me, above all the places I could choose and all the journeys I could make? She closes her eyes for a long time. The lids are blue and slightly glossy.

"You understand what Jim meant, don't you, Drew?"

"Yes."

"There's no need for you to do anything."

"Is he going to the police now?"

"No. He has a hospital appointment. They're helping him with his mental state."

"Yes."

"You just need to give him a little more time. He needs to find that last bit of courage and I know he'll do it."

"What if that's not soon enough?"

"No, just a few more hours. A day. He's made up his mind."

"And he's being blackmailed by Clare?"

"Yes, but for Jim the price is lower, the consequence less."

"Did you influence him?"

"No. But he knows your circumstances and what might happen to your family if you were smeared. He likes you a lot. He persuaded Victoria that she could trust you. I told him you didn't have your phone when she tried to ring."

"I can't let him do this Hennie."

"You must, Drew. He needs to do it. He needs to sacrifice himself for Victoria."

"We are going to throw Jim under the bus?"

Throw him under the train I can't stop myself from thinking.

"The alternative might be horrible," Hennie says urgently.

While the sharp wheels of the diesel are in my mind, Hennie is caught up in the optical illusion mirrors again. She watches the people coming towards her and rushing by her shoulder. Her eyes close. Tired, or tired of me. Or perhaps, for someone so delicate about travelling backwards, the mirror has made her dizzy. In the tangle of window and mirror she looks still and serene. Right in front of me, stray hairs she has carelessly brushed in front of her mouth are stirred by gentle breathing, and her blue eyelids, finely lined, flicker slightly. I would gladly steal Jim's chance of sacrificing himself. I could summon, for the good, an unquestioning loyalty as strong as Clare's to Dan and Ulph's to Clare. Hennie does not want this, not a pointless gesture. She wants normality, an ordinariness we have only glimpsed, but which is a solid foundation for dreams.

"Just do nothing, Drew, and things will sort themselves out."

It is important to her that I know we are not conspiring against Jim, which is why she showed him to me on the train. To honour Victoria, I need not ruin myself and my family. I need only do the right thing. I have not thanked her.

"Hennie, you are very clever."

"Well, I just thought *who else is vulnerable in this?* Jim was so pleased to hear from me."

It was a phone call I should have made myself. I had no idea that Hennie and Jim were close enough for this. It must have been a friendship forged in the few weeks of adversity they suffered together under my regime.

"Drew, I must go. I'm at work, but I have a non-existent dental appointment. Just time for some shopping before I key in."

She kisses me, and I am left alone in my new place. With all urgency lifted I can stare into the mirrors to conjure her likeness. I need not worry any more. She has done this for me.

Chapter Twenty-three

We almost lost Gabby. Susie carried her for twenty-eight weeks and then in comfortable Norfolk we were stalked by vultures for a month. Susie's anguish was total and yet I found ways to comfort her, and so comfort myself. I held her hand as she reached into the incubator and so we had a little chain. But alone at home, or at work, I could never deal with the threat to that tiny, undefined life. It was a weight, a pain, an indescribable sensation like falling. Is it terrible that I feel exactly like this now? I wait and can do nothing. Things I have no control over may yet ruin my eldest daughter and her precious sister. Jim is hesitating, and nothing has happened. Perhaps things are working out unseen, but I was expecting a thunderclap. I watch every local news bulletin, but they are all bypasses and council budgets. Surely this cannot have been set going without a ripple? Hennie does not know and urges me to wait. It is something that I cannot share with Susie, to confide that I am in the same helpless freefall as during the life and death struggle of our new-born. Jim does not answer his phone. When I had left Hennie and Jim I had gone from coffee shop to coffee shop; exalted, free. Then later I had visited all the bars on Hennie's mad agenda which were open that morning. Now the come-down, the hangover, the remorse. When I am waiting for something, I can always pinpoint the exact second when I know with certainty that it is not going to happen. I am not alone in this I'm sure, because I talked about it with Victoria once. I had been late for a meeting, and she said she said she had not given up on me, not quite. So we shared that sense, which may be commonplace or rare. I wait for that second to tick over.

Peter Kirk

I now know that Dan's wife, Freya, works for my company in a different office. She had a birthday last week, and everybody in the filing team sent their best wishes. I also know that Clare now has a new puppy called Leo. This is from Facebook. Hennie has committed Facebook suicide, as I did when the realisation of the power of social media began to overwhelm me. Strangely, Victoria and Nadia, who are really dead, live on here. Victoria's last posts are from a year ago and are relentlessly positive self-help slogans and desperate competition entries. Nadia's profile always had an otherworldly quality, with sparse cryptic comments, snatches of quoted poetry and photos either blurred or with the camera pointing the wrong way. I have a ghost profile now too.

I love Hennie so much. A strange adolescent yearning which is often more of a torment. We have not been intimate. I still do not even know exactly where she lives. She has told me that the address on file at work is an old one so that no one can ever find her. Perhaps this is not true, or perhaps she cast off and is drifting slowly towards Lowestoft. I like the idea of her being slightly Romany or piratical, and we have talked about it when our spirits have been high, or we have been trying to find comfort in stupid things. I have known Hennie for barely two months, but I cannot think of when I first knew her. I mean in part that I do not think of it because it is embarrassing and painful. It reminds me of Jim and the shameful drunken evening. It reminds me that I was hoping for Nadia, not Hennie as my bargain for Victoria. I associate it too with another night out, last year. Dan and I in cubicles five minutes after five on a Friday night. The smell of deodorant, and clean shirts over the doors. In the women's toilets, I imagine, Lucie excited too, calling to her friends. My birthday had coincided with my arrival as manager. The evening had crystallised into a mellow haze in celebration of myself and my new position. Dan had cajoled and encouraged me. Everybody friendly and drawn together by the shared experience of their jobs and the certainty of their role within the department. It seems ridiculous now. Even then we must have been working in a cesspit. And I must stop myself thinking of Ulph presiding over the corporate governance of the child molesters, because perhaps he joined as a mere club-member in this alternative order, and the true organisational head was amongst us, toasting my birthday. I think back to Clare, laughing awkwardly in the pub as she welcomed me, asking after my children, and Dan, pleased with himself to have recruited me. I am not proud of what happened later that night, but it was fun and innocent and spiced what I then imagined was the squeaky-clean day-to-day life in the company. Lucie was eighteen, myself thirty-eight. She did not know me then, and perhaps she thought I was going to be useful to her, a professional contact higher on the organisational chart. At any rate we had used my new managerial entry card, had raced each other up the stairs to some forbidden office, and had looked down on all of Norwich. If I was confounded by her indifferent reaction to me in the next few days, then perhaps that is why I wrote the confessional note to my wife. From that moment, and true to my anguished words, I did not find Lucie attractive in any way.

I was not attracted to Hennie at first. Impossible to imagine now when I am thrilled when the sea or sky come close to matching the colour of her eyes. How did this happen? Her willowy frame was not what I wanted then, but I have got used to her, or else I have been taught to appreciate her beauty. How are we attracted to people? We see in someone's face a beauty that we imagine reveals what is beneath, the soul of the person; we think we see something that speaks to us alone. But mostly men are beguiled by the same thing. A hint of softness and kindness. Symmetry and freshness and big-eyed innocence which remind us of a child's face. Features that suggest someone you should cherish and protect. Jim, of course, loved someone for a fault; Victoria, contrary and precious. A soul so different to his own that he just had a desire to let his spirit pour down into hers. But the reverse had happened, and the flow was the other way. I have loved someone for a fault too. In the revolving door I adored Nadia for her desolation and helplessness.

When I rang Hennie yesterday she had said,
"Just let Jim go to the police—the *real* police."
I would gladly beat Jim to his self-sacrifice, for Victoria, let alone for Hennie. Hennie does not want this, but Victoria has shown the way. I do not think that Jim will harm himself. He is safe with Vicky's family, and I will contact him, and Hennie will help him. I was only alarmed for him in the train when the sharp wheels were in my head… But I do not know. If Jim's stricken brain is still capable of feeling half of what I, rational, am feeling now then he may choose to drown himself in Victoria's memory. Meanwhile, while all these diversions are going on, I fear for Chantelle and Molly. And my second ticks over and I know for sure that Jim is not going to the police.

So every moment is for me like when my tiny child was in jeopardy. How can I share this with Susie? Either it is an obscene comparison or a truth that will shock her to the bone, that Gabby and Pippa might be in real danger.
"Jesus!" I say. My curse shakes me back from my thoughts, and in moving my lips I remember that I have spoken out loud seconds before too, saying,
"Susie, Susie, Susie."

Tesco, John Lewis, Poundland; as if this was a normal trip to the city centre. For every person smiling another rude and impatient. The middle-class melee and panic of Marks and Spencer no gentler than anywhere else. I let a pushchair pass, and someone is at my shoulder, elbowing ahead… I have

Pictures of Our Children

stopped dead in an aisle, buying nothing, seeing nothing. I rush out. I can delay this no longer

Chapter Twenty-four

I was at home with Ulph. At home with him, as he was at home with the minutiae which build insurance contracts, and which build insurance companies. I felt no more nervous with him than on the occasions when I had been in his place, across the table, investigating. This is different, and something is wrong. I have an urge to look behind me, which can only mean an urge to escape. When I do whip my neck around there is another officer by the door, standing straight, unsmiling. I have blurted out my message like a child in a nativity play, without pause or meaning. I have said that I need to speak about child abuse. Now something is wrong, and I cannot second-guess the processes that are being applied to me. I am being made to wait for a start. Nothing is quick like the mock, slipshod procedure of Ulph. Also, there is a fascination with my address and where I can be found, and what I am. There is the strangeness of a foreign country and the jeopardy of a foreign country with unknown laws. I could believe any depredation of the man in front of me. Small quick eyes. Ulph upright; this man slouched towards me so that I can smell the reek of tobacco from his jacket. Ulph insurance respectable; this man seedy and untrustworthy. I do not know whether he does not understand the situation, but thorns and tripping roots are put in my way.

"We'll get to that," he says, until my urgency is trained down to silence. And then suddenly a bit of office business, something I do understand. A woman enters, and I see that she is carrying an ox-blood cardboard file. She does not acknowledge me and lays the file on the desk. She waits while the detective reads; presumably, he is not struggling with incomprehensible lines of numbers, then leaves without speaking, the file still on the desk. There should not be a file.

"Now what do you have to tell us, sir?" Not much paper—two typed pages. But there should not be anything. Jesus, has Jim jumped before me? "Sir?"

Something has gone wrong, but now we are on to the business of the day. I have to think of the heads of my unilateral agenda. Who to incriminate? I realise that I am giving a formal statement now, but even in this plodding reconstruction, I am having to think faster than I am comfortable with. There is more to worry about than I imagined, and I wish I had prepared written notes as I had when I visited my doctor. But it is clear where I should start; Dan, and his wife too. Looks like hawks in the supermarket, beaks and claws.

"You were friends with this man?"

He should not know this. I give Dan's address because perhaps this is what he wants.

"When did that friendship end?"

"As soon as I suspected him."

"Did you take any other action when you first suspected him. That was some weeks ago."

"I told my immediate manager, Clare Ball. She did nothing because she is part of the abuse ring. She protected him."

Clare next on the list of course, but as I speak this transition seems too smooth and the explanation somehow weak and inadequate.

"You believe she was a part of this?"

"She organised parties, swaps. Perhaps she was the hub."

"You know this?"

"Yes."

Well, it has grown in my mind each time I think of my phone conversation with her in that damp coastal field. When she had sounded excited and just slightly drunk, when Dan had almost run me over in his eagerness to reach Chantelle's house and pick up and deliver a child like groceries.

"Are you talking about first-person abuse or the sharing of images?" The policeman asks.

"Real abuse I'm sure, but ultimately it is the same..." Yet I pull back. He stares at me, making it clear that he does not want to be lectured on the implications of crime, even if he has chosen words that suggest an X-box game. Now I have to think where I am in this. Ulph next on my list of those to accuse.

"The stakes are obviously high for Clare because she introduced me to someone who she said was a detective."

"Sorry?"

The almost unplayable trick of derailing a conversation by pretending not to understand.

"In an office at our work, Clare and I met with a man who I thought was a policeman."

"He said he was a policeman?"

"I believed him to be a policeman. Clare led me to believe he was a policeman."

"Sorry?"

"His name is Christopher Ulph. I now know that in fact he's a compliance manager with our company in Sheffield."

"Would a compliance manager have been interested in your conduct at that point?"

"My conduct? No."

And with this pressure of misunderstanding comes a strange urge to moderate, to protect myself.

"It was some sort of conspiracy, or a debt he owed to Clare, but I can't be sure that he was involved in the pyramid."

"What?"

"The pyramid. The club that shares children like profits from a selling scam..." Immediately I know this is too much for him and I stop. I must say nothing that I am not sure of, and so I do not mention Jane. I always had a suspicion that was something odd with Jane, even before I knew about Dan. A whispering closeness to Dan and to Clare that I did not understand. I remember my surprise, on my own induction, to find that she was not one of the protein shake initiates. I felt then that there must be something else, some other club bond. But I must be careful, and the most important thing is who should be protected.

"There's a girl called Chantelle."

"A girl?"

"A woman. A woman and her daughter Molly. Two years old."

"How do you know Molly?"

"I don't know her. I worked with her mother."

"You were her manager?"

"Are they safe?"

He looks at me blankly. I struggle with the address, although I could point it out on Google Earth.

"It was Chantelle's collapse that first alerted me to this. Her daughter was kidnapped. Dan almost ran me over when he was collecting her."

"You were at this girl Chantelle's address?"

"Watching. I'm sure Molly was in the car. I can give you the date. Jim might not have known about Chantelle and Molly."

"OK."

Jim is vulnerable too, although I do not know in what way Clare might move to harm him. I must forgive him for the mess he has made of this.

"You have spoken to Jim Crane? He's under a lot of pressure."

"I am not prepared to discuss who I have or have not spoken to."

So we are on to Victoria, who has somehow become a miscellaneous, any-other-business item on my agenda. I had resolved to mention her, to do the right thing for Jim, and even if he has been here before me, and whatever damage he has done, I will honour that. But this is shaded down too, though she is a hero to me now, running from Dan on that roof, her stubborn resistance mistaken for illness.

"Jim told you about Victoria Samuels?" I prompt, but he looks purposefully blank. "The young woman who jumped from the John Lewis car park last month. She was hounded to suicide by Dan and Clare."

This creates no ripples. Jim would have been even more emphatic, and almost certainly it would have been the beginning of his story, but it does not resonate with this man. He is only interested in me.

"What was your relationship with this Victoria Samuels?" he says.

The less about me this is the better. I would struggle in any event to define my history with Victoria and my feelings about her. It is not good to be working out what I must say as I speak, and I stutter.

"I was Victoria's manager... No, Dan was her manager at the time she died."

"You seem nervous."

"Pressure is being put on me."

"What do you mean?"

"By Clare. She has stolen my phone and put obscene images onto it."

I do not use the plain word though any idiot might guess at it. A little time to examine my motives as the process lumbers on without stopping at this station. Perhaps I have not openly say blackmail so as not to divert the investigation with this side issue, and yet perhaps I am driven to cut short my time with this wretched man. Now I have stopped we begin the process of verification, as everything is read back to me. I only wish that I could start again, like sometimes you can do on voice mails when your speech or your memory or your resolve have failed. Then suddenly something new.

"You know a young woman called Lucie Hammond?"

"She's my manager."

"You're confused, sir. I'm asking about Lucie Hammond." First pretending not to hear and now a deliberate misunderstanding. "Think, sir."

But Jesus, he has it right. Dan is my manager, and Lucie is nothing to me again.

"Has she been here?"

"You had a relationship with this girl."

"Not exactly a relationship. It was my birthday—"

"You were her manager at that time?"

"Yes."

"And you had sex in your office?"

"It was consensual. She's nothing to me. If she is implicated in this, I know nothing about it. But have you spoken to her?"

"Did you show her any of the images on your phone?"

"There were no images."

He is silent for a long time, staring at me. Eventually, without saying anything he leaves the room. I have an urge to grab the file and the detective's brand new notes, but the officer is still at the door.

"What happens now?" I turn and ask.

"We'll see, sir. It's the weekend."

I think that they are unsure whether to let me go. They have been confused by the file somehow, as surely as I am confused by files of pension reconciliations. I stand, but at the same moment the detective returns and says,

"Are you planning on any travel?"

"No."

"There are more enquiries to be made. If there are any developments, we can find you at the address you've given?"

"Yes."

"I have to tell you that most likely outcome is that we will resume on Monday under caution and you will have the right to have a solicitor present."

As I sign the statement I do not know what I have done. The document is confused and incomplete, but perhaps it is enough that I came here. Shallow, I always find comfort in short term gains. I imagined a cleansing shower of release and justification when this was over, even though I knew the real test would soon come. In fact, it feels as if I have been baptised in slurry, and still the storm has not broken.

Something is wrong. We never leave Poppy in the hall, but as I slowly walk up the drive her nose is up against the glass door. She has sensed me, and I am committed to doing this now. A desperate scrabbling and barking which goes unanswered. I search my pockets and slip my key into the lock. A squeaking somewhere between pain and joy. I am as pleased to see her as she is to see me.

"Where's your mum?" I whisper, "where's your mum?"

Then the living room door opens a fraction. In this narrow frame is Susie. She has been recently upset, and there is a fizzing embarrassment which she cannot hide with a smile.

"I'm sorry I let myself in. I didn't think you were here."

Great efforts to prevent Poppy from squirming into the living room.

"Oh, Drew."

"Can I come in?" I say, stepping back, so it does not look as if I am intent on sliding past her like the dog.

"Yes, of course." Her pale skin is blushing red, a colour I know from finding surprise presents and innocent thanks for unwanted gifts. "Someone's here, Drew," she whispers. "It's fine."

Patting and rubbing, we try not to trap Poppy's nose in the door. I turn, and standing by our mirror is Hennie, business smart.

"Hello, Drew." She is beyond blushing. Perhaps that was the first stage when she came here, but now her face has been drained of blood.

"Gabs and Pippa are playing upstairs," Susie says, flustered. I can sense that she is aching to check on them yet does not want to leave us.

"I'll get us another coffee." But even this is too far away for her. Perhaps sensitive to this Hennie hovers by the open kitchen door. Hennie looks at me briefly, then stares into the kitchen.

"What's happening?" I say, but she continues to watch the coffee being poured.

Susie hesitates, but my cup is placed next to Hennie's, and so we are on the sofa together. Susie takes the armchair. She is Saturday casual but sits bolt upright on the edge. It is Hennie in her suit who seems close to collapse, curling up and closing her eyes. I cannot see both women together. I expect the lead from Hennie, but it is Susie who speaks first. Of course, her professional training has prepared her for this, and she has had time to collect herself.

"Drew, we're so worried about you. Hennie came to see me because she cares about you too."

I wonder how long they have been together. Long enough for some hurried explanation from Hennie that my wife does not understand? Long enough for some female bonding so they could share stories about my failings?

"Susie, I'm fine."

"Drew, we have to look at this objectively," she says in her concerned and patient voice. "You haven't been at work and to be honest, some of your behaviour has been erratic. We need a way forward. We'll help you—"

I spin round to Hennie. "I don't need help, but I need loyalty. What have you said? Would you have told me about this?"

Hennie screws up her eyes further, and I have to turn back to Susie.

"Hennie only confirmed what I had been worried about, Drew. Only that. Can I ask what medication you're taking?"

"Nothing."

"Let me go back to your GP with you—"

"Susie, it's a game, I needed to lay low for a while, and I'm still getting paid. You're still getting paid!"

I will Hennie to come to my aid here, even though Susie might be hurt.

"It's gone too far..." Hennie whispers.

"Are you looking after yourself?" Susie says. "I'm not sure. We need to see what can be put in place to help you. What happens is that things slide little by little so that you hardly know that it is happening. Then when the change back is made, you remember what it was like before."

"Susie, you sound as if you are about to assess me for suction handles in my shower."

I have hurt her badly.

"No, Drew. What I mean is that you've been plunged into this and you are in no position to understand what is happening. Your reasoning might be impaired. Hennie and I can see the situation, and because we are fond of you, we want to help. Imagine what it must have taken for Hennie to come to see me, and I have no choice because you're the father of my children!"

God help me if I hoped to come back to Susie and be treated as a hero today.

"You think that I'm paranoid? Well I went to the police today. I did the right thing, even though I am being threatened by those I exposed. I came to let you know that."

A barely stifled groan from Hennie. I tell it as if I am telling a story. From the pressing, hostile crowds in the city which crystallised my decision, to the soiled reality of signing my statement with the policeman's scratchy ballpoint. Every detail against me and the manner of my telling it confirming that I am mad. Gradually I turn my back on my wife because she understands less and less of this.

"When I got to Ulph on my list I don't know whether this real policeman did not believe anything I had said, or whether he was secretly laughing at me. But I did it, and there is nothing else I can do for Chantelle and Molly and Victoria. When I had finished I became sure I was going to be arrested, and I think I will be arrested soon."

Pictures of Our Children

Hennie turns away from me.

"Drew, I'm scared," Susie says. "Stay here for a few days, for as long as you like."

"I don't know whether I can be anywhere just now," I say. But I think I want to be on an anonymous boat on the Broads. "Susie, I came to warn you."

For comfort she wants to run upstairs. "I must check on the girls."

Perhaps she sees that Hennie is now too distressed to be any threat.

As soon as she is gone Hennie grips my shoulder.

"Christ Drew, what have you done?"

"The only thing I could do. We talked about this last night."

"We agreed you'd wait."

"I think Jim jumped before me."

"You fucking idiot!"

"Christ knows what he told them. He must really have it in for me again."

She makes a grab for something on the coffee table.

"Local news." She spits and waves the TV remote.

I put a finger to my lips. Often, I think that if I need to advance my imagined illness, I only need to observe people who are supposedly balanced. The manic careerists at work, the people who crave attention on social media and now Hennie, shaking and all her insecurities written on her face.

I hear Poppy becoming distressed in the hall.

"Clare will hurt you; she'll hurt you Drew."

"I'll go back to the police to make them understand."

"Don't do that! I won't let you do that. I'm linked to you, Drew, I wish I wasn't but I am." She jabs a finger upwards. "And that girl loves you."

"Let's be calm." I whisper and she lets me take the remote. A physical softening. The hard tendon of her wrist relaxes as I stroke her arm.

"Drew, I'll look after Susie. Go somewhere for a while."

"Don't let her believe I'm ill."

"That's the least of your worries at the moment. Think!"

This plan is drawn in the seconds available before Susie returns. Poppy, locked in to protect Hennie from her innocent love, scrabbles madly like some tension-building gameshow countdown. Then Hennie, holding her ears, speaks.

"Go now. Grab some stuff from your flat and book into a hotel. Text me where you are and what name you are using. I'll come; I promise I'll come."

The door opens and there is a rush like after a rollercoaster drop. Gabby and Philippa are crying silently. Gabby rushes to me. Pippa, carried by Susie has a smile for Hennie. It is difficult to leave the house. To say goodbye to my daughters and console Susie. To contain the bewildered dog.

Chapter Twenty-five

Grab some things. One of the things I have grabbed in my mood of confused elation are my good headphones. I listen to Schumann until the time when I become anxious that I might miss a step or a knock. Life has become something different. I am in the Maids Head Hotel in the centre of Norwich, and in a definitely non-Tudor extension. But the timber framing and nice reception will be there for her as she arrives. I do not know what Hennie intended, perhaps something more out of the way of local news. Neither do I know how long I will be staying here, but I have chosen a room well above my means. She cannot mistake this.

I love Hennie so much. This is the excitement I feel now; she is propelling me away from work and failure. In the past I have disappointed my daughters if they were looking to me for inspiration; I could never live up to Susie. Now my world has changed to precarious adventure. I have done the right thing, and they will be proud of me when they understand. An extraordinary thrill about Hennie. I cannot lay claim to her in any conventional sense, but her crystal-clear mind is full of me and working for me. We will plan on her boat, later. From my window on the third floor there is a view of an exciting strip of pavement. I watch though I do not know if she will come this way. Street lights come on, and the strip becomes even more magical. Then towards dawn, as I shift my gaze to the dark cathedral the second ticks over and I know that she will not come. I have been robbed of sleep when I need to think clearly.

"Sorry, sorry, sorry," I say and try to take the envelope as gently as I can, as if this will make up for what has gone before.

The girl behind the desk looks genuinely crushed. I have said something like;

"Did you even try to let her know where my room was!"

Of course, she was not on duty during the night, although she is too apologetic and upset to say this. I make a show of clumsily opening the envelope as if the contents might excuse my behaviour, or divert her. A key falls to the floor. The note reads

"Hi Drew.

You can go to Jim's flat.

Love

Hennie x"

I cannot listen to music here. In this squalor I watch Dan's videos. The latest one revolts and excites me. He pretends to be on big bad city streets rather than in sleepy Norwich; perhaps he has learnt this from the busy, dramatic thumbnails that steal views from his channel. He shouts orders in a jumpy montage of clips. A cyclist in front of him swerves to pass between the curb and a bus, the blinking yellow left turn light smeared by rain on the lens. Dan barks orders.

"Don't go down there!"

Follow him, Dan, follow him down that tunnel of death you self-righteous prick. Go that way every time.

I accept that Hennie will not come here. It is difficult even to imagine her in this infested place. She has rung me twice every day since I have been here and has been gentle and encouraging. But in this mess I have never been able to recreate the comfort of Clare whispering on my pillow. When I am in bed, any warmth seems to be incubating a nest of fresh bugs. Hennie sends good wishes from Susie, but I have spoken to my wife briefly. She will come if she can get someone to look after the children, but it occurred to me that it would be like a medical home visit. I told her this, and she had laughed and said that she would bring the suction handles. I think that

Pictures of Our Children

Hennie is looking after her. I imagine them together now; with Poppy the dog, who loves the family, still exiled in the hall. I do not know what lesson Hennie meant to teach me by sending me here, giving me this golden key. There is a plan, but I do not press her. Possibly she means to go to the police herself, and I do not want to find myself talking her out of this. She will save me, but for the moment I am stuck in this hell. I cannot believe that prim Victoria ever came here either, still less was in the bed. The cooking facilities are dirty and possibly dangerous. The gas fire is no less treacherous. There are real creatures here. Woodlice parade across the bathroom floor and spiders hang above it. Once, on the cistern, a small slug. This is not the bachelor pad of a carefree young man who does not worry because he spends no time here. It is the nest of someone who no longer cares what happens. No different to my own flat.

A loud knock. But first a shuffle like carol singers gathering. A shout, but this can be nothing to do with me.

"I'm not Jim Crane," I say to reassure myself. Neither his friends, his landlord nor his dealer can touch me. I open the door, and a light is in my face.

"Who is Amy!"

Amy? Amy and Tom, who lived across the street, who we got to know when the frequencies of our baby monitors became tangled and who heard Gabby crying. Amy, who was made to sit next to me at my new primary school. Whose fingers flexed like cat's claws as she threatened to squeeze them into my ugly face.

"Who is Amy!"

Two phones and a Go-Pro. Now a woman's voice.

"How old is Amy?"

"What do you mean?" I say. Then a series of competing shouts.

"You're live on Facebook, for our protection and your protection."

"How old is Amy!"
"She's fourteen! She told you that she was fourteen!"
"Stay still!"
"What does that say! Read it to us!"
"You were going to meet her in Chesterfield!"
"Fourteen!"
"You're under citizen's arrest. Section 24a"
"Filthy nonce!"
"We're not here to harm you!"
The woman's voice again, struggling against the shouts.
"The girl doesn't exist. You were talking to me the whole time. I have all the chat logs. Do you understand?"

I shield my eyes and can see the woman more clearly now, drawn and anxious as she struggles to flick through a sheath of papers. They are ordered with pastel markers, in a sweet efficiency like Hennie's. When I first catch sight of the face behind her, I think it is a mask, but as he leans from the shadows of the hall, there is a floating visage of yellow skin and a black forked beard.

"I have three decoys on you. A fourteen-year-old and two fifteen-year-olds!" he says, as if he were their pimp.

The urgency of the people behind the cameras is propelling the woman close to me.

"Jim, is this your penis?" she whispers. "Dick pics to a fourteen-year-old, Jim. Our secret, you told her!"

"I'm not Jim Crane," I say.

"How many times have we heard that!" someone yells. But there is confusion amongst them, and the woman almost drops the papers in an effort to find a normal reference picture.

"This is what we do!" A squeaky male voice. "We're very good at it. We've travelled over a hundred miles to get you."

"You're vigilantes?"

"We're Creep Commando—"

"Keep filming!" Forkbeard orders. "Has the call been made to the police?"

The echoey hall does nothing for their synchronisation, and they talk over each other in northern accents, but it is the woman who takes the lead.

"Do you know where Jim is?"

"I don't. He's leant me his flat." I am anxious to be scrupulously honest. "Well, a mutual friend gave the key to me."

"Ring the bastard's phone!"

I show them my phone. After jerky, conflicting instructions as to what I should do, I hold it out to them to gaze at, like an icon. For a while they are all silent, even after it is clear that this *coup de theatre* has failed.

Then, "His friend is in there!"

"Den of nonces!"

I turn to the woman. "Please check inside. There's only me here."

I would like the chance to talk to her, to understand what is happening, and I need a friend in this. The men fall over themselves to prevent her from stepping past me, though she seems the most reasonable and strongest of this bunch. I feel sorry for her, for the filth she cannot escape.

"Don't be sheltering him!" someone yells.

Despite the clamour of men wanting to be seen to protect her, the woman has shown no sign of wishing to enter the flat. She stands perfectly still, brave enough.

"Guys, we have the wrong person here. We'll go."

It is now that I feel the group's raw aggression, stripped of any justification. For the first time, I sense that I am physically in danger, and I move to shut the door. A sharp bell. Loud. Just one chime.

"Wait!" The woman is staring at me, then at her phone. "Drew?"

In an instant I am seized by fear, as if it were a synthetic emotion triggered by a fairground ride or a virtual reality jump-scare.

"It's Drew, isn't it? Another team have recognised you just now from our live stream. You've arranged to meet a thirteen-year-old in London."

"Not me—" I say.

"Fucking paedo!"

"Do you understand, Drew? They have a decoy that you've been grooming. This is your photo?" The woman holds out her phone.

Often, when I know my photo is being taken, I will think of someone special as if to fix the moment. Let's say that I was thinking of Susie here. The photo was taken in an office, but I am smiling.

"It's my work ID photo."

"What is your employer going to say?" someone sneers.

The woman sighs. "I won't show you, but it seems that you both sent exactly the same cock shot. You'll have to fight your mate Jim for copyright."

"Den of fucking nonces! I told you!"

I struggle to understand what has happened and try to test myself to quell my fear. Someone has stolen Jim's phone and has deliberately taken bait in a chat room. My stolen phone is clamped to different bait. I assume all this and yet it is possible that a few moments ago Jim's phone rang in his pocket in his uneasy refuge with Victoria's family.

"My phone was lost. I know who has it now."

"How many children are you talking to!"

A door opens on the landing above. A stranger who I only know from his footfall on the ceiling. Returning late at night after shift work, and the ping of his bathroom light early in the morning. A snatch of an Eastern European language if he is on his mobile as he passes my door. The woman calms the shouts, and he does not come down. She dials a number on her phone.

"Ali, can you send the chat logs over, Hun?" Then she turns to her companions. "There's a mountain of them. They've been talking for two weeks. We'll leave this to Alison and her team. They're local... Drew, don't say it but is this your address?" I nod at the screen. "They'll pass what they have on you to the police. I do this because I have children of my own. I do this because they must be protected. Guys, we have nothing more to say to him."

"Your life is over you fucking scumbag nonce!"

Just as my mind is at the mercy of rogue emotions, my body burns and trembles as if a pyramid milkshake has poisoned it. I am sick into the filthy toilet.

Chapter Twenty-six

I watch the trains glide over the Hohenzollern bridge. Almost never a moment when the tracks are clear; sleek white expresses caught by the speed restriction, and red S-Bahn services slowing for Cologne HBF. I know almost nothing about German locomotives and must look up all the different classes. I drink beer late into the night, and the strange caged fires at the tables provide comfort like the lights of the trains. Perhaps I am destined to come back to this place until I master the ticket machine at the airport station, always crowded with confused tourists. Köln HBF is what you need to type, umlaut over the o, and be ready to validate the ticket in the separate machine. This time I forgot that it does not take twenty euro notes and the queue behind would have been happy to see me arrested as a fugitive.

I cannot listen to music here; not Schuman who tried to drown himself in the Rhine, not any of the German masters, not anything. My hotel room is functional and clean, but it is my mind that is cluttered. In this place I watch videos; videos where the sweet anticipation of meeting turns sour for predators. Sometimes there is an immediate chase, but more often there is a glacially slow realisation that no girl or boy is coming. Denial and then self-denial. *I knew that she wasn't thirteen*, they say, helping to build the overwhelming case against them. *I wasn't going to meet him*, they say, cornered in the meeting place. If they are clever enough to realise what they face they stop talking. If they are sly, they say that it is an illness and that they need help. *Sorry.* Perhaps twenty of these one after another, and they are all seedy, selfish men. Maybe the paedo hunters are heroes, but they face little resistance from these dick-pic saddos, and after all, they do not go after drug dealers or gangsters involved in organised crime. Dan and Clare are far out of reach of stings like these. They have their own marketplace: boutique and exclusive. But I would give anything to see them caught in the moment when they realise the game is up. Perhaps what I have done is more courageous than the adventures of the mavericks in station car parks, though no one will see or understand. Watch videos is what I do in this room, and I am driven to watch more until I feel queasy and sated.

"Hello, who's calling please, and how can I help you?"

Oh Gabby I love you so much, perfect little clone of a call-centre operator, but you will slough that off even before you are a teenager and be free.

"Gabs, sweetheart."

A stream of snapshots and ideas about her life today. Not selfish because she knows that it will please me. She finishes with,

"How can I hug you?"

Susie is close to the phone now; I can sense her before I ask, breath close to the receiver and a kiss on her daughter's head.

"Oh God, Drew, how are you?"

"Fine."

"Is that true?"

"For the purposes of this conversation."

"Did you teach Gabs to answer the phone like that?"

"Might have done."

"Prick!"

"Thank you."

"Gabs it was lovely how you answered the phone," she says to our daughter.

"Is everything OK with you?"

"Obviously, as long as Gabby is here with me. Pippa is fast asleep on the bean bag, I wish you could see."

"Susie, I need a favour."

"Yes, of course."

"I'll tell you where you can find an emergency key. Can you go to my flat?"

"You never invited me when you were there."

"I was never comfortable in that place. Don't worry about anything else there, please."

"Drew?" Concern begins to take over her gentle voice.

"My M&S Mastercard has expired. I must have received a replacement in the past few weeks. Perhaps I didn't open it."

"You're living on credit?"

"Just don't worry, Susie. Will you look for it for me? I can survive here until everything is sorted out."

"Of course I'll do it, Drew. Is it all I can do? Imagine you going back to Cologne."

"I like it here."

"I like that you're there, in a strange way. Do you understand? I was so happy in Germany. I know that since then Pippa has completed our family, but I don't think I've been as happy as I was then."

The old town is not old, of course. The original city was reduced to rubble by bombing, and the bridge was blown up by the German army trying to stop the Allied advance. Both the bridge and the city were rebuilt so naturally and perfectly that it is strange to find yourself thinking about what happened. Susie and I would sit in the Town Hall Square listening to the carillon and overjoyed that this world would belong to Gabby, and pleased with ourselves for showing it to her so young. Everything was wonderful until the cathedral and the bells. Then Susie would kiss me and ask what was wrong, but I could not tell her.

Creep Commando, these are my paedo hunters. By appointment. Always they operate with the same level of chaos and self-righteous misunderstanding. They have plenty of models because the Internet is teeming with these gangs. I get the impression that many of the people involved are unemployed, now entitled to use the language of professionals and seizing that chance.

"You're under citizen's arrest, section 26a!" they always say; but once, brilliantly,

"You're under Citizen's Advice!"

I leave it a long time before I dare to watch my own bit-part in this pantomime. I do this in stages. After three tries, I get past the moment where the woman says my name. Perhaps you can see the fear in my eyes, but I say nothing, and so say nothing stupid. From other videos, the woman's name is Gemma, or Gem or Gems. You can catch that she has extravagantly curly hair, but I have had the privilege of seeing it in life, and it is dyed dull autumnal red. She fascinates me, because there is a hint that if things had turned out differently for her then she would not be on all these doorsteps. The others with her would have found them. She whispers about her children and gives the impression that if she trusted you a little more, you predator cunt, she would open up about some shocking abuse that haunts her. Below my video is the swamp of the comments section, and I dare not look at this.

As the compelling exotic trains on the bridge become strings of lights a text comes in. It is from Susie, and my head is light from Kolsch and it is so overwhelming that I cannot take it in at first. Three kisses, one assigned to each of the drawings. Gabby and Pippa, and then both my daughters together with Poppy the dog. The sketches sing out from the screen of my cheap phone. I have a million photos, but these will stand for all of them. A moment captured—what is that? Here Gabby shows both vulnerable innocence and a hint of challenging intelligence which will blossom. Pippa radiates a serenity that suggests that she and those around her will lead a blessed life. The pure joy of the dog might stand for the people whose lives these girls will touch, but in fact Poppy is crazy most of the time, and it is this that has been caught, presumably from a synthesis of leaps and springs and smotherings. Hennie has made these. She has created my girls, and in this she has laid herself bare too. A casual order, second nature to her, where random lines come together to perfection. Running under the surface, a deep love for people and for life, but also a yearning for children she can never have. The drawings give me the answer to the question I did not dare to ask Susie. Hennie is looking after my family as she promised, and these days, I like to think of them together.

So, the front door of my flat is famous. Dark Angels of the East are a rather different outfit to Creep Commando, and I am familiar with their work now. They are tighter, with more of a distinction between the investigator-accusers and their security, who lurk behind. Therefore, they do not talk over each other nearly so much. They follow almost masonic rituals, pointing the camera to the floor before the sting and filming in portrait to narrow the field of view. They attempt to protect their identities, although they never quite succeed. And tonight, for me, they have been infiltrated by a lesser unit.

"We are doing this in collaboration with Creep Commando," a woman whispers into the microphone, clearly irritated. "Get sharing."

The camera swings. Purple leggings and papers that must have my name on. I don't see her face, but someone says, "Here Ali," as they hand her the chat logs. I do not see Gemma, and it is Ali's show. She becomes more and more bad-tempered.

"Don't say names!" Then, "I don't know how this fucking filter got on here, and I don't know how to get it fucking off!"

The filter says *Sunday Funday* and I can't help but laugh. The woman hands off this bomb to one of the men on security, and expects him to sort it out. The phone is passed from hand to hand, revealing every face in this crowd in turn, and resting on an unsettling close up of a forked beard, but the filter remains. If the fat yellow text is to be believed for its cheery electronic persistence, I am seeing this attack on my door a day after it has happened. An increasing frenzy as the door is not opened. Security line up to make an assault on the bell and woodwork.

"I know you're in there!" Ali yells.

"No you don't", I say, "no you don't!" and somehow I am pleased that they have been deceived and humiliated, and that they have done this to themselves live on Facebook.

"It will go better for you if you open up and talk to us."

"That's not true!" I say, "how can it be?"

"Open up!"

"Never!" I shout, and perhaps I would have yelled this had I really been behind my door, and I am suddenly excited. But then my mouth dries. A sound I know. Faint, but potent to me. The sound of locking myself into isolation, a struggle with the ill-fitting key, rattling and grinding. Susie blinks into the light. Of course she is doing my errand, and yet it takes me a moment to realise this, and I confuse my wife with an intruder. Murk behind her and searing beams in front.

"What is this?"

At first, as I recognise her, I think she is going to fight, the arrow pulled back; but she crumbles. Resistance is an illusion of the stark lighting, hardening her features and the booming hall, amplifying her voice. She is tiny against this horde of people, some steroid-pumped, some obese.

"He's not here! Go away please," she shrieks.

"This man is vile. Don't protect him!"

"Wait," the woman says. "Are you his partner, his wife?"

"I'm not telling you!" Susie cries as if surrounded by bullies in a playground corner. She collapses against the door, and there is a hint that her bottom lip is pushed out like a child's. The man behind the camera seems to have a momentary crisis of confidence about whether he should be filming, and pans away catching Ali full-face. His hand jumps. Perhaps he will tell his leader that he did not reveal her features, was not filming an innocent third party, and that he thought that the filter was off. There are shots of the concrete floor now but somehow, like a glass at a séance someone's hand moves the camera so that again it points at my wife.

"Ring the phone!" a man shouts, as someone always does, clever and triumphant. "He's in there!"

"Good luck with that," I shout at the screen.

The ringtone on my old phone was *Dance of the Sugar Plum Fairy* from *The Nutcracker*. Not much of me in truth, but a sacrifice on the altar of self-deprecation. I like classical music: how weird and stupid. Suddenly there are giggles as this sound floats from the hall. Susie looks round, shifty and understanding no more than I do. She seems ready to find and surrender the phone as the team stare like greedy gulls.

"Christ, Susie don't give it to them!" I say.

The group hover, turning their heads to the sound, pleased with what they have done. They know that they cannot cross the threshold, and have said so in a dozen videos, but I can sense that they are now beginning to question this rule and wonder just how important it is. Susie's hands go up, perhaps in total surrender, perhaps to signal that she does not have the phone on her person. It cannot be far inside, planted there, posted there. The team seem ready to stretch their necks and peck beyond the boundary.

"That phone is ours now!"

My wife is immobile, unable to comply with any instruction. Then Alison, remembering the masonic code of the paedo hunters says,

"We can't come in." She sounds conflicted herself, but everyone relaxes just slightly. Susie only has to say that she is my wife and they will change towards her, I know, but she stands mute and paralysed. The work is done by Ali, demanding one of the group's phones and flicking through Facebook or Instagram.

Pictures of Our Children

"You're his wife, aren't you, with two young children. Sweetheart, I'm sorry for you."

Hennie would have fought. I can see her, every nerve tight, spitting, "Fuck off!"

Susie's assailants leave. I spit, "Fuck off!" Four hundred kilometres away, and twenty-six hours after everyone has gone.

Another package in another hotel lobby. The woman smiles, but my stomach churns as I take it. Plastic bubbles pop when I press down around the shape. Only one thing that it can be, and it is a bomb, an IUD made to maim. Please let there be more drawings or a note with a kiss to accompany it, to nurse me. I take the envelope outside to rip it open. Susie has sent just my credit card and the phone; no words. Light plays on the greasy screen and the smeared pattern. Before I can retrace the plain square that Clare found, the picture of Hennie illuminates. Clare has taken off the lock. Oh God Susie, could you have searched this?

I use the card to book into a new, worse hotel. I watch the available balance dwindle, and I do not know how long I must be here, or what I am waiting for. Ever since I left work my moods have been super-defined, because I have been freed of the dampening routine. I sit on another new bed, and suddenly I have courage, a shaft of recklessness that I always ought to let illuminate the duller feelings. I take up my phone, not to try to contact Susie yet, but to dredge through the sewer of the comments under the video of me at Jim's door. Nothing will hurt me now; all the spite will be directed to the incompetence of Creep Commando, and perhaps someone will champion my innocence. I close my eyes and flick my thumb up.

"Well he looks like a fucking creep."

"Does he have children?"

"For God's sake take them!"

Peter Kirk

As I walk across the bridge I am protected from the trains by a wall of metal. Not part of the bridge; it stresses and compromises the bridge. An armour of small components. These are lovelocks. Couples have them engraved or scratch on them, and click them shut onto the chain fence. Then they throw the key into the Rhine. A symbolic shared touch by both I imagine, at the snap and the throw. They are never retrieved, never prised off, and so this solid burden has grown from both ends.

Small sounds, like remembered scents, can be potent. A bridge straight through to the brain. My key squeaking in the lock and last night a small tune which elicited a Pavlovian response of pleasure. At eleven Susie sent a text. After days without contact she sent this to my old, infected phone. A message like a terrible wound that revolts me. Chimes that invoked happier days then this;

"Gabby and Pippa were interviewed by Social Services today. Well done."

I would rather crawl through all the porn that has been pushed onto that phone than read those words again.

I will drop the toxic phone so that it lands amongst the reef of keys. I move closer to the river, though it seems everyone wants to crowd to block my way, and peer over the parapet. Vicky, you would not have jumped here. You would not have cared about the choking water prolonging your agony, but you would have seen the tourists and the tourist boats and industrial barges and despised them as possible rescuers; a messy, panicked interference as you tried to give up your life. Nadia, I think you might have hauled yourself over the bejewelled fence to be cut by the padlocks and then by the sharp wheels.

I have reached the end of the bridge and turn. The city is in front of me, and the cathedral, black, looms over it. Once it was the tallest building in the world. Vicky would have been drawn to the cathedral, and you can get access to the tallest tower, I know that. A river to destroy a phone, a high building to destroy a life. And yet the phone is still in my hand, and my grip is becoming tighter. There is something. In every competent predator hunter video I have seen, someone warns that the phone will be evidence, and that nothing should be deleted. But if they are reckless they taunt the hunted, inviting them to delete everything because it can be recovered. Yet for me, there can be no evidence except in my favour because I am innocent. This friendly forensic mishmash might be scoured to implicate Clare. I text Hennie, cryptic in the hope she might ask what I mean.

My old phone has found me and might save me xxx.

I do not return by the bridge, so that the lovelocks cannot mock me, and all the inscribed names spit in my face. So that the real people cannot lock arms in pairs against me. Instead, I take the U-Bahn back to the old town. How strange that the love locks did not register with me when I was here with Susie on my arm, because perhaps she would have liked this nonsense in her girlish way. It is nonsense that I need at this moment, to recreate the heady unreality of the evening when I fled from Walsingham, dizzy and stupid enough to grab my best headphones and my passport. I have Hennie now. I will invite her, and I will do the whole lock and key thing, whether she comes or not.

The sleek multiple units in grey-white livery with red cheat lines are ICE trains. 330 kph into Europe on the fastest. There are four generations, and tilting versions. I will recognise them all and all the red, powerful Deutsch Bahn locos too.

Chapter Twenty-seven

I do not remember this the last time, the pull on my calf muscles and the sheer effort of it all. I focus on the thin handrail and the wedge of steps I can see in front of me. I have to do this climb. Claustrophobia was not with me three years ago either. Perhaps I have said *feeling a bit claustrophobic here* when people crowded around my manager's desk, but I think that was a joke claustrophobia and it was people pressing me and not cold stone walls closing in. Often there are echoey calls from people who are coming down from the top, unchanged by the experience. This is also a disruption that I don't recollect. If they are children or elderly I will surrender the handrail and hug the spindle of stone that runs up the staircase, gift of the spiral geometry. Beneath me I can hear the purposeful steps of some German tourists. To let them pass, so that I do not feel pursued, will mean an even more precarious balance, and smiles and an attempt at conversation due to fellow travellers.

Where was it? Where was the place we turned back? It felt as though we had done a climb, but we cannot have got much further than here... and I still do not know what happened. The sound of the cathedral bells had poured down the steps and caught us, and in an office three years later I had thought of it as a woman had fallen from a car park, and I had understood everything. Suddenly it is clear I am on new ground because ahead is a slab-sided passage more like the entrance an Egyptian tomb. The walls are covered in graffiti. Every surface on the climb has been defiled, but this is an easy target for the show-offs and the love-struck. Now here are the bells, massive and industrial and fenced like the dangerous trains. This machinery is for the city, their peals and knells settling softly on distant streets. Being so close to them we had been caught in a storm, a vortex; space collapsing in and time squeezed into a moment. There are benches here, but I hurry past and into the next staircase.

Don't tell me you're not coming. I mean don't tell me if you plan not to come.
This to Hennie, a woman who I know cannot be managed or taken for granted. Yet she has not picked apart my invitation. A few messages since then. Me trying to casually clarify my muddled instructions, Hennie chatting about Susie and my daughters. But I wish I had begged the unbiddable Hennie to come. Perhaps she is here, and when I find her we will sit by the bells, and hug and smile through the cacophony. I turn around to make sure she is not already laughing at me from the stone benches. I am more tired than I ought to be. Maybe I am not eating enough. Hennie would be good with this, urging me to some remedy safely removed from the rigour of medical science. But as I race the German tourists and the bells, I know that the second may tick over even before the meeting time.

Above the belfry. This is the strangest space. It is raining here, drizzle blowing through the huge unglazed windows. The interior of this tower is insubstantial, almost transparent, but alongside, its sister is black and solid. In front of me a modern iron staircase climbs into the rain. The steps are open, and you can look through them to the round stone platform. This staircase is only challenging for me because it is different to what has gone before. It is no more or less dangerous I tell myself. I don't look down, but my thoughts plunge and hit stone. I think that my daughters are almost certainly more clever than Norfolk Social Services. They will be sure that something is wrong, and Gabby at least will have struggled a little way towards knowing what it is.

Peter Kirk

Three years ago we had been stopped in our tracks by the bells. I was in the lead, and it had been my idea to climb the tower. I think we had lied about Gabby's age at the desk as we paid. I am not sure how long the assault lasted, and I know that this is ridiculous because the bells and the clock are all about time. If I say it stretched to minutes, I will be wrong because surely the bells' work is done in seconds. If I say it was over in an instant the long sequence of my thoughts as the bells still sounded will belie it. I was startled by the initial shock and gripped both rail and stone. Susie was secretly pregnant with Pippa then. I turned and looked at her, and perhaps there was a short time when we might have laughed together as you do in the moment of release after a scare. She was more beautiful than I had ever seen her, but as I stared, I noticed that tears were welling in her eyes. There must have been more than one bell sounding because later there was a dissonance which was as oppressive as the volume. Susie was not looking at me but at Gabby, a step below me. I looked down, and Gabby was impossibly beautiful too, perfect reflection, now crying like her mother. And as the sound continued to pour down my girl wept uncontrollably. I know hearing changes and fails, and that children can hear frequencies that adults cannot. Distress began to distort her features like physical pain. Perhaps it was the agony of a jarred eardrum, and yet I was, and am still, prepared to believe she was shielding her ears against a high whisper that was saying *this is what life will be.* Still the noise continued, and my daughter looked straight at me. With all my being I wanted to comfort and kiss her, but as I reached down, she took a perilous turn to her mother, and because they were on different steps was able, for as long as they both stayed still, to press her head into Susie's belly. Later I bribed the girl with sweets to win her back.

Pictures of Our Children

The iron steps become a tight spiral and screw themselves into the vault. Here there is a curious wooden pavilion and above it the void of the pierced spire tip. Then at last I am at the viewing gallery. It is enclosed with hooped iron which gives the impression of an old zoo or aviary. There is a strict one-way system, and I walk slowly through the rain, clockwise. As I follow the path round, it is as if I am tracing the seconds and I want to hold back, not savouring the dwindling time but hoarding it. Now, near the sacred summit I suppose, the profanities and aimless doodles have given way to familiar hearts and linked names. If Hennie comes I will carve our names clean on the black stone, and no one will remove them because the old masonry will crumble if it is scoured. The tourists are not stopping to deface the stonework today; everyone is hurrying past the telescopes and the views and jostling me.

The strangest thing is that I have not lost all hope. Rather my hope has been crowded into the last part of the path, the last seconds. I do not know whether this is some childish optimism or an intimation and dread of some terrible consequence if she does not come. I can see, though, the very place where my hope might die. Slower... I do not think Vicky could have jumped here because the drop is so protected. The landmarks of Cologne mark the clock face: the station, the town hall, the radio tower. Arrows mark the way you must go. If I can't surrender to the climb down or to the fall, will I try to stay here forever? Something has been nagging at my anticipation for the past few days. What if Hennie has so utterly misunderstood me that it makes everything that has passed between us almost meaningless? What if by an unforgivable misjudgement, like some embarrassed adolescent dating arrangement, she has shattered my dreams? What if she has sent my wife in her place...? But what? I would take that. I want it now... I stop and close my eyes. I sense the slightest commotion. And then I open my eyes to her, striding confidently against the flow. Hennie smiles, stretches out both hands and kisses me.

Chapter Twenty-eight

We lie on the bed in the filthy room, and I think I am the happiest I have been in my life. This has not been a rush to come together. Hennie has slept, chatted, slept again and begun to loosen the straps of her dress and scrunch down her tights. She is lovely. Now I watch her as she sleeps, eyes never quite closed so a flash of blue-green. Abandoned, mouth open, she sighs, snorts and wheezes. Her hair is still slightly damp: no dryer in this mean room. It is extraordinary, grown even beyond the extravagant length of when I first knew her. Often, at work, she would double it into some sort of ponytail. Now it tumbles off the edge of the bed. She droops one arm to the floor and turns her gently lined face upwards. Not like Susie, who covers her face and curls into a ball like a child. Susie: springing awake at every touch. I stroke Hennie's arm and kiss her, and she does not stir. And the thing that fascinates me most about her naked body is the scar. I run my fingers down it. This almost killed her and in a sense, defines her. It has constrained her life in a way I cannot imagine. Her soft belly and the crease of hard tissue. Something has been strange with me lately. I have been living retrospectively, at a distance. When I embraced Hennie at the top of the cathedral I was not in that moment, even though I had longed for it a few seconds before. I hardly know— perhaps I had felt her damp hair, and my mind had gone back to the time of our wretched first date. On the way down we did sit on the stone benches, and Hennie giggled and took my arm, but I had jumped at the first strike of the bells, as if I had wanted to recreate that moment with Susie three years ago. Now I have caught up. I touch Hennie, and the thrill is immediate and defined, and I feel the exact moment my hand lifts. I lived and felt the climax too... except that in that mix of pleasure and pain I thought of what had brought us together, the crime and the danger and that had seasoned the ecstasy. Except that I thought of Nadia too—not with me, but caught in the revolving door and all that had happened after. I do not quite feel guilty about that because it is part of our shared history, Hennie's and mine.

Being isolated for so long I can barely string two words of speech together, and I come at things obliquely.
"Listen, your ticket will be cheap enough not to worry about."
"No, Drew, not a good idea for me to stay."
"Delay a few days; I'll find something and come back with you."
"We need to think, think, think. Not much longer. What do we need...? A cooling-off period, a respite, a breathing space."
"So many things I'm thinking about... Chantelle."
"Chantelle and Molly are safe, Drew."
"You've spoken to Chantelle?"
"I've seen her."
"She's back at work?"
"No, I went to see her."
"At her house?" I have an urge to test her because I fear she is saying this to please me. "What was that like?"

She props herself up on her elbow for this, then her trick of screwing her eyes up before opening them wide. The effect is as if she is telling a ghost story.

"I'll be honest with you. The situation isn't great for Chantelle and Molly. I choose to live in isolated spots, but, Jesus, I couldn't live there. I sat in the kitchen, and it was like something from the nineteen-seventies, suspended in time because even then they knew the sea was on its way. Everything stifles Chantelle, she just watches her mum slowly succumb to dementia and tries to do the best for Molly. A very Norfolk type of depression Chantelle has, oppressive sea and sky. I don't think she was affected by what we know about though... nothing that sinister. Chaz and I got quite close when you sequestered us in the file room. It was quite an intense moment in that bloody kitchen. I think she would have told me."

"Thank you."

"Don't worry. You're a quiet hero, Drew. Just hold your nerve a little longer."

She relaxes, and I think she will sleep again, but she whispers something it takes me a little time to catch.

"I'm working for you."

I cannot help but think of that comfortable moment when I was in bed, and Clare's telephone voice was in my ear. Even the words become the same.

"Mr Ulph in Sheffield."

"What?"

"Mr Ulph in Sheffield. Mr Ulph, Mr Ulph, Mr Ulph..." As she sings this, I find it more difficult to believe that it is a name at all, or even a word. But, gloriously, Hennie believes it. "Leave this to me."

The last thing was that she took the engraved lovelock from me, clicked the mechanism a few times and, as if her decision was founded on this satisfaction she said,

"Yes, do this!"

I do not know the exact time she left me. A series of disturbances to my sleep and the impression of parting. A kiss on the lips, but I might have dreamed it. Again, my bed is a boat, on the Rhine or on the Broads. I knew that she might leave before I woke because of the logistics of the late flight to Stansted. My arm rests on an empty pillow, but I feel a wistful sadness, nothing like grief. So many consolations I am left with, echoing. She thinks I am a hero; she is working for me; she loves me. I am certain there will be a note, and I rush to find it. It is on the scratched grain of the dresser, not folded, open. *Dearest Drew* and kisses at the end. Only a second before I read it, but enough to catch the sense of division. Two paragraphs, each distinct. A subtle change of slope and script, but each as different in feel as printed fonts, and an unnatural space between the blocks. The first lines rushed and cheery.

Dearest Drew

Thank you so much. What a day! I wish I could stay even a little longer, but you will understand why I can't. By the way, I'm scared of heights!

Now the jump.

In our short time together, I wanted to concentrate on positive things, seeing you so together and determined. But one bit of news I must tell you is that Jim died last week. How can our little office be so cursed? But please keep strong.

Lots of love

Hennie xxx

She will be at Cologne-Bonn Airport now; on the low, hard seats, legs splayed. Her bag unapologetically on the next place to protect herself. Our little office. It takes a little effort to remember that I might be a part of this again. The insurance family. I do not think I am responsible for Jim's death. I gave him the chance to go to the police first, and I believe he did that. I protected him from Creep Commando. In the last weeks I have not been in the country to try to sort out his tangled emotions.

Chapter Twenty-nine

Two cries, mine and the man's, and the roar of a passing freight train. So the moment is lost, and the key falls from my hand without ceremony or thought. "Schnell!" I shout at the rider, but he does not turn, and I suppose he could not look back without losing his balance on the narrow bridge path. I might have stepped back, careless, and I've learned from Dan that cyclists believe nothing should impede their effort. Carried a little in the wake of the bike I am disorientated and have lost the lock. I wanted a photo for Hennie, but the composition on my phone's screen is ugly, a mass of competing locks; ours in the middle perhaps, but I am not sure. I may not send this, but the photo can serve as my memory of the idea of the lovelock. I prefer something else. I did not find this until much later. On the back of her note a drawing of the Hohenzollern—she would have seen the bridge from the cathedral, but to understand the structure she must have registered it as her S-Bahn from the airport rumbled over. Stretching almost all the way across the bridge is a train. No train I recognise, it is an imaginary train, but a plausible impression and seeming to be travelling impossibly fast, as the ICE expresses do. Now I think that she is gently making fun of me, and that there is no hidden meaning in the depiction of the bridge. Almost the first thing I said to her as we made our way down from the top of the cathedral tower was to thank her for the beautiful drawings of my children, but I don't believe she interpreted this as a plea for help to get back to my family. I did ask her to negotiate with Susie to unblock me on her phone, but that is a modest ambition.

Instead of the photo I send Hennie a description of me on the bridge, struggling to turn the key as I had selected such a rich field of locks rather than have us isolated on the edges. Then I smuggle in a concern that has been growing.

Hennie, should I look at the pictures on my old phone?

The answer comes at once.

Go for it!

Perhaps she hasn't understood what I meant, this response is so casual. But she is the one in Norwich, and perhaps in Sheffield too, and she is the one who might be in real jeopardy for pursuing this. I have been thinking about Jim. I cannot find much in the Norwich press, but he died in the flat where I had been confronted by the paedo hunters. The unspoken word is suicide. It shocks and scares me because I witnessed the whole descent. Victoria and Nadia were already broken when I first knew them.

My burner does not seem to be flaring as brightly as the others. I may call the waiter over to see to it, but perhaps the real source of heat is the radiant electric fires on the walls, and I am not close to one of those. After my near collision with the bike my clothes became drenched with sweat, and now this has cooled. It was the same when Dan almost hit me with his car at Chantelle's house, and I froze as I summoned the courage to go to see Susie. What happened that night, and what was I thinking about with Chantelle? She has always been safe. I should have gone back to my hotel from the bridge, but the phone signal is weak there, and I am waiting for something. For one night only I am back on Facebook, and I am longing for a friend request to be accepted. Now it comes. Jane. I think we were friends once, but she purged me; now she cannot resist the chance to do me harm. Jane; soppy-fierce mother of the insurance family, archivist of corporate conviviality, relentless chronicler of work-related fun. The folder is called Department Summer Party. Yesterday I saw something in Nadia's photo. I cannot pretend to myself that my compulsion to scour every other image of that day is driven by the same forensic curiosity that led me to blow up the image of Luca, and drag it through reverse imaging software. It is simply that I think that Hennie might have been there because I noticed a tall figure in the background. Perhaps it was just a suggestion, a reminder of Hennie, but I am hungry to find anything. When I had first seen the photo I had carelessly fallen back to my default position of offended self-righteousness, and had assumed that it was an event I had not been invited to. But thinking clearly this was not the case. It was a barbecue before my time.

So, what was I doing on that glorious summer day? I was riding trains; trying to keep my feet as the brakes caught, leaning from the doors into fresh early morning air, marking tickets with my adopted signature. They were short trips mostly, shuttling between Norwich and the coast, but I saved all those miles and coming home to Susie it was as if it was as if at the end of a very long journey. Revenue is king, of course, but, in gentle Norfolk, it was easy to adopt some matter of fact or stern persona to get payment or an address. Terry, who trained me, would, on leaden winter mornings, announce things like,

"We are due to arrive at Sheringham at ten forty-one where the temperature is a balmy thirty degrees centigrade. Before that, on the left, you will be able to glimpse the legendary Hanging Gardens of North Walsham..."

Sometimes these stupid things fitted me too, and I would promise lavishly stocked dining cars as if from the golden era of the Scottish expresses. Yet there was always the possibility of a situation where I might be tested. I did not dwell on the chance of disaster, but away from the trains, I let myself believe that I would do well. Then two things happened. I met Dan in a pub after months without seeing him, and he put into my head the idea of going back to insurance, but as a manager. He had not dangled it in front of me exactly, but had given me the confidence to see it as a possibility. And a train had moved; crept forward a centimetre, not even that, a slight judder. But the doors had been open. Nobody hurt, nobody even noticed except me and my driver, and we did not report it. In my job interview with Clare I emphasised the people handling skills involved in the of the role of train guard, the technical knowledge necessary, and the ultimate responsibility for safety.

The very first picture in the folder is of Hennie. Of course it is. I knew that she was at that barbecue because I am tuned to recognise her image no matter how blurred or pixilated. Now I am treated to a portrait that is unequivocally the woman I love. Jane is a terrible photographer, but she has been presented with a gift of a subject, bathed in perfect light. Hennie talking to Danuta, both radiant and enjoying each other's company. The impression is that they have been sharing some confidence or indiscretion just before the camera clicked, and are embarrassed in case it has somehow been recorded. Hennie's hair is pinned up, which I have never seen before. I eagerly swipe up, but am disappointed because the next shots are of people I only half recognise, minor players from other teams. I harvest these photographs, though, taking screenshots in case they have a significance which I have not recognised, or hide a shadow of Hennie. Then Dan, then Clare, their brazen smirks defying any efforts by Jane and the poor camera to hide them in shadows. Then I see Hennie again. In my excitement I skip a frame and have to thumb back. A flash, the illusion that this picture of the sun might harm my eyes. Hennie's figure distilled into an exquisite silhouette. She is holding a child. Suddenly there is a tingle in my scalp which I do not understand, but I know that people seek these sensations by watching long videos of women talking to them softly. ASMR. I have found all these thrills in a single frame, unbearably poignant in a way that only I can understand. Whose baby is this? No girl as young as this in the album I have already seen, and now it is back to pictures of people I might have said six words to in my management career, possibly about accounting. Then a shock. I have

Pictures of Our Children

another picture of Nadia and Luca, Nadia holds her son, but someone else is wheeling the pushchair and it is Victoria. The women are close enough together to give the impression that they have linked arms. Another tingle in my scalp. So they were friends, and without any process of deduction or thought, I know that the payment slip which bookmarked Victoria's file must have represented a reward for headhunting her friend from the law firm; the bounty that had destroyed them both. A little later, in another photograph the womens' roles are switched, with Nadia pushing the pram; but they are no less physically close. Luca is laughing, on his way down from being held high by Victoria. Nothing between these women when I had seen them on the morning I had been lost in the basement; no smile or acknowledgement, and I had been curiously disappointed. Even now, a sudden inexplicable emptiness. But this is what I pretended I was looking for, some insight or some strangeness. If I am to collect all these clues I must work quickly, before Jane decides how best she can hurt me. The last of the folder, and now you get the proper sense that these pictures are in time order. The sun gets lower and is even more troublesome to the camera and photographer. There is a change in composition too. The families have gone, and people stand around drinking beer from bottles. Rather than simply recording her subjects you can see that Jane is interacting with them, all gossip, innuendo and lewd comments. They grin back and make silly faces at her. The very last shows Dan and Clare. Clare holds a bottle, and her head playfully rests on Dan's shoulder, cross-eyed to acknowledge that she is tipsy. So innocence has turned to evil. As I screenshot this Jane plants on my timeline an interchangeable arrangement of trigger words, like the title of some click-bait website;

Paedo nonce fucking kiddie-fiddler piece of shit. Then, *Everybody wants you to die.*

Peter Kirk

In the past days the greatest temptation and torment has been my old phone. I take it from my pocket now. I have seen some of the images before as Clare flicked through them in John Lewis. I had thought then that they seemed to go in order of horror, and had turned away. But sometimes glimpsed sights are more disturbing than fixed and steady ones. I push the button and open my eyes. There is no going back now; I am breaking the law, the children's suffering deemed to be for my benefit too. My digital fingerprints are now on these atrocities, but the movement of my thumb, instinctively trying to cover the nakedness and the unspeakable acts is not recorded. Is this the currency of the group, these dead and empty photos where the subjects are indicated, displayed, exhibited? Mostly the children look terrified, but none are crying. Those later shots must have been discarded, I realise, the images easier to manipulate than the subjects. I wait for the nausea to set in as it did in John Lewis, but it does not come. Something worse comes: the ASMR tingling. A comforting tickle, like someone playing with my hair. Jesus! It feels like the thrill associated with Hennie, and it must be about her; the excitement of being out of bounds made keener by knowing that Hennie is with me in this by saying, "Go for it." Or perhaps it is anticipation; an unconscious belief that I really am going to find something important in this cesspit, or it is a wish for that thing, or a divination of what is to come. Every girl and boy is set against a bland background for anonymity and for better showing, and there is no artistry in the photos. No child that I recognise yet from the barbecue pictures. Still the excitement plays just under my skin, a slight tug at my hair then release, a knuckle catching the nape of my neck. My scrolling speeds up— Stop! Luca sits on a table. He is as good as gold, bewildered, but compliant. There are six images of him, and in each he is focused away from his abuser and towards his right, exactly as if an effort is being made to distract him with a toy or a funny face—Fuck! Can he be looking at his mother? The buzzing in my head rises to an intensity that is unpleasant: thank God for that, thank God! Now suddenly the scene in the basement makes sense; Victoria had collided with me as she scurried away from Nadia. The thing I had not imagined in my recall of this strange encounter was primal hatred. This was the animus of that ballet, with Vicky hugging one wall and Nadia slipping sideways against the other. Probably both women had just been released from a confrontation which Clare had staged for her own amusement, or to intimidate them. The world has shifted a little for me, but I find that I cannot despise Nadia as Vicky did. Nadia was at the bottom of the pyramid. Guilt had frozen her in the revolving door, and guilt had swung her hand as she drove into the bridge. I look at the pictures of little Luca for a long time, and now force myself to dwell on children I do not know, out of respect. There are a lot of them, and they are all very young. Perhaps not every child will wake up crying tonight, but all will be ambushed by this at some time in the future. Sometimes the children are being attacked from both sides. Always non-descript sleeves; jewellery—tokens of affection—removed so that the men and women are unidentifiable. Stop! Another child I know! A child I know, a child I love almost. Molly. I have never met her, but I remember the circumstances when I learnt of her existence, as if she was joyously born in that moment. There is only one precious frame; perhaps she screamed for her mother. I loved Chantelle a little bit too in that office, because she had taken me so much by surprise. It is unimaginable that Chantelle should have been complicit in this, but why did she deceive Hennie, telling her that her daughter was safe? I know the circumstances of this picture. Dark behind the windows now and if any date stamp had survived it would have recorded a time when I was hiding in the bushes at Chantelle's house, afraid to do anything while the girl wept. More than this, I can pinpoint the moment that Chantelle met this terror, the night I had left her alone to be picked off by Dan. The ASMR buzzing is gone; in an instant, whether it was excitement, fear, or anticipation. It is replaced by nausea and trembling, even before I understand what I am seeing. A shape, no more that, has hit me. I do not know the child in this photo; it is a circle behind her that commands all my attention. And this is what I was being led to. I seem to know before my brain processes it. Rising nausea, then cold fear. A circle, a window, the porthole of a boat. The unknown child could only endure one more image on that sunny day, river and sky behind her. Then this is the end of the filth Clare had injected onto my phone. The next picture is summer in Cromer. Kites and sandcastles. Gabby and Pippa.

Chapter Thirty

"Hennie." I cry as I run, "Hennie, you have no boat!" When my steps are not muted by grass and fall hard on the river path I shout louder to compensate, as if I want to be heard in this mad denial. Hennie has no boat because it is only a joke between us, an obsession of mine, and that is why she finds it funny and perpetuates it. And perhaps what I saw was a faux porthole on a new-build on some soulless estate in a suburb of Norwich. Except that the later photographs showed a row of portholes. Except I was sure there was a river and bank beyond the little victim's prison. But if Hennie does live on the river it might not be in the boat that I saw in the images, because there might be a hundred antique vessels on the broads. Caught up in these things, I turn to run up into the city, and I am taken by surprise by the children's fountain. I don't know if it's called the children's fountain, but I stumble into its stepping stones, pools and cobbles and recover like a clown. "Hennie, you have no boat!"

Another machine that queries me in German. But this one has a line directly into my life, a wire straight through my routine and habits and my failings. I stab at the union flag, but the options do not open up; I do not think that it can give me a balance, and I must make a bid. Two hundred would be enough in this moment, and I care about nothing but this moment. The pit that is early-in-the-month direct debits will not yet have swallowed up everything, and anything to come after that does not matter. I push the buttons, and there is a tension-building pause as if before the announcement of a TV vote. A message I do not understand, but no fake counting sound. Try again, another service, whatever the text means.

A hundred Euros. The slot machine reels spin and nothing. The bastards have not paid me.

My phone credit drains like blood.
"I've given you the address! Just protect the woman and her children who live there! Just save them because the children are in real danger! Don't you understand! It doesn't matter where I am. I'm nowhere, nowhere, but I'm coming back to see my wife and children, and after that you can do what you like with me—!"
My connection to the Norfolk police dies.

My feet are on grass again, and I hear a shout directed at me. Is everything about me outlaw and outsider now? I am being chased from the turf above the Philharmonie by earnest volunteering citizens, shooed like a chicken in case my footsteps disturb the concert in the underground hall below. But I am not intent on disruption, I have just forgotten that this lies below me, though I have reason to know all about it. I turn and swear at them like the crass marginal person that they imagine me to be. When I walk through the doors of the Philharmonie I am no more welcome. I am challenged, and I have to defend my right to enter by waving my ticket, and even then am not sure I have permission to stride into the foyer. It is the interval, and elegant couples order Aperol spritz and sec and cherish and guard the traditions.

The man at the counter has perfect, obliging English but does not understand what I need.
"The Brahms and Schumann tomorrow. That will be very special."
"But I don't want it!"
"Oh, Sir, I am so sorry that I cannot help you with this. It may be that you can arrange something privately, although we cannot accommodate it…"
I snatch the ticket back, and I break away, angry and frustrated. Good concert tickets in Europe are ruinous, but

Pictures of Our Children

this is what I had wanted as soon as she had left. Life rushed back into me, and I was recklessly happy. I become aware that someone is pressing at my shoulder and tense to resist the assault of a pickpocket. But he is a student, surely; very young, open and smiling. Again, perfect English that shames me.

"I understand how devastated you are that you cannot see the great man conduct these masterpieces. It would mean so much to me too… Forty Euros, perhaps?"

"OK, thank you."

If I were in my right mind, I would put this on Facebook as people do, his delight and my generosity.

"Hennie?" he says, and I realise that I have accidentally repeated my mantra in front of him. *Boat* he would have understood perfectly, but I cannot explain the rest and hurry away, crushing his notes in my hand.

I am saying Gabby's name aloud too. A year ago, I had a dangerous urge to play the guitar. Out of some logistical necessity I took Gabby to my second lesson and now she outshines me in every way and can sing as well.

The next transaction is not like the one for the concert ticket, though both have been decided by desperation and crushing fatigue. If the concert ticket was like pressing money into the hand of a beggar, negotiating the Ryanair site seems more like the currency markets. In between I have stuffed cash into another hole in the wall and am a player again. One seat left at this price! Fuck you! I cannot wait. Ten euros either way is meaningless to me. I press the button, and now a terrible calm in which I can do nothing.

Hi Amy I'm Drew
Hi Drew I'm fourteen. How old are you?
I'm thirty-nine.
OK!
Are you a decoy?

Peter Kirk

What's a decoy?

It is easy to think of Pippa as some serene princess, wise in unknown ways. What goes on inside her head is as mysterious as the mind of some beautiful, friendly pet. But I think she would love and trust anyone.

Cologne-Bonn Airport. Let me never come to this place again. It has some recent comforting places in my thoughts, but all of this is meaningless now because they are associated with Hennie. I had imagined her in the departure lounge, graceful on the rows of seats. I had pictured her at a distance, as if I was about to surprise her. I must abandon every image now. The memory of her blue-green eyes, concerned but smiling, as I sat under a table. The sun-drenched silhouette of her holding some borrowed, random child. Going through security I am frisked for a single coin in my pocket. They have no idea what I am carrying. No machine can detect what is on my phone, and no proper human can understand it.

In front of me on the plane, a little boy screams and cannot be comforted. I think *Good for you, good for you!* Gabby had sat smiling and awestruck, savouring the experience.

Chapter Thirty-one

I write my address and hand it over, and my nominal home has no more value to me than the scrap of paper. Perhaps the guard senses my contempt for what I have given her, and she hesitates; but the brakes begin to catch for the next Essex station, whatever it is, and there are doors to be opened, and she has little stake in this transaction. The thing is this. In the customs channel at Stansted, I had started shaking because I was sure that the doors would snap shut and trap me. Then stepping out, and a sense of freedom. Then a second after that the realisation that nobody cared about me.

"Thank you, Sir."

"You'll get the penalty fare before you can commence proceedings," I say, and I think perhaps she does care a little.

Please let me do this job again. Its gentle rhythms, medium-thick rulebook, and the sense that I was always journeying back to Susie. It suited me. That train did move with the doors open, I think, but my passengers were a long way from danger on that Norfolk track. So much better if me or my driver had reported whatever indiscretion or concentration loss it was. Then it would have been dealt with by a hearing, not the kangaroo court of my conscience; and that would have saved the deaths and ruined lives that really did happen on my watch, under my guard. I once told Victoria that insurance could be as noble as painting or music, and I think as I said it that I knew it was a lie, but I am sure now. I was so lacking in imagination that I was shocked to see a photo that showed her happy. No obituary for Jim that I could find to match the overwhelming ones for minor pianists or tenors. He was good at his job, but his work file was given over to the casual mistakes and indiscretions that I logged, and will not mention his love for Victoria and the help he tried to give her.

The guard passes again with her little hammer for emergencies and her whistle, which is almost redundant and ceremonial and I think she smiles at me. I allow myself to doze, and in this sleep I do not think Hennie has a boat because that would mean she had coldly won the trust of Molly, and it would mean that she had groomed me just as surely. I am jolted fully awake at Norwich. Two of my three sets of keys are for places in this city, but I do not want to go to either of them. My own flat, where Susie was hurt and Jim's place where he kicked away the chair.

I travel on, and, on the line on which I used to work, I recognise the next guard slightly. He takes my promise of payment readily and does not probe my changed circumstances. Whatever my skill in stealing train rides, I must walk to Walsingham from Sheringham, the limit of the proper railway.

My key bites but does not turn. My fingers bleed, and the metal bends so that I can no longer withdraw the jagged shank. This is your lovelock, Susie. Where are you? I fiddle with the tricky catch on the side gate. I think what is in my head is finding something in the shed to sell, or else living in that shed for a day. Someone has crept behind me, and I spin around. The elderly man's eyes are sharp enough to have seen the ruined key.

"Do you need a locksmith young man?"
"How would I prove I belong here?"
"I don't know about that."

He knows very well who I am. We have been neighbours for at least five years. Not directly opposite, but in the line of fire from behind their curtains. Once his wife had cooed over Pippa, and it was a time I needed to talk to Susie and be with her privately. Just leave me alone and let me think. And now his wife has joined him, shuffling up my drive and causing him to start whistling a brain-dead greeting. I borrowed a strimmer from them once. We were with them one boxing day; smothering religion which Gabby did not understand, but she had understood the generous present of a doll and the love and attention.

"What can you tell me?" I bark.

"Your wife has had to go to Wales to see her mother. She's ill."

"Susie's mother is ill?"

"Yes," the man agrees. And now, not spontaneously, but as if it is a conspiracy between them, hatched with coughs and twitches, it seems that they assume I will go back to their house with them, and that they will stay here until I comply.

"You can ring her if you like," the woman says.

I squint at her.

"It makes no difference to us," the man adds. They do not move.

"Fuck off," I say and run.

In the middle of nowhere, at the limit of my breath, I ring Wales. A long time before the landline is answered, and enough confusion over voices that I do not know how to start the conversation.

"Are you OK... How are you?"

"It's Stella, Drew."

"Yes. How are you?" The enquiry more measured this second time. She does not sound ill.

"I don't know how I am; that's the truth. An inconvenience."

"I'm in Norwich..."

A pause and a sense of great effort. "Drew, can ask why you are ringing us?"

"I need to speak to Susie..."

Silence. My anger rises... But this woman has been on my side. She backed away from the grand wedding plans once she had realised how stressed her daughter was. She had thanked me for telling her. She had behaved with courage and dignity on the death of her husband. She likes trains. I recognise enough of her daughter in her, and I see more plainly what I love in Susie.

"Drew, I'll try."

Her steps recede, and I listen for Susie making her slow way to the phone or my daughters' laughter. Absolute silence. The house is big and quiet, and Stella rattles around in it. I can smell the polish and the feel the frayed rug sliding slightly as I knelt beside Gabs and Pippa a couple of Christmases ago. Susie would have known a few houses like this with the overheard phone in cold halls. Impossible to guess whose steps trail back to the phone, but I greet them, "Susie!"

"She doesn't want to speak to you, Drew."

"Tell her to ring me! It's important!"

"Drew, we have things to think about here, things to discuss, separate from the storm that you have created. You'll understand and respect that."

Oh God, Stella. I push the red button and understand at the same moment.

Why am I driven to re-enact experiences as if that will be a comfort? Here are the marshes where I watched Chantelle's house through plastic binoculars, no less crushingly isolated in full daylight, but I shiver until dusk for the full effect. Here is the exact spot where Dan almost mowed me down as he kidnapped Molly, and I walk in the tyre prints. Now the front door and I am just as cold, and my clothes are as damp. A hard, sustained knock to rouse them, as if it was their fault I have been waiting silently on the step for ten minutes. Nothing. Perhaps they are used to secret knocks here. No light behind the door, but then a minute crack and two round eyes in the darkness, absorbing not reflecting. Then I am in the hall, and Chantelle's mother is behind me, gently not understanding, not even looking at me. Forgive me for bundling past you; it was me who opened the door wide. I think I may have caught your hip in a soft blow, or else it was the cutesy doorstop I felt resisting my push. You have forgotten the boundaries of your own home.

Chantelle sits at the kitchen table, Molly on her knee, sleeping. Her daughter's hair streams down Chantelle's back, and the colour is so well matched that the strands are indistinguishable. With Susie and Gabby and Pippa, the light and the dark skeins form patterns. The room is exactly as Hennie described, and I relied on her description to find it. Plain wooden chairs and a slatted table. Everything scoured clean but fighting back. Knife scars on surfaces and mould in the recessed drawer handles. An ambition of rustic harmony; at some point someone has hung pictures of impossibly fat farm animals on stick legs, no more belonging in this arable wilderness than on a modern estate. Chantelle does not scream; she makes no sound at all, as if infected with her mother's quiet acceptance of everything. Opposite her is a plate of crumbs and so, unwashed and unshaved, I take the chair next to her.

"Chantelle I'm sorry."

"Hello, Drew."

"You must go to the police."

"I can't, Drew."

Chantelle's mother has now followed me or else remembered where she should be. A clatter and she has opened one of the painted cupboards which is stuffed from top to bottom with Jacob's cream crackers.

"It's OK, Mum," Chantelle says gently at this gesture of hospitality.

"Please trust me."

"I know you weren't part of this, Drew. You were here the same night as Dan, but you weren't with him." She looks up to her mother for confirmation of this which does not come. "You have children of your own; you showed me their pictures, kindly."

My sweaty skin prickles at this spurious reasoning, and I wonder if even now she does not know the full horror of the situation.

"Please tell the police what has happened. Is there anybody who can help you? Molly's father?"

"Rat," she whispers, and smiles briefly at the simplicity of the situation. Then she blushes like a schoolgirl with a secret. "Drew, I have a friend from work who knows what has happened. They trust her, but she's against them, and it's all about to blow up. She said just to wait."

Processes I do not understand again, the weird ASMR buzz as I listen to the girl.

"She says that Molly will be safe, and I won't have to do a thing, and the police will catch everybody—"

"Who?" I demand, and for the first time, Chantelle looks as though she might actually be terrified of me.

"She said not to say anything."

"Please Chantelle!"

"She was awful to you, I know, but it's Jane."

"Oh God, don't trust her! You need to tell the police everything."

"I can't."

"Who's threatening you?"

"Everybody, Drew. Clare says she'll stop my pay. Dan talks about... horrible things. Hennie says that she'll report me to Social Services... Drew, I can't be separated from Molly; I just can't..."

"I'll do everything I can," I say.

As I leave Molly is waking up, and Chantelle gently takes her hand and waves it.

"Goodbye, Drew."

"Goodbye, Molly."

I flee the stifling, doomed house, but when I stop it is me who is in the mud and shit of this nineteenth-century bucolic hell-hole, who must find myself, and find somewhere to go. The full emptiness and hopelessness of grief has caught up with me. In that haunted kitchen, Hennie did not help Chantelle; she threatened to have her child taken away. There is only one thing I want to do. No one expects me to be rational, so let me fall back into this mad comfort. No one can expect anything else of me. Let me embrace this strangeness.

This feels more outlaw and difficult. I have had to buy a ticket for a close destination to get past the barriers at Norwich station. The guard looks at me with distaste, and I realise I am looking more and more like a criminal.

"Let me give you my address and a promise of payment," I plead. "Please don't put me off the train."

By mistake, I take the key to my flat from my pocket, not a pen. In the face of this he must treat me with care and sympathy. Begging train rides: my special power.

Who are you?
I'm Drew. How old are you Amy?
I'm twelve.
Are you really twelve?
Don't you want to be my friend if I'm only twelve Drew?

My phone dies, and this dangerous conversation is frozen. Jesus.

I love this place a little. Shitty and smelly Port Talbot dignified by distance across Swansea Bay. Swansea itself out of mind in quaint Mumbles, then the beaches of the Gower where Susie and I have walked, making gentle fun of her father.

"Oh Drew, Oh Drew." Susie's mother is pale and terribly thin. She looks me up and down—I have my own signifiers, I suppose. I wanted this to be wordless, without explanation from me. Instead, I am besieging another woman on her doorstep. Eventually I say.

"Just Gabby and Pippa then, just for a minute."

"They're not here, Drew."

"Where are they?"
"They're being looked after by Susie's friend."
A movement in the hall, a door opening and a head poking round.
"They're with Hennie, Drew."

Chapter Thirty-two

We hit a hundred and ten on the M4, Susie's teeth gritting and her eyes wide. On the M25 there is coiled-spring anger as we stop and start. But it is at dawn is on the roads of Norfolk that her fear and urgency fully transfer to the machine. As she overtakes a tractor on a blind bend, I grip the seat.

"Don't you trust me!" she spits.

No, Susie, I don't trust you. Not your angry, tired hands on the wheel, and not your judgement with Hennie, who you used against me and who now owns us both. It is all I can do to stop myself saying this, but it would mean disaster. Every time we speak there is a new transgression, a reckless tug of the wheel, a stab at the brakes.

"What are you going to do?" she says, gauging the impossible stopping distance in front.

"What do you mean?"

"Where shall I drop you?"

"Susie, I'm with you. We'll search together. "

"Well, I'm going to the police."

"But you told the police everything, and you've sent them the pictures for the local news."

"They'll use the ones in the matching party dresses for Laura's wedding."

"That's taken care of now. We can trace the river back to Yarmouth."

"For fuck's sake, Drew! She lives in a house. This fucking wherry is in your fantasy!"

"A line of portholes! I need to do something."

"OK, I'll drop you at fucking Brundall, but I'll tell the police what stupid thing you're doing if they ask where you are!"

This is enough for now, but a few miles later, fighting nausea, I make myself say,

"I'm sorry about your mother, Susie, I really am. She was always on our side."

"Fuck you!"

So complete is her collapse now I wonder if I could fight control from her if I needed to. But the A11 is straight and true if she wants to get back to her children. As we speed past the place where Nadia died I say,

"Imagine Gabby and Pippa are on the back seat, Susie… Let me drive."

"No! You fucked up! When you thought you were in control fucked up!"

At Brundall station, she stands on the brakes to teach me a lesson. I close my eyes to recover. "Susie, your phone, unblock me."

"For today," she says.

I know that as soon as I slam the door the wheels will spin and screech, but in a moment of calm, she fiddles with her purse, and forty pounds passes between our shaking hands.

I do not understand boats. Nor do I understand art, but this is all about shapes. Modern cruisers have windows in crazy, unpleasing shapes if you take the panes in isolation. I am looking for the line of perfect circles that I saw on the photographs. The river is not a straight path to tread relentlessly. There are cuttings and moorings and marinas to search. I try until late afternoon but do not find the alarm shape of those portholes.

There is a road overlooking Great Yarmouth Station. Here, on the damp grass, sits a man. He is echoing the travel announcements, loud enough to be heard over all of the long platforms. But he is getting it wrong. The service about to leave for Norwich will go via Acle, not by Reedham and listen to his timings and you will miss the train. The type 37s and their coaches now setting off will never be able to fit at Berney Arms Station, and so will not stop there. And all this has a strange physical effect on me; my arm starts beating with every mistake. Why does this poor man's presence upset me so much? Yes, I am back on the railway again. I need to think, and I need to sleep. I cannot even say Brundall is searched and clear, and there are a thousand more hiding places on the Broads. My childhood bed was sometimes a boat, but it always became a train again because I did not like dreams of what was beneath the dark surface of the water. But in this train I cannot collect my thoughts because a mother is allowing her seven-year-old to run up and down the aisle. When eventually I sleep, I am in a train full of children, climbing on the seats and swinging from the luggage racks, noisy, squabbling and selfish. Intent on instant gratification, but always racing towards their destination and a golden future.

I must be careful of showing the face of my phone. I have not looked at the images since that night in Cologne. I think I know them, but surely my revulsion would not have allowed me to study each one for more than a few seconds. Elastic time would have convinced me that I had seen every important detail and clue. I still do not know if Susie is aware of this horror on my phone, but I must navigate it for her to save our daughters. Between each image I pause and close my eyes. The most harrowing picture for me is of Molly, who waved me goodbye and smiled. I do not want to open my eyes again to this. I jolt awake, and the reflection of my screen is clear in the window. My sweat prickles and cools and I whip my head down and bury the phone in my lap. Who might have witnessed me casting this pornography? A man looks away as I jerk my head up but a middle-aged woman holds my gaze, and I rapidly flick my thumb over the screen. I have landed nowhere safe in my camera roll, and as I frantically look down I see it. Away from the magnetic pull of the naked figure, away from the lodestone of obscenity, I see it. I see it in all the photographs which catch the portholes. I see it through the leftmost one whenever my eyes can shift from the subject. A shape. An object. It strikes me as the mast of a sunken boat; nothing natural lies at that angle. I pinch my finger and thumb and flick them out. What comes towards me is a fallen crucifix; something so odd and jarring that I know it must be important to me. On the bank I am sure, not a withered insect on the glass. Then a hint of skeletal struts, setting my teeth on edge. On this photo, a profoundly shocking image and then this little shape, disturbing in a way I do not understand. Could this shape, away from the focus, have added to the ASMR tingling as I sat by the Rhine? Do I know it? Sorted from the trees and the clouds, I am sure it is a mass. Not a drowned ship supporting a mast, despite the sinister feeling of a submerged hulk. A tower supporting a beam. A mill. When I connect to the internet the search is kind to me, as if it is an extension of my memory, finding something I had always known. Not a mill, but a ruined wind pump.

Brograve! I text to Susie.

An out of the way place for this monstrosity. Norfolk coastal. No roads there.

Brograve Wind Pump! The boat was there!

This may not be helpful now because Hennie would have driven her boat to that isolated spot to escape attention because of the parties. Now she could be anywhere— No she couldn't! Jesus, Jesus, Jesus! My daughters!

A branch snags my ankle and I fall. I do not think I have fallen like this since I was a child. Running, then helpless; then self-adjusting and head up and landing on my knees. Everything I have landed in soft and wet, and my phone falling safely, well in front of me and now like a beacon. I laugh and then cry. I pull myself up and run again, over to the right like Dan in his videos; away from the mud and the shit and the river. Like Susie, part believing I am in control, part not caring. Fifty-fifty. Running then walking, elated then sobbing. Everything will be fine because Susie will have got my message and the blackness and silence here mean that everything was resolved long ago.

I see the pump now. It catches me by surprise, closer than I thought it would be. Obviously, I can neither see nor visualise things properly, otherwise I would make myself an artist, like Hennie, with all the power and kudos that gives you in representing the obvious. The creepy pump is here, but I cannot work out the angles or what comes before what, so I cannot trace back to where the boat might be. I know shapes though, and this one chills me. I continue to run, mixing up perspectives and stopping because I do not trust myself. It is not a visual clue that stiffens my spine: it is a sound. It is not something that I have heard before, but an extrapolation, a guess at what this might sound like. Our dog, Poppy, is in real distress. Among all the practicalities that did not get talked about, I had assumed that Susie had booked kennels, but no, so complete has Hennie's campaign of infiltration been that she has pretended to love our pet. It slowly comes to me that these echoes across the broad mean that Susie and the police have not been here, because the dog would not be left to howl if everything was settled. My instinct is to call out, but I make myself stop and listen. A great distance, beyond the tower. I pray not on the wrong side of the river.

It is not a wherry. This lie had brushed my consciousness, pleasing in its playful extravagance. It is almost big enough, which probably sparked the mocking exaggeration amongst her friends who know about these things. It is called Stream of Light and is a lovely thing. I can see the individual strips of wood from which it was made. I have only to whisper now and Poppy's whines will become squeaks of excitement, and there is no point in stealth. But as I am about to call my childrens' names I see her. She is wearing a long white dress and a cream jacket, and her hair is up, ringlets tumbling about her ears as I have only ever seen on the barbecue photos. This boat is some sort of capsule in this rural slum, and I watch, transfixed. The smell of the wood mingles with the smell of water; water spilling over the banks, salt from the sea, and a mist of rain carried by the warm breeze. When I call her name she is not shocked to see me or else does not show it. Perhaps she is expecting someone else and only has to make an adjustment to accommodate me.

"Drew, come aboard."

"Where are my children?"

"They're here Drew, come and see them."

I am reluctant to go near the treacherous bank and she extends a hand to encourage me, but still I cannot see what I am supposed to do, and she moves to the right spot at the edge of the deck, smiling, arms still extended. I reach out and feel her cold hand just as the marsh beneath my feet seems to give way. A moment of imbalance, then imagined jeopardy, and she grips me tighter. Then safety as her arm is around my waist. On this raw wood deck she is barefoot, her nails painted blue. I can imagine my daughters' excitement at seeing this boat. The whole impression is of wood, dark but shiny, reflecting lanterns tied to the rails,

"She's beautiful, isn't she?"

"Where are Gabby and Pippa?"

"Come and see your daughters, Drew."

But first here is my dog. She is tied to a modest wheel, no more than the steering wheel of an old car, and her lead is taut in this world of taut ropes. She has bitten on a ball for comfort, but this has rolled out of her reach.

"This is torture for her," I say, but at once she relaxes into licking my hand. The cabin to which Hennie leads me, up and down short ladders, is dark. I can hear my daughters' soft breathing before I can make out their gentle shapes. In fact, Gabby—on the top bunk—is almost breathing into my ear.

Pictures of Our Children

Then a jarring, sinister detail in this peace, an arcade of shiny black circles; it is in this part of the boat where the portholes are. I notice that I am slightly unsteady and perhaps my daughters have been rocked to sleep.

"They're fine, Drew," Hennie urges and tugs at my sleeve. We clamber up to the wheel again, and I face a new onslaught from Poppy. I find that I want to gauge my dog's reaction to Hennie, but the woman holds back, and the excitement is all about me. The wheel jiggles with the movements of the lead. If I were Hennie, I would have pointed the nose of this boat towards freedom, not tangled myself in this maze of water. Hennie is hanging over the rail, pointing.

"Brograve Pump. The shape. Can you see it?"

"I know what it is!"

"It's incredible. The landowner was a haunted man. He made a pact with the devil, trying to keep his creditors at bay and the sea from engulfing his fields. Eventually the devil comes after him and tries to blow the pump over—see how it leans!"

"I hope you haven't been filling my daughters' heads with this nonsense."

"There are many worse fairy tales, Drew," she laughs. "Don't you ever enjoyed being a bit scared? There's something about the shape; even you must be able to see it."

"I found you by this shape!"

She turns, puzzled. "Come with me, Drew, tell me."

She leads me to what I think you would call the saloon; polished oak and maroon upholstery.

"Isn't she beautiful?"

"Yes," I say when I have processed what she means. She has said this before, but I was thinking of something else.

"She's a nineteen-thirties broads cruiser, amazingly restored."

"Not a wherry."

"Not a wherry, but huge. Bless you, Drew. Not a wherry."

She touches my shoulder, laughs and shakes her head.
"Do you have a house?" I say.
"Yes, but I've forgotten where."

Dear God, this is as cosy as a caravan, not the adventure I had imagined when I had first known about the boat. Like family holidays when I was a child, and sure enough, a sharp shower starts to beat against the windows as we talk, and ends with drips on the roof. Good red wine, uncorked and left to breathe. My children are safe, and it will end here. Soon my wife and the police will come, and I need do nothing more. I have relaxed, but Poppy has not, and her plaintive yelps are painful again. How is it that my children can sleep through this? Gabby would have insisted that Poppy sleeps with them— I jump to my feet, hitting my head on the low ceiling.

"What have you done to them, Hennie!"

"It's Calpol, Drew, it's Calpol. They caught a chill yesterday." She kisses my head like the perfect mother. In this saloon the windows are long and rectangular. I push past her to be at my daughters side', where the portholes are. I shake Gabby's arm and kiss her and she smiles, and although I do not think she knows I am really here, it is enough. Hennie gestures at Pippa as if she is anxious for me to go through the process again.

"You see, they are safe. I wouldn't harm them. Let them sleep; they've had a busy day. They have such an affinity with nature. We've identified all the birds we've seen and dipped for creatures in the water. They don't get that from you, do they?"

"Bloody bugs, I'd kill them all."

"Let's talk, Drew, please." She grabs my wrist and does not drop it as I comfort Poppy again, but I am still not sure she has an affinity with this member of the animal kingdom. "Tomorrow we'll row the tender across Hickling Broad."

I take it she is talking about the tiny, vulnerable boat lashed to the side, and I shudder at the thought of my children in it.

"How can there be a tomorrow?"

Pictures of Our Children

"Let's sit down again."
"Yes," I say, but hesitate.
"The toilet is at the back, Drew," she smiles.

Anxiety and the pain in my stomach are inseparable now. Here wet and dripping copper pipes press on my back, and the air is sharp with metal and polish. The only relief from this claustrophobia is the circle of a copper framed mirror. How long must I stay and how many times must I come back here?

When I find my way back to Hennie she has topped up my glass and another bottle is open, and I drink, thirsty, taking gulps of complicity. A gentle nausea is overtaking me from the subtle rocking of the boat.

"I enjoyed Cologne, Drew," she says, resting her head on the cushion.

"But why did you come?"

She rolls her head from side to side. "Because I'm fond of you."

"I think it was to delay me, to persuade me to stay out of the way."

Now she looks me in the eye.

"Yes, exactly that , Drew, but I did it because I'm fond of you. It was foolish of you to come back. You should have waited a little while, because I think you are still in danger from the police and the vigilantes. I came because a little bit of my heart wanted to see you, because I love you despite myself..." She pauses and then driven by embarrassment she screws her face into a smile. "And despite you resolutely wanting to meet on the tower when I have vertigo."

When her features relax she looks vulnerable and more beautiful than I have ever seen her; ghostly face and pale lipstick.

"Well, you have got me back now. I hate the Broads," I say.

"My flight back was delayed, and I had to make up a story for work. I told them I had to visit a sick Aunt, just to protect you. Oh God Drew, you should have stayed in Cologne with your bridge and your trains."

"I was at Great Yarmouth this morning."

"Yarmouth? I loved our day there."

"I was at the station. There was a man on the road overlooking the platforms. He was echoing the announcements, but everything was wrong. Platform numbers, times, destinations."

"How long were you there for?"

I do not answer, and she seems concerned. Eventually I say,

"I think it worried me so much because I used to be a train guard."

"You never told me that. I wish you had. I never thought that you were quite right for insurance… That's a compliment…" Suddenly she leans forward and moves to take my hand. "Oh Drew, was it you on the station, calling the trains?"

"No, Hennie, it wasn't me. But it brought me into a cold sweat because I have no doubt that poor man thinks what he is doing is rational. You've driven me to the same thing, Hennie."

"I always tried to help you."

"And when you went to meet Susie you wanted to help me? Can you tell me that it wasn't a plan to get close to my family?"

"Well, yes, Drew, I was desperate to see your daughters again."

So many times I have been secretly angry with Dan for paying more attention to his phone than to me, and, dear God, Lucie was the worst… This isn't quite like that. It is almost the reverse. I know there is no phone signal in this God-forsaken place, but perhaps there is a wisp of Wi-Fi. Hennie wants to focus on me, but her eyes dart to the screen and her fingers flick it. Then her hand closes around the phone, and she squeezes it and does not pull it to her breast but holds it away. She is trying to unpick arrangements.

"Are you cancelling the party?"

"What do you mean?"

"Who is coming?"

"Nobody, Drew."

"Do you know how I found you?"

"I imagine you walked every footpath by the side of every broad and river in Norfolk."

"Not quite."

"With your plastic binoculars."

She moves to touch me again, and my arm beats up and down.

"Do you realise how I found you! Brograve Pump through the portholes of this boat, and I knew you'd come back to this quiet place because you had Gabby and Pippa!"

Hennie stills my hand. "Calm, Drew. No harm has come to them. No harm. They're my friends."

"Hennie, I have terrible pictures of children on this boat. Each child posed in front of the portholes and the shape of that ruin as the tell-tale!"

She does not speak at once and then is taken over by a helpless anxiety.

"What were the date stamps on the photos? Two months ago? That got out of hand. I wasn't here for most of that."

"Who drove your boat to this lonely spot?"

"What was the date stamp? What was the date?" She frets about this as I have seen naturally anxious people fret about an admin error at work, but it is strangely shocking in her. Can it be that she has only at this moment realised how deeply she is implicated?

"Show me the photos," she says.

"I don't want to see them again."

"Drew, I do know the time you mean. I didn't have the stomach for that either. It took something from the girls and boys, and I hated it."

"Who was drinking in here while that was happening in the cabin? Fuck! Who is on the way? Dan, Clare, Ulph? Tell me about the organisation."

"There is no organisation, Drew. It' a work thing. A common interest that bubbles to the surface. A WhatsApp group. No more organisation than arranging a meal or a drink. That's what I understand. People gravitate to each other as they would if they followed Norwich City."

"Who instigated this?"

"I don't know what you mean, Drew."

"Christopher Ulph, Dan and his wife?"

"You keep talking about Ulph. I only know Ulph as a creep from Sheffield who fancies Clare. You don't understand. A common interest. Not an organisation. A succession of people."

"Jesus, Hennie, the parties on this boat, who organised them?"

"They fell into place. The boat is an attractive proposition, like if you have a car at college you are always giving people lifts. I want nothing more to do with this."

"Who is coming now?"

"I've told you, Drew, no one is coming."

"Jane?" Almost a snort from Hennie, "So Jane is involved?"

"Yes, Jane is involved!"

Is she saying this to please me by agreeing to any name, or to try to dilute the wrong with an escalating count of those implicated? Then she says,

"I would guess that most of the children you saw in those wretched photos were brought by Jane. The supply chain. An endless source of ugly grandchildren. I hated her influence, and I hated the way she treated you."

"You talked about me with her?"

"Yes, and I stuck up for you."

So, there was another life for the story of how Jane attacked me, aside from inside poor Chantelle's head. Did this crystallise Hennie's reconciliation with me in the file room after our disastrous first date?

"Jane is high up in this thing?"

"There is nothing, Drew, it's so fluid."

"But the organisation kicks in if you're threatened. I've felt the full force of that."

"No, from what I know it's everyone for themselves."

Is she talking about Clare's cunning deception and Jane's crude manipulation of Chantelle?

"Who gave the very first party?"

"You're asking me things I just don't know. I wasn't there. The first party might have been years and years ago. I've found I hate all this."

She stands up, flustered and trying to pour more wine. Then she drops her head and slowly sits next to me, close. It was like this when I first knew her; always standing just a hand's width from me. Now I look at stray strands of hair adhering to her cheek by drops of perspiration and the sweep of her long lashes.

"Listen, Drew, what you think about me is in some ways true. How can I explain? I'm not sure myself. What is it? Some other sexual orientation—"

"Jesus, Hennie!"

"Not that then. Not that. Something more. A fetish, but a common one. God, I'm sorry, but you know above anyone how complex and fragile the mind is. Something the same with me. Think, Drew. Images, drawings. Or an old photo of someone who has now grown. A cartoon or a loving drawing of a child. There can be no harm in this. These are my things. Drew, you don't know how common this is. An illness in that I didn't choose it, but beautiful sometimes."

"Jesus! Are there more drawings of my children I haven't seen?"

"No, Drew, honestly. But if we were together, this could be normal in some way. I got almost nothing from those parties. Nothing I could stomach at any of them in truth, I've learnt that. There are degrees. I love your children, and I've loved them from that first day in Great Yarmouth. I keep thinking how precious Gabby is because she was nearly lost and what a life Pippa will have. Together we could fight for them and protect them, because even now this could be untangled. How much more harm is done to children by criminalising a natural reaction? Police involved; social services involved. But if I need help, help me, Drew."

"You stole my phone. On that day when we trailed from pub to pub in Norwich, when I fell in love with you beyond escape, you stole my phone. In that moment of relief when I shared everything with you, you betrayed me. You gave the phone to Clare, and she injected evil into it and set people on to me."

"Honestly, I didn't know what Clare was going to do with it. She has her claws into me, as she has her claws into you. She threatened me through work, a work thing, not anything else."

"Three people dead because of this." Nothing from Hennie. She cannot be struggling with the names, but I call them for her, "Nadia. Victoria. Jim."

"Nadia I don't know about. I think she introduced her son; I'm not very sure. Poor Vicky was brittle and felt Nadia's death so deeply because they had fallen out. Jim I feel terrible about because I think we could have helped him. But in any workplace it would be the same. Vicky misjudged it, but it's common, almost normality. How many of those predator hunter videos are out there? But sometimes it's innocent. These last few days I've found so exciting, just teaching them new things. Mostly it's not sexual, please believe me… You know that this is something that I will never naturally be able to share in, don't you, Drew, so it's torture and joy in equal measure if I think of it."

"It's something I'll never understand."

"Are you sure? Where is the borderline? Big eyes, frail limbs; aren't they the child-like things that men find attractive in women? A natural gravity towards young and fresh."

"I wanted no more than you, Hennie."

She looks down breathing hard.

"Do you find Chantelle attractive? Of course you do because we teased each other about it once. She looks so young, we said. Can you separate the quality of love I feel for a child from the quality of love you feel?"

"For my daughters? Yes, I can, don't you understand?"

"I don't know. But if I don't, isn't that marginal too? In the spectrum of human affection that is a subtle distinction. Sometimes I might see it; sometimes I struggle with it."

"Wouldn't your mother and father have done anything to protect you from a predator?"

"Well, that's so far into the land of childish confusion that I don't know how to answer it. My parents died when I was six years old."

"I'm sorry, Hennie, you told me about the accident."

"Hardly an accident, Drew, it was a farm attack. They were fleeing for their lives and had hidden me."

Twice, I think, when I had started in insurance straight from school, I had seen matching pairs of car accident death certificates, and I had projected the circumstances of these onto her. Distracted by this, I can only think about how the money for this boat must have flooded down by inheritance, not an aspirational pyramid.

"I'm sorry."

"My guardian didn't care in any way about me. But every night I went to sleep, I knew my father loved me."

I move on before I have understood this.

"Did you steal Jim's phone too? I thought Jim had gone to the police before me, but that can't be right because he would have talked and talked about Victoria. The police didn't know her name, and the only thing they wanted from me was about Lucie. Did you tell them some lie to implicate me and to divert them?"

"I was frantic when that happened."

"Who did that?"

"Dan went. Dan, Clare, Lucie. It must have been Lucie as well, mustn't it? Drew, yes I spoke to Dan when I was afraid you might crack and go to the police, but he panicked."

"And you urged me to hide."

"I did that for you."

"It only made me look guilty. And then my phone was posted for the police to find in a search."

"But everything stopped after that, and you don't know how grateful I was."

"The unforgivable thing is that you threatened Chantelle and Molly. I was with them. I know that you told Chantelle that you would report her to social services."

"I was desperate then. And I sat in the fucking kitchen, and I felt almost physically the weight stifling that little girl. I said something casually; I would never have gone through with it. I wanted the best for Molly. I wanted her in my care, to be honest. Now, in my senses, I know that it was a terrible thing to say. And you judge me for it. Oh God, Drew, are the police coming?"

"Yes."

"Not vigilantes to hurt me."

"Of course not."

"Drew, please listen. How can I explain? It's children's *futures* that I love."

Have I ever seen her cry? Yes, once, I think, when we were drunk and intoxicated with the idea that nothing mattered. When her tears had come because she had laughed so hard at a widower's grieving frustration. But then those tears had turned into something different; frail and compassionate. It is the same now, and it makes her complete: almost a choking, a danger, an illness. As I am thinking this she begins to shake, as if she had learnt from Victoria. Something she can never be free of, a weakness, an affliction.

"Don't judge me harshly," she whispers.

I stare at her; a vile, disbelieving attention that people used to give to the disabled; mongols and cripples. If I am willing her to show some sign that her display of weakness is fake, she does not. With every second her distress deepens, and becomes more frightening and compelling. She is fighting against it because she does not want to show this to me. This may be the last throes of some conspiracy, but as I watch her, I think that it may be how close she can come to loving someone fully grown.

"Please excuse me," she splutters.

"Of course, Hennie."

I imagine her in the copper toilet, gracefully bent over the tiny pan, then checking her face in the round mirror. I listen to my dog crying and barking, and a feeling comes over me that I am in charge of this huge boat. Then slowly, slowly, a wish for her to come back; a minute trace of loneliness. She has been too long and the second has ticked over. Visceral panic that I have not felt since I was nearly mown down by a car. I slip on the wooden ladders and deck and become entangled in Poppy's stretched, winding lead. The toilet door is wide open. I burst into the cabin of portholes, but there is no sound. I grope for the silk of Hennie's dress, but there is nothing. My phone gives its last life to illuminate my daughters' faces, pale lipstick shining on their cheeks. Another ladder and I am on top of the saloon, and I do not know if it is safe.

"Hennie!"

I scan both ways along the footpath, hoping to see a flash of white, my mind racing to the exhilaration of the chase through the traps of slippery reeds and the snares of roots. But there is a steady shape near the bow. Cream. Her jacket, abandoned. A flood of thoughts about her cold, bare shoulders. Another shape merging ever more completely into the darkness of the water. Her jacket and her body. I am here on top of the boat, and I cannot jump. I must go a little at a time, on my knees, clinging to the ladders, slipping on the deck, and then falling, to land in the little rowing boat. The boat is tied fast, and I cannot free the rope. But I think I always meant to lower myself into the water here then launch myself out. A terrifying cold and no footing just slimy vegetation and God knows what beneath. Then a paralysis of fear. I will myself to push forward, but dare not. The most movement I can make is to grip the side of the dinghy tighter and haul myself up a little, to escape the water and to see the shapes; her jacket and her body.

Chapter Thirty-three

I convince myself that it is my sodden clothes, not my failing courage, that stop me from striking out towards her, and every second it becomes more impossible. A weight I cannot overcome. I call her name to her shell, her ideal, and think of her tears. The time for saving her is passed, and all I could hope for would be to reach through her unpinned hair and lift her face from the water. Slowly a sense that my footing is becoming more secure. I am settling into the reeds, and there is an illusion that they might support my legs like stirrups; but if I relaxed I would feel the leaves split and I would fall deep into the river bed. I kick down, and my thighs ache above the pain of the cold, and the leaves tear and play higher about my calves. Something new. An idea takes hold of me that I will not be able to haul myself back into the little boat. When I dare to test this, it is true; the side of the boat is now a wall to be climbed, the hollow of wood no longer a refuge to fall into. I try again, and not only is my strength being sapped, but I fear that pain may break my grip on the side of the boat. I have not been eating and wine dulls my senses like the drug my girls have been fed. I discipline myself to keep still as I sink further into the slime; to build strength and to find a new grip on the wood. I try again and fail. The processes which paralysed her are killing me too. Always I have lived life at one remove. Now, when my hands are numb and useless, I imagine them on the rope. In my head I feel them unpicking the knots of the coil as if it is string on a parcel. I know that it is a puzzle that cannot be solved, but I am unable to escape from it. Things are happening more quickly than I thought. My mouth touches the water, and when my lips open to gasp the taste is not cloying slime, but a bitter iced drink. I yell,

"Gabby, Pippa!" as if my children could save me. But they are sleeping, through Calpol or excited exhaustion or whatever it is. I think of them serene and beautiful like this. Agonising practicalities have given way to the sadness that I have seen them for the last time. I am not quite calm; my hands are still on that rope in my mind, unpicking the individual fibres now, because the strands have become unravelled. I tilt my head back, and my ears go under and there is a roar in this deathly quiet place. Stillness, then roar as my head bobs. Quiet then a splintering crack. I know what this is, and I know what is going to happen. There has been a reckless leap into the little boat. I cling on as it dips, but then all of the water in the broad pushes it back up, and it is a force I cannot withstand, and my hands are torn from the side. It is like a small child on a see-saw flung upwards— oh God, we did this to Gabby once and don't let this be my last memory of her. Water presses on my eyes and fills my ears, and I hit the silt of the river bed. A new shock of cold and I kick. I surface, but my legs are no longer beneath me, and my head dips under again. I push down with my arms, and now every wave batters my eyes. Another push and I see the shape of the boat, but it is out of reach.

"Who are you!" I scream.

A pole grazes my hand and crashes into my shoulder. This does not feel like rescue. No pulling-in and my hands slide on the wood, and the pole is lost into the water. An oar into my stomach and I fight to grasp the slippery, turning blade and know that somehow there is a struggle at the other end too. The oar twists and splashes.

"Who are you!"

Still waves from the boat beat into my head. Then suddenly the oar is still and solid, and I pin it under my arm. Then it is pulled, then a hand, and I fall into Dan's embrace.

I have not been warm since the river. But now I am surrounded by my people. The incompetents, the losers, the lost. The peripatetic paedo hunters, the national menaces. Creep Commando. A surge forward as the door opens and I try to stop myself being propelled into Gemma and inhaling the artificially coloured confection of her hair. She hates me and does not want me here. I forced her hand.

Are you a decoy?
What's a decoy?
Are you Gem?
I'm Amy. I'm fourteen.
These people do not represent the constituency of gentle, family England. The comments below the videos are bear pits, and don't expect emails to be handled with the decorum and efficiency of an insurance company inbox.
Gem. I beg you. Real children are in danger.
Nothing back.
My children are in danger. You've seen pictures of them. Gabby and Pippa with their dog.
Nothing for a long time, then,
Tell me. I don't fucking trust you but tell me.
I had felt something close to elation then.

"Stay back!" Gemma shouts into my face as the door opens. Behind me a new recruit elbows me forward. His hand is bandaged, and I know what caused this.
"Fucking get out here bitch!"
Freya shuffles out, crying. Of course, she is alone now, bereft and fearful. Creep Commando seem lost. They have no props; no chat logs and their procedures and rituals are not geared to deal with persistent abuse of real girls and boys.
"Your husband has been put away, hasn't he," Gemma sneers. Yes. Dan's arrest had been civilised, as had mine.

We laid together in that little boat, Dan and I, cast off from *Stream of Light* in a moment of his mad impulse, exhausted and grief stricken. At every second we expected someone to come, unaware of Susie's collapse. Every time Dan spoke I screamed at him to be quiet, trying to hold on to Hennie's words. And yet we were linked. The papers reported that we rested side by side until the police lifted us apart. But the papers reported too, and I am quite prepared to believe this, that at dawn, when Gabby was found, she had her arm around her sister, comforting her.

Freya collects herself and mumbles, "Are you the police?"
A shiver of unease seems to go through the group now, as if they are all of a sudden aware that this might be a real interference with ongoing justice.
"We work with the police…" Gemma falters.
Blunt knives are dangerous. I saw what happened last night. The crowd bend almost imperceptibly towards Freya. Gemma spins around, nervous of half-understood legal principles and nervous of well-understood protection concerns.
"We are filming for our safety and for your safety."

I saw what happened last night. I think it had been when she had recognised me. I had met Clare's eyes for a second, and she had looked away. As if towards freedom, as if toward escape. Then people had pushed past me as if they had been waiting for this moment for the whole of their careers in justice, and I had turned away from Clare's cries as she fell onto her doorstep and crawled onto the gravel drive.

I could be more use here. I know what happened, and I carry the dead woman's testimony. But I step back, claustrophobic and nauseous. As Freya whimpers, I turn and run. The stream will be abandoned, and the remains hurriedly deleted. I will leave them to this; to Janet, to their uneasy drive back to Yorkshire, to Mr Ulph in Sheffield.

Pictures of Our Children

Susie takes my hand, but drops it too soon. It is a greeting, not unconditional companionship. Perhaps it is pity as she looks around, the white walls and the unmakeable bed. This is not a cell; I am kept here only by imagined obligations to people I love.

"What do the doctors say?" she asks softly and smiles.

"The doctors say nothing. It's just therapy."

She is not entirely being the efficient health professional because there are tears on her cheeks. There is something that I must say, though I know that it will go badly for me even before I speak.

"You promised to bring Gabs and Pippa."

"Drew, they can't see you like this. I can barely deal with this… We need to find a way forward for you…"

"Tell me about them."

Now her phone comes out, and our heads are together to share the images of our lovely daughters. I dare not ask about Susie's life.

"Has it been a good day?" Susie asks desperately when we part. I think she will have asked this of her clients a thousand times, trying to force the answer with a smile. "A good day, Drew?"

"Yes," I say.

So I will tell you that this is a chemical imbalance in my head, the processes working secretly in ways that I do not understand and cannot control. Sometimes clawing at my physical wellbeing, sometimes laying on me silently so that there is nothing, nothing, nothing I can do to find hope. Good days and bad days. Always open to be ambushed by this thing. Nothing I can do. But it is always worse when I think of Hennie.